LIGHTS OUT SUMMER

"In Zahradnik's well-plotted fourth Coleridge Taylor mystery (after 2016's *A Black Sail*), Taylor, a journalist who works for a small wire service in New York City, ignores the Son of Sam story everyone is closing in 1977 and instead goes after the largely ignored murder of Martha Gibson, a 24-year-old black woman who was shot dead in her Queens apartment. Gibson earned a college degree from City College, and worked her way up from secretary to a sales position at a company headquartered in the Empire State Building. When her boss sexually harassed her, she quit and took a job as a maid for the DeVries family on Park Avenue. The police aren't interested in Gibson's apparently senseless shooting, but Taylor gets several possible leads from Martha's drug-using sister, Abigail, whom Martha was supporting, as well as members of the DeVries household. Zahradnik nails the period, with its pack journalism, racism overt and subtle, and the excess of the wealthy at places like Studio 54, as he shows how one dogged reporter can make a difference."
—*Publishers Weekly*

★ ★ ★ ★ ★ "*Lights Out Summer* is a gripping multiple-murder mystery overlaid with tremendous atmosphere and action. Here's hoping a fifth Coleridge Taylor adventure is in the works."
—*ForeWord* Clarion Reviews

A BLACK SAIL

★ "Taylor, while out to get the story and get back to the crime beat, is complex and has a good heart. Verdict: Fans of the late

Barbara D'Amato and Bruce DeSilva will relish this gritty and powerful crime novel."
—*Library Journal*

"The pace is of necessity quick and varied, Rich Zahradnik's characters are well established and interesting, and the plot is intense and convoluted. There is a wonderful retro dime novel flavor to the protagonist and the telling which really suits the New York City setting. And Zahradnik's knowledge and use of the huge variety of watercraft is smoothly researched and presented. Gritty, tough, and well done—this one's a treat."
—Diana Borse for *Reviewing the Evidence*

★ ★ ★ ★ "Coleridge Taylor is a character fans can firmly stand behind. His dogged pursuit of the truth and commitment to helping others while exposing his foibles is what makes him so sympathetic and complex. Zahradnik ratchets up the action in this novel, which quickens the pace and keeps readers engaged [....] a truly enjoyable read."
—Keitha Hart for *RT Reviews*

★ ★ ★ ★ ★ "A beautifully written crime story; absorbing, fast-paced, and laced with literary gems that will make the overall reading experience fun and enjoyable for fans of mystery and murder."
—Divine Zape for *Readers' Favorite Reviews*

DROP DEAD PUNK

Finalist, *ForeWord Reviews* 2015 Book of the Year Contest
Gold Medal, mystery/thriller eBook, IPPY Awards 2016
Finalist, mystery, 2016 Next Generation Indie Book Awards

★ ★ ★ ★ "*Drop Dead Punk* provides hours of engrossing entertainment. The protagonist's choices, both good and bad, illustrate the depth and complexity of this utterly relatable

character. As the action develops and intensifies, the pace moves from moderate to fast. The 1970s New York City backdrop seems well researched. Book two of the Coleridge Taylor series is a thoroughly satisfying read that will keep readers guessing until the end."
—*RT Book Reviews*

"The New York City financial crisis of 1975 provides the dramatic backdrop for Zahradnik's frenetic sequel to 2014's *Last Words*. When police officer Robert Dodd starts to chase a mugger in Greenwich Village, Dodd's partner, Samantha Callahan, is unable to keep up. By the time Callahan catches up, Dodd and the mugger, who turns out to be punk rocker Johnny Mort, are both lying dead in the street after an apparent exchange of gunfire. Coleridge Taylor, an investigative reporter for the *New York Messenger-Telegram*, begins probing the oddities of the crime. When the newspaper folds and leaves Taylor without a job, he stays on the case. As he learns more about Mort, Dodd, and Callahan, he becomes convinced the shooting was a setup, but it's unclear who may have been the target. Taylor, who lives for the big story, makes an appealingly single-minded hero."
—*Publishers Weekly*

"As you follow the story and uncover the clues, finally reaching the end, you come up for air. It was the writing, how the author kept me curious and anxious for the characters, especially Taylor, and excited to get answers to my questions, plus how easily and quickly the story flowed, that got this a high recommendation from me. 5 Stars."
—*Laura's Ramblings and Reviews*

"The author's description of the gritty world that was New York in the 70s, as well as his research into the near bankruptcy of New York in 1975 was spot on and really added to the character of the story. Callahan's struggle with being one of the first woman cops in New York comes up repeatedly and gives the reader great insight into what must have been a very difficult time for women on the force. Add in the author's real-life experiences as a reporter for over 30 years that seep through the pages, and you have a definite winner."

—Ellen Feld, *Feathered Quill Book Reviews*

★ ★ ★ ★ ★ "Author Rich Zahradnik has done an amazing job at creating characters that the reader will truly care about, and if that's not a sign of a great writer, I don't know what is. Any reader who enjoys mysteries, an exciting read, a little bit of romance, or simply a great read will love *Drop Dead Punk*."

—Tracy A. Fischer for *Readers' Favorite Reviews*

LAST WORDS

Honorable Mention, mystery, *ForeWord Review*s 2014 Book of the Year Contest
Bronze Medal, mystery/thriller eBook, 2015 IPPY Awards
Finalist, mystery, 2015 Next Generation Indie Book Awards

"The tenacity of the main character will resonate as he overcomes barriers and reclaims his former life. [....] A fast-paced, deeply entertaining and engrossing novel. *Last Words* is the first book in a mystery series featuring the intrepid investigative reporter. Readers will be glad these aren't the last words from this talented author."

—Robin Farrell Edmunds, *ForeWord Magazine*

"The sights and sounds of the city in that day ring true to those of us old enough to have gone through the seventies. The author deftly uses the gritty landscape, the cops on the take who will do anything to those who even remotely consider crossing them, and the smell of fear that blanketed the city. From the very first sentence to the stunning end, readers will likely struggle to put the book down. Fast-paced and riveting, and well worth the read."

—Edie Dykeman, *BellaOnline*

"Despite his literary name, Coleridge Taylor is the 'Columbo' of beat reporters, suffering no fools and pursuing the facts at all costs. Set in 1975, the discovery of a deceased kid, presumed homeless, sets in motion Taylor's chilling odyssey."
—Claire Atkinson, senior media reporter, the *New York Post*

★ ★ ★ ★ "Mr. Zahradnik did a great job portraying the color and culture of the time. If you want to read about a slice of New York history during the 1970s then you'd probably enjoy this mystery for that reason alone. It's fast paced and the dialogue is natural sounding and I felt true to that era."
—*Long and Short Reviews*

"Rich Zahradnik is a superb craftsman. Like a painter, he adds layers of detail to a canvas he loves until he has created a picture that enthralls. *Last Words* has both beguiling landscape and revealing portraits and is a picture worth all its thousands of words: Rich in intrigue."
—Jeff Clark-Meads, author of *The Plowman* and *Tungol*

"*Last Words* sizzles like the fuse on a powder keg. Hero reporter Coleridge Taylor is gritty and unstoppable as he plumbs the mean streets of New York City during its darkest days."
—Paul D'Ambrosio, author of *Easy Squeezy* and winner of the Selden Ring investigation prize

"The story has a lot of twists and turns, which kept this reader on the edge of my seat waiting to see where the next turn leads. It was an exciting story right up until the end, and what an ending! For everyone who likes mystery, this book is for you."
—*Ann's Reading Corner*

"In 1975, as New York City collapses into a financial and violent sinkhole, journalist Coleridge Taylor dodges bullets and bounds from borough to borough to find the killer of a seemingly homeless boy, a crime that the NYPD can't or won't solve. *The*

Bronx is Burning meets *The Poet* in Rich Zahradnik's *Last Words,* a taut debut novel that keeps you guessing until the very end."
—Vito J. Racanelli, author and journalist

"Captivating [....] It is obvious from his writing that Rich Zahradnik is familiar with the setting he describes so well. Coleridge and Voichek are likeable, classic characters, and I enjoyed learning Voichek's hobo language. *Last Words* is not only entertaining, but also informative about a past era."
—Michelle Stanley for *Readers' Favorite Reviews*

"Zahradnik develops characters of all types and sizes in this novel. He gives readers a real sense of New York in the 70s via his cast, and the way that they view things. Top this off with an amazingly well developed and very interesting main character and you have a winner."
—Pure Jonel, *Confessions of a Bibliophile*

"I didn't realize how much I missed seedy gritty corrupt crime-ridden New York City of the 1970s till I read Zahradnik's debut thriller. *Last Words* captures the palms-out politicians, the bully cops, the not-so-hapless homeless, the back-stabbing reporters of a city on the brink. The pace speeds up; the whispers and clues and leads all come together for a big empty-the-revolver and fling-the-vodka-bottle finale. Well worth the trip back in time."
—Richard Zacks, author of *Chasing the Last Laugh: Mark Twain's Raucous and Redemptive Round-the-World Comedy Tour* and *Island of Vice*

"Like any great crime thriller, *Last Words* keeps the pace frenetic, dangerous, and surprising at every turn. Zahradnik delivers an intelligent, flawed hero in Coleridge Taylor while showcasing the darkness of New York in the '70s that devoured the weak and unsuspecting. A visual, visceral debut from both the author and his lead crime reporter."
—Diane Becker, Producer, FishBowl Films

Lights Out Summer

Lights Out Summer

A Coleridge Taylor Mystery

RICH ZAHRADNIK

CAMEL
PRESS

Seattle, WA

CAMEL PRESS

Camel Press
PO Box 70515
Seattle, WA 98127

For more information go to: www.camelpress.com
www.richzahradnik.com

This is a work of fiction. Names, characters, places, brands, media, and incidents are either the product of the author's imagination or are used fictitiously.

Cover design by Sabrina Sun

Lights Out Summer
Copyright © 2017 by Rich Zahradnik

ISBN: 978-1-60381-213-9 (Trade Paper)
ISBN: 978-1-60381-214-6 (eBook)

Library of Congress Control Number: 2017937046

Printed in the United States of America

In memory of Mom & Dad,
who never thought this was a bad idea.

———————◆———————

Also by the author

Last Words
Drop Dead Punk
A Black Sail

ACKNOWLEDGMENTS

———◆———

I'M INDEBTED TO two books on the Son of Sam murders, *Son of Sam: Based on the Authorized Transcription of the Tapes, Official Documents and Diaries of David Berkowitz* by Lawrence D. Klausner (1981) and *Son of Sam: The .44 Caliber Killer* by George Carpozi Jr. (1977). I learned about the 3X killer from the wonderful *Police Reporter: Forty Years One of New York's Finest Reporters* by Ted Prager (1957), as well as much of what it was like to do Taylor's job in the earlier decades of the 20th Century. I found the book on a little stand at the Brooklyn Book Festival, one of those treasures you hope to discover in such places but almost never do.

For specifics on other events during 1977, I relied on *The New York Chronology* by James Trager (2003), *New York Year by Year: A Chronology of the Great Metropolis* by Jeffrey A. Kroessler (2002) and the *New York Times* archive.

Since in a previous book I killed off an imaginary newspaper, I should note in this modern era of dying papers that the *Long Island Press* was quite real, starting as the *Long Island Farmer* and lasting 156 years. It was based in Jamaica, Queens, when S. I. Newhouse newspapers folded it. RIP.

Associate Publisher and Executive Editor Jennifer McCord and Publisher Catherine Treadgold have my deep appreciation for their expert editing, support throughout the publishing process, and guidance in all things making and marketing books.

As Taylor's journey has continued, I've enjoyed the great support of family and friends. Thank you to Tom and Cathleen Zahradnik, Julie Bramley, Mary and Tony Mathias, Bob and Jennifer Zahradnik, Kevin and Jean Rodd, Nancy Burger, Marianne Gilland, and Clay Bushong. My wife Sheri and son Patrick were with me before my life in fiction started and have stayed with it all along the merry way. They have my love and gratitude.

CO-ED'S KILLER
MAY STRIKE AGAIN

—*New York Post*, page 1, March 10, 1977

3 Murders of Women Since July 29
Believed Actions of Same Gunman

—*New York Times*, page D12
(bottom corner of the last page of the paper),
March 11, 1977

CHAPTER 1

———◆———

POLICE COMMISSIONER MICHAEL Codd, the six-foot-tall, 200-pound Chief Straight Arrow of the NYPD, never let anything faze him—a gentleman in the midst of chaos. Even when having to lay off thousands of cops. Even in the face of New York's soaring murder rate, corruption scandals, and rampant mafia violence.

Today, Taylor detected a crack or two in that façade as Codd discussed the murder of a woman in Queens. This wasn't your typical New York homicide. One person doing another in because of passion, fury, greed. A whole lot of greed.

The victim was the third killed by a single man in the past sixth months using the same .44-caliber revolver. The first homicide occurred back a ways, on July 29, 1976. The cops had connected the dots because of the current victim, Virginia Voskerichian, who was shot to death two days ago on March 8.

Mayor Abe Beame stood next to Codd during the press conference at the 112th Precinct in Forest Hills, Queens, to announce this news.

Taylor took down the details as Codd and the mayor doled them out. The point of the news conference was to enlist the public's aid in investigating the "senseless murder" of three women, said Beame. The first had happened in the Bronx and the second and third in Queens, half a block and about a month apart.

Whatever the goal of this press event, Taylor knew the mayor would show up to any occasion recorded by a camera now that he faced a difficult—impossible?—re-election campaign in the fall. Five Democrats were coming after him in the primary race. Beame was, after all, the man who'd almost bankrupted New York.

At the word *senseless*, the guy from the *New York Post* got up and ran out of the room, probably to tell his desk he had a big one coming. The *Post*'s reporter, short and dark-haired, returned two minutes later. Taylor didn't know him, which meant he was probably one of those imported by the paper's new owner, Australian press baron Rupert Murdoch. This story would suit Murdoch's strategy for the poor, ancient *Post*. Dive down-market as fast and as hard as possible.

Codd said police figured out the same gun was used in the homicides of three women after ballistics were run on the bullet that killed Voskerichian, a twenty-year-old Columbia University student who was walking home from the subway when she was shot in the face, a textbook held up to fend off the large caliber bullet. The gun was a Charter Arms Bulldog .44. Everyone wrote that down.

At this revelation, one of the two *Daily News* police beat reporters ran out for his call to alert his city desk. The *New York Times* reporter didn't move and probably wouldn't. He'd be lucky if his story made it into the paper.

"All New Yorkers have been shocked," said Beame.

Taylor doubted they were shocked yet, not in a city with a couple thousand murdered a year and the news of the connection only being given out this minute. Tomorrow would be a different story, as people read that the same man had murdered three women at night in two boroughs for apparently no reason. The circus was coming to town.

Phones were provided for the reporters—all the better to enlist the public's support, of course—and Taylor called in to the City News Bureau and reached Cramly, the small newswire's dyspeptic rewrite man and de facto editor.

"Take a page of copy to facsimile to the radio stations," Taylor said. "Everyone's here and this is getting out fast." Taylor read out six paragraphs he'd already written in his notebook.

"You think this guy's really hunting women?" Cramly said.

"That fact hasn't been established. It will be one of the many blanks the tabloids will fill in for us tomorrow morning." In fact, Taylor could hear the *Post* man next to him, the strangely stretched vowels of his Australian accent stretching the facts as far as they would go without breaking.

Cramly returned from the facsimile. A whisper and the slightest crackling came over the phone as he puffed one of today's cigars. "That wasn't bad." Even a compliment sounded like a complaint in Cramly's creaky voice. "Give me the rest for our newspaper clients."

Taylor did that, adding police were trying to link four injured since July by .44s, but so far, those crimes had not been connected using ballistics. Voskerichian had been shot at 7:30 p.m. Christine Freund, 26, had been killed sitting in a parked car in front of 1 Station Square in Queens on Jan. 30. A male companion wasn't hit. This all may have begun—police weren't sure—last July 29, when the same Charter Arms Bulldog revolver killed Donna Lauria and wounded Jody Valenti in the Pelham Bay neighborhood of the Bronx.

"The commissioner gave a description of someone they want to talk to, but wouldn't call the man a suspect. He's five feet ten to six feet, twenty-five to thirty years old, medium build, with dark hair combed back."

"A lot of those in New York."

"Cops want to talk to anybody who knows anybody owning a forty-four pistol."

"Probably a lot of those too."

"Fewer than men of that description, but yeah. A whole lot of guns in New York. All shapes and sizes."

"What are you going to do now?"

"Find a story."

"Find a story? You've got a fucking story."

"I've given you everything from the press conference. P.T. Barnum is setting up his tents. The *News* and the *Post* will put twenty reporters each on this, which means the Associated Press will get all those stories as will our clients. Our stations and papers want something they're *not* getting from the AP."

"You're supposed to be the hotshit police reporter."

"I can't stay ahead of forty others unless I'm on something they're not. That's not even counting the sideshow boys from TV and radio. I go after the stories no one else is doing. There's going to be even more of those now."

"We'll talk when you get back."

"Sure. Talk."

Taylor hung up, scanned the detective squad room that had been used for the press conference, and saw a guy working at a desk in the far corner. As Taylor arrived, the detective, with a bird-like face and horned-rimmed glasses, was talking on—more like at—a phone.

"I understand your concerns, ma'am," the detective said. "That's why we're making this announcement. That's why we're putting more people on the street." He listened. "Yes. Yes, I'll have someone come over and talk to your neighbor. Yes, feel free to call me back. Detective McCauley."

"Started already?"

"All-news radio put it right on. Phones are jumping. Neighbors who look like psychos. It's not gonna stop. How can I help?"

"Wondering if you got anything?"

He chuckled. "You're kidding, right?" McCauley looked behind Taylor at the chairs used for the news conference. "Weren't you listening to the big tops?"

"I was. What else is in?"

"Never fucking understand reporters. They want what you don't have. Don't want what you do have."

"This forty-four guy will get covered. Don't worry about that."

McCauley pulled a file off a stack. "This came in same night as Voskerichian. Martha Gibson. Twenty-four years old, Negro," he looked around to make sure it was okay to use his preferred word, "lived in a building in Richmond Hill. She came out of her sixth-floor apartment to dump trash down the chute. As she was heading back, a man bolted out of the stairway with a gun. She screamed and turned to run. God knows where. She was shot in the back and died on the way to the hospital."

"Robbery?"

"Purse and cash were in the apartment. She didn't know the killer."

"She talk before she died?"

"In the ambulance. Talked to a uniform riding in the wagon. Couldn't ID her killer. Last thing she said."

"Bet the gun wasn't a forty-four."

"Got that right. Thirty-two."

"What's the address?"

McCauley read off the street address: 115-99 89th Avenue. "Apartment Six Thirteen. Survived by her sister Abigail at that address and her parents in Bed-Stuy."

"Anything else that night?"

"Really? What's your angle on this?"

"I'm a police reporter. I do police stories."

"Yeah, and you want these when you heard we got this nut running around?"

"You been on a case when the press funhouse starts up?"

"More than once." He shook his head. "More than once. I already got my sergeant crawling up my ass, and he's got his lieutenant crawling up .... You get the idea. Not comfortable."

"Another thing happens is stories get missed. Even with

you guys working the cases, the press runs as a pack, chasing the one big bad guy. Victims deserve to get their stories told. The *News* and the *Post* are going to do a bang-up job with the victims of this forty-four guy. Probably too good. Families' privacy invaded. Photographers in backyards. They won't need my help with that."

"Whatever floats your boat. Here's the other from that night. Sixty-Ninth Avenue, the other side of Queens Boulevard. Tommy Noxon, sixteen, shot at six in the morning. Dead on the pavement."

"Thanks. I'll let you know if either ends up a story."

McCauley looked like he couldn't care less as he picked up his ringing phone.

Taylor walked out of the 112th Precinct, a big building because it was also Queens headquarters for the NYPD. The Eyewitless News van had already parked and men were pulling out wires and doing other TV sorts of things. The NewsCenter 4 van turned onto the street. All three rings of the circus were almost in place.

The temperature danced around 50 under a sharp blue sky, positively balmy after the second coldest winter on record in New York. He turned toward the Forest Hills subway stop, happy to breath the air of Queens—borough of his birth—and be done with the press conference.

There were two kinds of journalists in the world. Those who loved press conferences because they liked the protection of the herd. Everyone got the same quotes, the same facts.

Then there were those like Taylor—a minority, but he wasn't the only one—who loathed pressers. Men and women who wanted the story no one else had. He didn't doubt that journalists would get all sorts of scoops out of the .44-caliber killer, climbing over each other to get them. That wasn't the same as nailing the story no one else knew about. Like he'd told Cramly, chasing the man with the Charter Arms Bulldog revolver didn't make sense for the City News Bureau. City

News was a secondary wire service set up to give radio stations and suburban papers stories they weren't receiving from the Associated Press, which moved all the stories from its members, including the three New York papers. Sure as shit, the AP would stay on top of the story Beame and Codd put into the world with their announcement today.

CHAPTER 2

———◆———

A T THE FOREST Hills-71st Avenue subway stop, Taylor caught the E train. He'd have a short walk to the bus and then another to the late Martha Gibson's apartment building.

On the subway, he pulled the *Times* out of his Army field jacket. The coat was almost too heavy for today's weather. The cold of the winter had gotten so deep into his bones, he was still layering up, always finishing with the winter-issue military jacket, a gift from his late brother Billy. *Still* listed as MIA in Vietnam. Taylor knew he was dead, not missing. He wore the jacket until it was too warm to keep it on—a physical way to remember Billy. He needed it. His memories of his brother were fading. Clear scenes had become cloudy. Images of Billy at different ages were blurring and falling off into whatever hole swallowed memories.

He'd read the *News* over breakfast this morning because it had the best police coverage. The *Post*, the city's sole remaining afternoon paper, would be on the streets in a couple of hours, probably when he got back to Manhattan.

The *Times'* lead story—under a three-column, three-line all-caps head—was the invasion of three buildings in Washington by Hanafi Muslims. They'd killed one person, wounded 13 and held more than 150 hostages. Small bands of gunmen had taken over the B'nai Brith Headquarters, the Islamic Center and Mosque, and the District of Columbia city hall. Among their demands was cancellation of a movie about the prophet Mohammed.

International terrorists. All the domestic terror groups on the radical left. They and their bombs, kidnappings, and takeovers were a grim smear across the decade. How did so many grievances come into the world?

On the other side of the front page was a story reporting Beame had found the money to pay almost $1 billion in short-term debt and avoid default. Again. Taylor shook his head but held in a laugh so as not to become this subway car's reigning nutcase. The city had been threatening default since the fall of 1975, when then President Ford told the city to "Drop Dead," as the *News* neatly put it. Ford reversed himself, and the feds had been bailing and bailing ever since, like men in a rowboat with a hole they couldn't plug, with schemes and money shuffling and default deadlines and court rulings along the way. Taylor didn't think New York would ever be out of financial trouble—or not for some long time—nor would the city go belly up. It was simply an ongoing government-sanctioned Three-Card Monte game.

He'd had a big murder and police corruption story that was tangentially connected to the crisis in 1975, but even then, he couldn't get a handle on how the game was being played.

Martha Gibson's apartment building was six stories of redbrick at a corner, similar to the other buildings in the area. Those little white flowers that were the first to bloom in spring—snow-somethings—were sprinkled like snow itself in well-tended beds next to the building, their heads bent to the ground like they were embarrassed to be the first thing up after the long, miserable winter. A mix of contrasting bricks in the façade above the roofline—some sandstone-like, some even lighter—was the one thing that differentiated the building from its neighbors. Was it a decorative touch or did the builders run out of red bricks when they got near the top? It was the kind of question he'd never get answered; all sorts like it popped into his head all the time. Some ended up gaining a telling detail in a story. A few sent him after the big story itself. Like why was Martha Gibson gunned down, shot in the back, after throwing away her garbage?

Also at the top of the building, in the multi-colored part of the façade, were three seals or coats of arms set into the brickwork. He couldn't make them out—not even what they were made of. What house royal claimed 159-99 89th Ave?

No doorman, but a buzzer. He pressed the button for 613. Queens wasn't much of a doorman borough. That was for Manhattan, across the East River. Taylor could list many other differences between the two. He'd been born and raised in Queens and owned his first home here (firebombed by dirty cops; he'd been forced to sell when the contractors disappeared with his insurance money). Now, he and Samantha Callahan lived in a Murray Hill sublet, which probably meant another move was in their future. They'd had to take that place when their Brooklyn Heights landlord kicked them out to make room for a brother-in-law's family. He'd expected to hate living in Manhattan. Turned out the opposite. Manhattanites cracked him up. They were the best free show in town.

The lock buzzed. Taylor opened a front door of black wood with wrought-iron grillwork. He crossed the lobby to the elevators.

He'd been living the gypsy life for the past two years, and was now in his fourth place in his fourth New York borough. Only Staten Island remained. As he pushed the button to call the elevator, he shook his shoulders with an exaggerated chill at the thought of getting stuck on that island borough located closer to Jersey than New York. Where you commuted by ferryboat if you worked in Manhattan. He couldn't count ten stories—any stories, forget good stories—he'd covered on Staten Island. Even the crime was distant, different out there. Maybe because the cops and the mobsters lived cheek by jowl, and that kept things quiet. Taylor didn't care. He didn't want any part of the place.

The elevator rose to six.

Am I crazy doing this?

His gut tightened in answer to the question.

If he had a job at the *News* or the *Post,* they'd think he was completely nuts to care about Martha Gibson.

Maybe. It wasn't that he *couldn't* compete. He didn't want to. The .44-caliber guy wasn't the kind of story that had made his name. Victims no one cared about. Victims people had written off, or hadn't bothered to write a single word about. Telling those stories—that had been his business.

Still, the tightness running through his stomach felt like a warning. Could he still make a career out of what he was best at? For six months through the end of last year, he'd tried to get a job back on a big newspaper. The economy sucked. Taylor had disappeared from every editor's radar since his last paper, the *New York Messenger-Telegraph*, went out of business in the fall of 1975, right as the city's near bankruptcy and the recession were crushing businesses left and right. There were no journalism jobs when he looked. He started moping. His moping had driven Samantha crazy. It had even driven him crazy. He'd made a promise to himself and to Samantha. He'd quit the search, work at the little wire service, and do his kind of stories. His boss (and friend) Henry Novak didn't care, as long as the radio stations and suburban papers were happy to get what they couldn't from the AP or steal from the big dailies. Cramly complained. He always complained.

Taylor told his stomach to quit bitching. He'd made his decision. He had a story to do. The pain stayed. His stomach never listened.

The elevator doors opened. He walked around the hallway

until he found what he was looking for—the shadow of a murder. There was no chalk outline or police tape. This hadn't been a homicide for the movies. No big deal here. A large elongated stain in the light gray carpet marked where Martha had done her bleeding. Gray and red together turned into a muddy color that looked more like murder than the red of blood itself. A big dried splotch. A sickly, sour odor of death and dirt hovered over it.

On the right wall, four narrow slashes of red—from the fingers of a hand?—ran from about three feet up to the floor, looking like the start of one of those modern paintings that weren't of anything. His guess was that Martha Gibson had put her hand to the wound, gone for the wall for balance, and fallen to the floor. Detective McCauley had said Gibson was shot in the back. Unless Gibson reached around to the wound, the bullet must have exited from somewhere in the front of her torso. A .32 slug traveling all the way through the midsection? Killer had to be awfully close. Pretty much pointblank.

He walked from the bloodstain, checking the left wall and then the right. The hole was midway up on the right, circled in pen. He assumed the slug had been removed by the cops.

Taylor paced off the steps from apartment 613 to the trash chute. Fifty, and the trip went right past the stairwell door, which had a shoebox-sized window in it. The chute and the door were fifteen paces apart, and Gibson had dropped five paces farther on, give or take the difference in Taylor's and Gibson's strides.

The killer could have seen her through the window, jumped out after she dumped the garbage, and fired at extremely close range. The landing in the stairwell was clean, pink-painted cement. He walked down and back up, huffing a little as he reached the top. He'd found nothing along the way, which was no surprise. The cops would have done a good sweep of what was the likely escape route.

Taylor returned to Apartment 613. Aside from the steel

numbers attached with brass screws, the light-blue metal door had a wreath of plastic flowers surrounding the doorbell/peephole unit, a true New York signifier.

We need to know who you are before we open our doors.

Taylor pressed the bell once.

CHAPTER 3

———————◆———————

M ARTHA'S SISTER, ABIGAIL Gibson, answered the door.
Her eyes were reddened and sleepy looking.

"Everyday People" by Sly and the Family Stone played on a
stand-alone 8-track sitting on a milk carton.

How's it possible that song's almost a decade old?

"I'm Taylor with the City News Bureau. Doing a story on
your sister."

"I was here." She used one sleeve to wipe her nose. "Happened
right outside."

"See anything?"

"No, nothing." She found the couch and lolled back in the
corner, eyes closed. "Just the noise. The Fourth of July noise. I
came out. Gone. The ones that did it, gone. She was near gone."

"Did your sister work?"

Abigail paused to think, or do something. The song "I
Want to Take You Higher" came on next. *Stand!* was such an
amazing album, with "Don't Call Me Nigger, Whitey" pushing
hard against the tune playing now, like the jig was already up
on the sixties when the LP came out in the spring of '69.

"She worked." The subject of Martha perked her up a bit, but there was something off about her. "My sister was the smart one. A real hard worker." Her voice lowered. "Not like me. She got out of Bed-Stuy. Got her *bachelor of arts*," the last three words pronounced like they were mystical, a prayer, "from City College. If only that was enough. You can try and do it all but … was hired right after college by Manning Corp. Offices in *the* Empire State Building. Went from secretary to sales in two months. That's hard with all the prejudice. 'Course she was promoted to call on their Black clients."

"Was she well liked at Manning? Any enemies, anyone angry at her?"

"She lost that job a few months ago. The boss man in charge had this habit of putting his hands on her. All over. She told him to stop. I told her to put up with a bit of it. Teasing him along some. It's what happens if you want a job. Didn't she want to stay out of secretarial pools? Nope, not Martha. He came on real strong. She said no. He fired her."

"Real strong?"

"Groping. Six sets of hands. Dirty suggestions. What men do. Like I said, she was expected to put up with it. Should have. Wouldn't. He booted her."

"What's the boss's name?"

"Ricky MacDonald."

"Was she working when she died?"

"Martha wasn't one to give up. With her bachelor of arts in history and economics, she was hired as a maid by the DeVries family on Park Avenue. Eight Twenty-Seven Park. Big old apartment. College degree stuck cleaning toilets. She wouldn't let it get her down. It was paying our bills. She kept visiting offices for interviews, offices that pretty much said no soon as they saw her. She knew why. Racial prejudice. Wouldn't admit to it. Mr. DeVries up there on Park Avenue was nice to her. Sent her to a couple of jobs he heard about. The wife there was tougher—wanted everything done one way and only one way in her house. There's a son and a daughter, grown and living at home. The son sounded like a brat. Martha told me there were some dark secrets in that family, but she wasn't sure what was going on. Or probably Martha didn't trust me to know."

"I know this part is painful—"

"It's all painful. You new at this job?"

She was right. It was all painful for the family. There were phrases you were simply supposed to say anyway.

"I'm sorry. I know it is. Did the police tell you how she died?"

"Some bastard ambushed her dumping the garbage. Shot her in the hallway."

"The killer lay in wait and came out of the stairwell after she returned from the chute. He must have been targeting her. That means a plan and a motive. Who would want to murder your sister?"

"No one." Abigail began weeping. Her head tipped to one side like she couldn't quite control her neck. Taylor looked for a box of tissues, but saw it was on a side table next to the couch. He waited.

After wiping her eyes, she said, "Makes *no* sense, someone doing that to her. She picked this neighborhood because it was safe. She worked hard to stay here."

'Makes no sense.' The unending chorus of the families of the murdered.

Abigail went to a small black table crowded with pictures and handed him a portrait of a pretty, Black woman in a black graduation gown looking over her shoulder as people did in such shots. Her smile was on the edge of laughter, like she'd cracked up right after the shutter snapped. The eyes, a deep brown almost-black, were in on the joke, crinkled at their corners. Her hair was parted in the middle, wavy and thick, falling down around her shoulders.

"You don't understand. Martha didn't make enemies. She didn't make mistakes. Her high principles wouldn't allow her to stay at Manning. She moved on. She was going to get another office job. She was going to do whatever she wanted."

Abigail had probably been sitting here for two days, waiting for someone to tell this to. "I don't have a job …. She was taking care of me."

The phone rang. Abigail went to the kitchen to get it. The low mumbled conversation lasted a couple of minutes.

"That was her boss, Mr. DeVries. He wanted to know if I was okay. If I needed anything. I said I couldn't think now. I'd let him know."

Shows a lot of concern for the sister of a murdered maid. Is that normal?

Taylor didn't know. He didn't know much about big Park Avenue apartments and the maids working for the families inside them. The police beat rarely took him to such homes. Maybe this DeVries was being a good human being. Good people lived at all sorts of addresses in New York City. Still, he circled the name and address in his notebook. A visit to the victim's workplace was always worthwhile.

He lifted his head from the pad, and as he did, Abigail, who was absently scratching her lower arm, yanked the sleeve of her thin red sweater all the way down, holding it in place with her fingertips. Before she could get her arm covered, Taylor caught sight of bruised blotches—the ruptures of needle tracks.

Drugs got you killed in New York City. Easy. All the time. Mess with the wrong pusher. Owe too much. Turn snitch or get accused of same. He observed Abigail with fresh eyes. He'd taken her for too thin and not thought much of it, but there were hollows in her cheeks and dark patches under her eyes. She'd been slumped on the couch and slow in her speech, which he'd thought was grief. Those were also signs of being high.

"You live here too, then?"

"When I'm not at my boyfriend's."

"When is that?"

"Here two or three nights a week. My boyfriend never comes over. Martha wouldn't allow it."

Without the thinning of the face and the dark areas under the eyes, she resembled Martha—as far as you could tell from a photo. Abigail's hair was pulled back, so it was hard to guess at length.

"Do you think you two looked alike?"

"Some say. We didn't think so."

"Could a killer have been gunning for you?"

"Me?"

"Lotta guns and gunmen circling the heroin business."

"Get out of here." She stood, swayed, steadied herself.

"You have a habit. That's clear. Do the cops know? Where'd you buy your smack?" She walked over to the door and pulled it open. "If it was a case of mistaken identity, the killers will come back. You're in danger."

"Get the fuck out of here. You didn't come to help anyone."

"I'm trying to figure out what really happened to your sister."

Taylor stood for a moment near the doorway, hoping she'd have a change of heart. There was a three-shelf cherry bookcase next to the door. An economics textbook. Books on the Napoleonic Wars and Elizabethan Britain. *The Invisible Man. A Raisin in the Sun.* A calculus textbook. *Native Son.*

He moved closer and brushed his fingers across the spines. Some were emblems of her college education, one that had been hard won. He doubted the books by the Black authors had been taught at City College. He knew all the titles and had read a couple, back when the riots in Harlem first broke out, hoping to better understand the anger. It was one way he'd tried to get underneath what was going on. It'd helped a little, but not enough. He'd needed to talk to Black people in their neighborhoods—not just the cops and those arrested. Even down at the level of a police reporter there was a White city and a Black city. He knew too little of the Black city.

What was Martha trying to learn or understand or affirm by reading these books? He'd like to ask Abigail.

She didn't have a change of heart. She jabbed a finger toward the hallway and he stepped outside. The door slammed.

He might have asked his father, the City College English professor, at least about literary views on the books. Too bad his father was in a coma, dying from liver failure. Standing in the hallway, he wrote down the titles. Maybe they meant Martha was interested in how she fit—or was supposed to fit, or was supposed to avoid fitting—as a Black in New York City—or anywhere for that matter. That was a topic Taylor knew nothing about. In reporting, there was one answer for ignorance. Interviews, lots of interviews.

Virginia Voskerichian, the latest victim of the killer using a .44-caliber gun, had been getting her college degree, still attending the much more upscale Columbia, coming home from classes when she was shot here in Queens. There seemed to be as little motivation in Martha Gibson's murder as in those killings done by the guy carrying the Charter Arms Bulldog .44. Someone wanted Gibson to go away, and she had.

He walked the scene one more time and took detailed notes about how he saw the ambush happening. He'd need to check his take on it with the cops, but it was always a better plan to try and confirm a theory than to ask the detectives cold what happened and hope they were in a generous mood. Detectives liked knocking down reporters' theories or taking them in other directions. He learned more that way, even when he was dead wrong.

Always make 'em feel smarter.

He walked the stairway one more time, for the hell of it, and came across more nothing. He called into the office from a payphone in the apartment building's lobby. Novak got on.

"This is some stuff about this forty-four guy."

Here we go.

"It's something."

"What have you got?"

"I filed everything with Cramly. I gave Cramly stuff I don't usually put in a shooting story. You think they've made an arrest in the last hour?"

"What's your angle?"

"I don't have an angle. I'm looking into a woman murdered the same night. In the hallway of her apartment building. She was single, working, trying to make her way in the city. College degree but stuck in a maid's job. No one else has this one."

"But this crazed gunman—"

Taylor exhaled loudly. "The police find a cigarette butt that's related to the story, they'll announce it. The AP will put it out and our clients *all* have the AP. I don't jump on bandwagons. You know that. I report surprises."

"Taylor's always Taylor. Okay, keep one eye on it for me please. I don't want to hear from our clients."

"You won't. Remember half the stories in the *Post* are made up now that Murdoch owns it. Might as well be crime fiction, though the *Post* stories are probably better written than most crime fiction. No flipping out because the *Post* has some fantastic story. Fantastic because it's fantasy."

"Okay, all right. Stay in touch. File soon."

"I always do."

CHAPTER 4

O NE OF THE two doormen at 827 Park Avenue said he
would have to call up to the DeVries' residence first.

*Residence. There's a word I've never used to describe a place
I've lived.*

The other doorman was hailing a cab for a straight-backed
old woman in a purple coat. Both men wore white shirts,
striped ties that looked like they came from a prep school,
crisply pressed blue slacks with gold stripes down the side, and
jackets with more stripes. The uniform made Taylor wonder if
doormen had ranks. Maybe he'd spent too much time dealing
with cops.

When the doorman asked what Taylor's business was, Taylor
said, "Reporter. I'm doing a story on Martha Gibson. She
worked as a maid for the family."

The doorman looked taken aback, but it was hard to know
whether it was because of the mention of the dead woman or
of a news story.

Mickey, that was the doorman's name, walked Taylor across
a lobby of polished brass with wood furniture that it seemed no

one ever sat in. Evenly spaced lamps provided evenly spaced lighting. Mickey pushed the button for the elevator.

"Which apartment?" Taylor said.

"The Eighth Floor."

"Number?"

"The entire floor. Each family owns a floor."

"I guess *residence* makes sense then."

Mickey left him at the elevator without comment. Taylor stepped in, and the operator closed the outer door and the inner iron gate and slammed the elevator's control to the up position like he was driving at Daytona. The mirrored, ornate elevator began to climb. Taylor pushed his hand through his short brown hair a couple of times to neaten it. He was a comb-once-a-day guy. Did it matter? He doubted an Army field jacket made the grade at 827 Park Avenue.

The lift opened directly on a foyer—no hallway or door. The elevator *was* the front door to this place. A man dressed to the nines—maybe the elevens—greeted him. Was this *a* butler? *The* butler?

"Mr. DeVries will be happy to meet with you. Do you have a card I can take in to him?"

He held out a sliver tray.

"A business card?"

A nod.

Taylor had run out six months ago, and Novak hadn't ordered more. Probably couldn't afford to. Taylor dropped his NYPD press credentials on the tray.

A minute later, the butler returned and offered the pass back. "Follow me, please."

They walked through a couple of living rooms, a dining room, a room Taylor couldn't figure the purpose of, and finally entered what must be the library. Bookshelves stained a rich oak brown extended from floor to ceiling. Books were jammed horizontally in the spaces above books. Books were stacked neatly on the floor.

A man with thick gray hair that still bore traces of its original black rose from one of three leather reading chairs.

"Edmond DeVries, Mr. Taylor."

He squeezed Taylor's hand firmly. DeVries wore striped gray slacks—his legs were even longer than Taylor's—and a pink-striped dress shirt with light-green V-neck sweater. He was tall all the way up.

"Taylor will do."

DeVries smiled.

"Was that an actual NYPD press pass?"

"Actual as they get."

"I remember the ones they had decades ago. Stuck in the brims of the reporters' hats with *press* along the top of the card. They still show 'em in the movies."

"Gone a long time. Not many of us wearing hats anymore."

"Shame, the death of the man's hat." He settled back into his seat and stretched. His penny-less brown penny loafers were polished to a high shine. "Please have a seat. I'm sorry about the mess."

The stacks of books didn't qualify as a mess in Taylor's world. Taylor would need to own a lot more books—a lot more anything—to make any sort of a mess.

"What is the City News Bureau?"

"A local wire."

"Do you remember *Wire Service*? TV show in the fifties about the Trans-Global Wire Service. Every week followed one of three reporters on a story with life or death consequences. Dane Clark was in it."

"I do. Bit before I got into the business. More glamour than I'm used to."

"I loved so many of the early TV shows. *Bonanza, Perry Mason.* How about *Justice*? Legal Aid Society lawyers helping the indigent in New York. The medium was new, so the networks were willing to experiment. Now they've figured it out, and the shows aren't as different, as interesting. The new is gone. Well, an old man's opinion."

He turned and pointed to a reel-to-reel tape deck with boxes of tapes stacked next to it. "See those?"

Taylor nodded.

"My collection of radio shows. The original *Gunsmoke*. The original *Dragnet*. Plus *The Shadow, X Minus One, Night Beat* …. I could bore you forever. Now, here was the first, true experimentation. The very beginning of drama over the airways. Whatever they tried had never been done before. I have to buy them from the few collectors around. They'll all be gone soon."

If asked to guess beforehand, Taylor would have said Edmond DeVries of 827 Park Avenue spent his evenings at the ballet and the opera, not listening to tapes of old radio shows and reminiscing about TV from the fifties. Stereotypes had a bad way of making you wrong.

The smile faded from DeVries' handsome, strong-boned face. "We were very sorry to hear about Martha. It's a terrible tragedy. How can I help?"

"Someone went after her. It's like she was targeted. Would anyone from her work life have reason to want her killed? Her sister doesn't have any ideas for me."

"Lord, I can't imagine. She was a good employee. A great one. Friendly. Helpful. We had no problems."

The butler came into the room. "Would you like anything, sir?"

DeVries checked his watch. "Hmm. One thirty-five. A little early. Still in all, tragic loss demands we bend the rules. Will you join me in a bit of an Irish wake for Martha? The Irish do know how to bury their dead. Whisky and wailing. In my family, we're only allowed to dab at the eyes a bit."

"I'll have a beer if one's available."

"We can offer all sorts, sir," said the butler.

Taylor was too embarrassed to ask for a seven-ounce Rolling

Rock—his preference—because he doubted they had it back in the big fridge in the big kitchen. Sticking to little bottles of beers was one of his drinking rules—Rule Number One, actually—insurance against his father's alcoholism.

"Anything you have will be fine."

The butler went off.

DeVries returned to the topic. "I really can't think of anyone or anything I know of that would cause someone to attack Martha."

"Her sister mentioned you were helping her with job interviews."

The gray eyebrows rose. "You think that had something to do with her death?"

"No. Reporter's curiosity. Helping a good employee go elsewhere isn't the usual practice."

"Martha was quite the smart one. A college degree. I knew she had to make money, and that's why she was here with us." A small smile. "I also believed she could do better, so made a few inquiries. There's so much prejudice in this town …." He left the last hanging like Taylor should automatically understand what happened to those job interviews. "Martha's sister could come up with nothing?"

"One idea came from her, though she didn't offer it. There might be drugs involved."

"Martha on drugs?" A shake of the head. "I don't believe it."

"No, the sister. She's an addict. The two women look enough alike. Drugs draw violence."

The butler entered and handed DeVries a mixed drink and a newspaper folded on a larger silver tray. Taylor received a long-necked bottle of Rheingold.

DeVries set the paper aside and sipped the drink, staring off into the distance, somewhere beyond the bookshelves.

"Could have done so many things. A terrible way to die."

They drank in silence for a couple of minutes. DeVries picked up the *Post*, whose first edition had been hitting the streets

in the past half hour, and read out the front-page headline,
" 'Co-ed's Killer May Strike Again.' Good God, it sounds like a
promise. Have you heard about this?"

"I covered the press conference."

"What's the story?" He set the *Post* aside.

"Killer's targeted young women so far. Three murders since
late July linked to the same gun. This one will be getting a
whole bunch of coverage."

"Yet you're doing a story on Martha?"

"Happened the same night. Makes sense to see what
happened."

DeVries didn't ask why. His look said he got it.

"You know, my family used to be in the newspaper business.
We had a stake in the *New York Sun* until it went under in
1950."

"The 'Yes Virginia' editorial."

"Indeed, a front-page editorial affirming the existence of
Santa Claus in exquisite language. Yet, it said more. Affirmed
the idea of hope. That paper did some good things. We were
also investors in the *Messenger-Telegram*."

"With the Garfields?"

"A minority stake."

"We share that connection, in a way. The *Messenger-Telegram*
was my first and last newspaper job—last, so far, at least. Hired
there when I was seventeen. Walked out when the paper died."

"The youngest generation of Garfields were great editors,
but not so good at business. The economy didn't help. We lost
our investment in the *MT*. Ah well, only money."

"Yes, *only* money." The man who'd spoken was in his late
twenties, early thirties. He was a less-handsome carbon copy
of Edmond DeVries—like a carbon that had been blurred. He
leaned against the entrance to the library. "Throwing away
money that's supposed to stay in our family."

"This is my son Charlie. Proof that breeding and education
do not beget manners."

"Oh, screw that old stuff. Mother called. You're to go down and make sure the new suit fits for tonight."

"Taylor is doing a story on Martha."

"What do *we* have to do with it?"

"Just getting all the facts about her," Taylor said.

Charlie laughed. "There can hardly be any facts about her death around here."

DeVries escorted Taylor to the elevator and gave a quick wave as the door shut. While the car descended, Taylor had an odd vision of how that nice, intelligent man spent his days: sitting with his books in the library, waiting for someone to come talk with him about his many different interests. His son Charlie probably wasn't one of those people.

Chapter 5

FATHERS AND SONS. Were they always a mess? Okay, so maybe the DeVrieses weren't a mess. He'd only had the one encounter. Maybe they got along fine most of the time. An apartment that took up an entire floor and the money to back it up. That could help you get along with most anyone.

His next stop was Roosevelt Hospital, where his own father lay as his liver prepared to fail after a lifetime of serious abuse. The Professor hadn't opened his eyes the last three nights. This wasn't a loss, really. For as long as he'd been conscious since his admission two weeks ago, he'd somehow mustered a look of angry disgust directed at Taylor—and Samantha and the nurses and anyone else.

Credit Samantha, who he'd lived with for more than a year. She visited every night Taylor did, though he'd told her she could stay away. She said she could take it. She was made of strong stuff, stronger than his father, who'd drunk his way through life's problems, little and large. Problems? In '75, Samantha had to deal with the killing of her father and the revelation he was a corrupt cop. It was why she'd been forced to leave the NYPD and become a private investigator. They'd met then, when Samantha was a story for Taylor. She was far more than that now. Taylor clenched his fists, palms sweaty. Why did thinking poorly of a man who didn't love him still make him guilty? He didn't want to face the anger tonight, and he felt all the worse for that.

He and his father hadn't had any sort of relationship since Billy died in Vietnam. They'd stayed away from each other. The drinking turned into multi-day binges. Somehow, the Professor had kept teaching.

Taylor's childhood had been worse. Scalding abuse, delivered in an educated man's vocabulary, followed by long silences when *everyone* had to be quiet. A misery. If it was a really good drinking session—and, therefore, a really bad night— they'd all get to hear the complete recitation of "Christabel" or something else by Samuel Taylor Coleridge. Been forced to listen. Billy would fall asleep, get smacked awake. His mother would clean the kitchen with the care of someone disarming a bomb. Taylor would listen to the words like they offered a code that would help him figure out his father. They never did.

At the end, before this final stay in the hospital, even Taylor's efforts to help his father, his efforts as the man's only living relative, were rebuffed with fury and abuse.

He walked in the hospital's front door and signed in as a visitor. A news story was always his escape from the guilt and the pain. Where should he go with this murder? One approach he often used was to profile the victim, so the world—or the small part of it that read or heard his stories—would know who was lost. He didn't have enough on Martha Gibson for that yet, much less an idea for why she was killed. The latter was the key to his best stories. Readers and listeners wanted some kind of closure. Made sense. Without it, all he was giving them was a well-written obit. He needed to report the cause, what was going on, and if possible, who.

So, next steps?

He stopped to write in his notebook before heading to the elevator.

Interview the sister again to see if there was more to the drug angle. He'd have to get in the front door first. Was it a case of mistaken identity? A woman murdered over drugs when she wasn't the addict? An irony, yes, but not the kind that would grab much attention in New York.

Martha'd had that white-collar job with Manning Corp, up in the Empire State Building. She'd been fired because the boss propositioned her and she wouldn't go along. Couldn't hurt to interview him to see the guy's head spin some. Sometimes an interview was worth doing for that reason alone.

Last, he had the DeVries family. Mr. DeVries didn't seem to know anything. The butler, cook, and others who worked in the *residence* with Martha might have heard or seen things DeVries hadn't. He'd bet DeVries would see him again, and maybe he could find a way to talk to the staff during his visit.

There was that one thing Abigail Gibson had said that stood out. Martha had told her there were "dark secrets" in the DeVries household, but she didn't know what they were. Or she wouldn't say to Abigail. That wasn't enough to interview DeVries about, but if he could get Abigail to recall something— maybe when she was less doped up—he'd have a lead. Or a dead end. To a maid in a rich household, a dark secret could as easily be a nutty great-aunt in the attic (or a backroom) as a murder plot.

He really wanted to go back to the Park Avenue apartment out of a reporter's pure curiosity. The DeVrieses lived in the antique-furnitured, libraried, doormanned, butlered part of Manhattan he never got a look at. He was a collector of any and all scenes of New York. How else was he supposed to describe the city—the crimes in the city—without seeing into all its corners? A habit of the job. No, more than that. A passion.

He closed the notebook. His interview list was finished, but had no clear direction. The muscles across his back tightened.

He'd loosen up at judo tonight, a class Samantha had insisted they both start ten months ago. She'd wanted him to do it because he'd given up carrying an ankle-holstered .32. The reason? He was a terrible shot. The gun was more a threat than protection. She, on the other hand, was studying the discipline because the police academy intentionally stinted on hand-to-hand combat training for female recruits, even though they'd been riding on patrol since 1972.

The Professor died sometime between the interview list and Taylor's ride on the elevator. It had just happened.

Samantha ran from the door to the room and grabbed Taylor in a tight hug. "He's gone."

"I'm sorry," they said at the same time.

"There's nothing for you to be sorry about," she added.

"Things he said. The way he treated you."

"I had a short run compared with what you lived through. Remember, my dad messed up my life. Peas in a pod, you and I. We're both getting through it." She stepped back and grabbed tight the sleeves of his dead brother's Army jacket. "You've still got family. You've got me. You've got Grandpop."

"I do. It's been you and Grandpop for a good long while now."

"And Mason."

"Right." A small smile. "The dumbest Labrador in New York."

"What's dumb when you've got love?" she said as they walked toward the room. "They said he went quietly."

"That was a change."

Inside the room, his father's mouth was slack-jawed open, the skin of his face gray and flaking, his thinning white hair still parted in the middle. Taylor wasn't sure what memory he wanted to carry with him of his father, but this wasn't it. He left the room after one look.

"I'll check with the nurse, and we'll get out of here."

At the desk, he signed papers.

The nurse handed him an envelope. "He said to give this to whoever took care of things."

"Right, *whoever*." Taylor shook his head. "Couldn't use my name. Who else would bother?"

The envelope read, "My Will."

Aside from the will, there was a short letter addressed, "To whom it may concern."

Getting close to no one.

> My body will be cremated at Carmichael's Mortuary on 98th Street. There were will no religious or memorial service whatsoever. My ashes will be kept at the Broadway Bar & Grill on 87th Street and Broadway. As is stipulated in my will, Bethany Griffin, the bartender there, is executrix and beneficiary. She was always quite kind with the buybacks—and that is truly a great kindness.

> A damsel with a dulcimer
> In a vision once I saw:
> It was an Abyssinian maid
> And on her dulcimer she played,
> Singing of Mount Abora.
> Could I revive within me
> Her symphony and song,
> To such a deep delight 'twould win me,
> That with music loud and long,
> I would build that dome in air,
> That sunny dome! those caves of ice!
> And all who heard should see them there,
> And all should cry, Beware! Beware!
> His flashing eyes, his floating hair!
> Weave a circle round him thrice,
> And close your eyes with holy dread
> For he on honey-dew hath fed,

And drunk the milk of Paradise.

In expectation my wishes will be closely respected, and these exquisite words of poesy will fall on the deafest of ears.

Malcolm T. Taylor

Taylor handed the note to Samantha.

"A Coleridge poem, I assume."

"Lines from 'Kubla Kahn.' Which is a fragment. Came to Coleridge in an opium-induced dream, but he was interrupted when writing the words down, and he could never finish. One addict quoting another. Maybe my father decided to be honest at the end."

"Or maybe he believed this line about 'milk of Paradise.' "

"Just as likely."

"He hurt you even at the finish." She shook her head, her pale cheeks flushing with anger. She grabbed his hand hard, almost violently, then released the pressure. "Naming his bartender to handle the will."

Taylor laughed, low and dark, as he flipped through the five-page document. "May have tried to hurt me. There's little money and all of that will go to pay his medical bills. He was always investing in the schemes of his bar buddies. Played the numbers. He didn't save. His pension would only pay out to my late mother. Made a point of telling me that once. He was off on sick days, about to move on to medical leave. So there's probably one paycheck coming, which will take care of the cremation. That is, after I pay for it and if this Bethany will give up the money. The apartment is full of books and garbage. More garbage than books. It will cost to clean it up. No, he didn't hurt me with this. He stopped hurting me long ago."

That's not really true. Long ago still hurts now.

He talked to the nurse about getting the body to Carmichael's. Back on the elevator, Taylor fiddled with the frayed edge of the field jacket's sleeve. His father's last will and testament really did cause him no pain, but the Professor's death opened a different pit of hurt. He missed Billy; God, he missed him so much now. Only he and Billy could really talk about this. He swallowed against a dry throat. Taylor had lately been going days, sometimes a week, without thinking of Billy, and the realization would jump him like a mugger. When Billy first went MIA, the sense of loss, a shadowy absence, a gap in his world, never went away. Relief in the form of an hour or two came after a while, which was probably for the good. However, there was a huge difference between getting on with your life and forgetting.

The death mask of his father was replaced by the memory of Billy's young face—ten years younger than Taylor's—proud and smiling. He wore the uniform of the 10th Mountain. Why was it getting so hard to recall all the many other memories—what Billy looked like after his second tour, after second grade? The kid *chose* Vietnam when most other kids chose just about anything else. Despite their age difference, they were always allies in the ongoing struggle to live through the Professor's drinking. Now, he wanted, needed, Billy back to go over it all— the verbal abuse, their mother crying early in the morning before they were supposed to be awake, Billy's decision to run to the bad war as the better option than dinner in their kitchen.

There was the good Billy represented. He missed the good. When Billy was a kid, there wasn't a story Taylor wrote that Billy hadn't read as soon as the paper got to the house. That continued any day Billy was home on leave. *My brother the big-time newspaper reporter* wasn't sarcasm. It was sincerely meant and the exact opposite of the Professor's verdict: a scribbler with a high school degree wasting his life. No, the last insult with the letter and the will didn't bother Taylor; everything before that did.

Samantha insisted on springing for a cab to get to their Murray Hill apartment.

Her warm body leaned against his side, her auburn hair spilling across his jacket. He kept few secrets from her. This, *this* wasn't a secret. This was only something he could talk about with Billy, the Billy he didn't think about for a week at a time now. All around him, people were forgetting the Vietnam War as best they could. The U.S. had pulled out in 1973, and North Vietnam had won the war two years later. Now, in 1977, people wanted to believe the war the U.S. couldn't win maybe hadn't happened. They danced out of the way of vets begging on the street. The veterans were failures, like the war, to be ignored, avoided, and despised. Didn't matter how much sacrifice. America only loved a winner.

Billy was the only witness to what Taylor had gone through with their father right up until Billy had gone off to war. There was no one left to acknowledge what kind of father the Professor had been—no hope of that. He could tell the stories, tell them even to Samantha, but not to anyone who'd lived through his wrecked and frightening childhood. The loneliness of that idea hollowed him out. *Billy's dead.* And it seemed like Billy was deader than his father, like there were different grades of death. He could do nothing for himself. Of all things, this kindled a light in the empty darkness inside him. For Taylor, it was always about telling the stories of victims—victims no else cared about. If his witness was gone, his duty to witness for others was all the more important. The stories he wrote to illuminate a life, and maybe, sometimes, bring justice.

IN SEARCH OF distraction, Taylor took out the Wall Street Final edition of the *New York Post* he'd picked up outside the hospital. Well, a drink would work too, but he'd skip even one seven-ounce beer the day his father died after a life of vodka mixed with not much else. On page four, the *Post* gave prominent display to the location of the funeral chapel for the services for Virginia Voskerichian and the cemetery where she'd be buried. Lower down, Mayor Beame said he was ordering a police detail assigned to the Voskerichian funeral to protect the family from curiosity seekers. The *Post* didn't see the need to draw a connection between touting the location and the assignment of cops. Murdoch's paper had the same sense of irony as Taylor's father.

THREE DAYS LATER, Taylor went to the Broadway Bar & Grill with a box of ashes and the will. He'd called ahead to confirm Bethany would be behind the bar. Samantha was working a divorce investigation for her employer, Raymond & Associates, Investigators. The investigators totaled two—Samantha and her boss, Lew Raymond, radio detective turned real-life detective.

Taylor was opening his mouth to offer to take care of cleaning out the apartment when Bethany snatched the will from this hand.

"There's not really much," he said.

"I'm the executrix *and* beneficiary?" She was chunky and wore green hot pants and a red-striped tube top. The bar had to be 80 degrees of humid steam heat. A little tropical paradise in March on the Upper West Side.

"You are. He appreciated all the buybacks. Drinking killed him."

"Is that right? He owed me twenty-five bucks."

Taylor didn't reach for his wallet. "He asked that the ashes reside here at the bar."

"I can't put them up there."

Taylor looked at the box. If there was one thing he had to do, it was take care of his father's last wish. It was a law of the universe.

"Somewhere else?"

She thought—and that looked like it took an effort—eying the box.

"I can take care of what he owed."

"I'm beginning to see possibilities."

"Fifty."

"In the back is a shelf with some old darts trophies. No one plays anymore. No one does anything but a shot and a beer anymore. Put it there."

Taylor wrote out a check while she watched with a smile that wasn't kind.

He drank one Rolling Rock pony. Took the whole beer for her to read to Page Three of the will.

He was at the door when she stopped him.

"Hold on. Did you read all this?"

"Yes."

"At the bottom of the paragraph that says I'm beneficiary, it says except for one thing."

"Yeah, I know. His poetry books. They're supposed to be mine. You can have them."

"They worth anything?"

"Big collection. Might get you to paradise."

"Is there any money?"

"Not really. Most of what's left needs to go for the medical bills. I'm owed three hundred twenty-five dollars for the cremation. I was hoping to get that from the estate."

"This isn't really much of a tip. I'll get back to you."

There was a call Taylor didn't expect to receive.

CHAPTER 6

———◆———

TAYLOR LOST MOST of a week before getting back to the Martha Gibson story. He had to deal with his father's death, taking one day off because Novak insisted, though he spent that day searching the Professor's apartment for anything of his brother's before Bethany got the key. He found three black and white pictures from a trip to Jones Beach, a high school yearbook, a medal he'd have to research, and the telegram saying Billy went missing. That appeared to be the complete collection of his father's family memorabilia.

Three workdays were chewed up pursuing a bank robbery, a mugging turned murder, and rewriting the usual collection of soft press releases into minor features. He turned one around on the Bronx Zoo, which was opening a Wild Asia section on 38 acres of undeveloped land, complete with a monorail tour of a habitat featuring elephants, lions, tigers, and rhinoceroses.

In Manhattan, something called the Big Apple Circus had set up for the first time under a tent in Battery Park.

"We're an old fashioned one-ring show," the ringmaster said in a phone interview.

You're not the only circus in town.

ABIGAIL GIBSON OFFERED the long-used New York greeting. She opened the door with the chain still on—not a good sign—and peered at Taylor through the two-inch gap with black eyes that had a telltale glassy appearance.

"Aren't you the dude who was asking the wrong sorts of questions last time? What do you want now?"

Her speech was slurred. Though he'd already been near certain after his last visit, her condition now confirmed for Taylor that New York's scourge of choice, heroin, was also Abigail's. Every third murder he looked into was connected to smack.

Shit, how am I going to get anything out of her?

"I want to tell the story of your sister's life, not just her death. I need to talk to you for that."

The door shut. Re-opened with the chain still on. "We only talk about Martha. Nothing else."

"Yeah, sure."

The chain came off. The door didn't move, so Taylor had to push. Abigail was already at a round plastic table, scooping up a big glass ashtray and heading to the kitchen. Taylor caught a glimpse of the hypodermic needle. He could guess the rest of an addict's works were in the ashtray. The Sly and the Family Stone album from last time played again. Was that a junkie thing, playing the same music over and over?

Best I can hope for is she shot up a good while ago. If not, she'll doze off. Or not remember anything helpful.

Taylor sat down on a white wooden stool covered with a pleated cushion. Abigail settled into a red canvas butterfly chair, more like was swallowed by it—the perfect place for a junkie's doze. Her face wore a slack smile.

"When I was last here, you said your sister talked about the DeVries family having dark secrets."

"That's all she said. Didn't I tell you that? She didn't trust me.

Not a bit." *Anger. Good, maybe that will keep her focused.* "She didn't tell me what was going on."

"Why didn't she trust you? Your habit?"

"You said we weren't talking about anything else. I'll kick you out again."

"Yeah, you can kick me out. You care about your sister's memory? Anyone else trying to figure out why she was shot?"

The anger stayed with her, giving her a more awake, alive demeanor than last time. "My sister was a snob with that college degree. Those months working up in an Empire State Building office made her the biggest of the big. She didn't change any after she got fired either. If you didn't measure up to *her* standards, she treated you different."

"She let you live here."

"She said she was trying to help me." *Wasn't getting far.* "Wouldn't give me any money, though. She didn't trust me, but I heard things."

"Like what?"

The smile changed, more sly than slack. "A phone call. It was someone from that family she worked for—"

"How do you know?"

"I answered. I know the way those White people talk."

"Who was it?"

"A man's voice. He wanted her to come out and meet him somewhere. She refused. She got anxious. She said, 'I didn't overhear a conversation at the residence. I don't know who was in there.' Her voice got low, but I was right around the corner there." Abigail pointed to the entryway to the kitchen. " 'I just want the job, not trouble.' She set the phone down, and she was wiping away tears when she came back in here."

"Did she say for sure it was a member of the DeVries family?"

"No. But I know how White people—"

"There are a lot of White people."

"Yeah, but she mentioned her job on the call."

Abigail's not stupid.

The lock above the knob to the front door snapped to the left. Taylor had put the chain back on. New Yorker's instinct. Abigail, struggling as if the butterfly chair held her in its clutches, finally got up and raced to the door like her life depended on it, took off the chain, and opened the door without checking.

A tall, slight Black man in flared jeans and a red-checked shirt with the sheen of polyester entered and stopped a step inside the small living room.

"Who the fuck is this?"

"He's that reporter I told you about." She turned to Taylor, who was already rising. "This is Jerome."

"Taylor with the City News Bureau."

Jerome passed close to Taylor, almost close enough to collide, and dropped down in the middle of the tan corduroy couch and spread his arms to claim the whole thing. Abigail went back to the butterfly chair.

"The fuck's a City News Bureau?"

"A wire service for radio stations and newspapers."

"Whitey news."

"We've got a jazz station—"

"You think I care about jazz, asshole?"

"I don't know what you care about. Just mentioning. What *I* care about is Martha Gibson's murder."

"The apartment goes to Abigail."

"I'm not worried about the apartment …." Then Taylor got it. "It's rent-controlled?"

"We're not talking any private family business with you. Like I said, this apartment goes to Abigail."

Taylor knew of serious fights—trips to the hospital—over who ended up with the lease on a rent-controlled flat. There'd even been a couple of murders. The locked-in, regulated low rents were valuable enough to make people crazy. Leases were handed down through families. Could that be the motive for the crime in the hallway outside a week ago? Taylor needed a read on Jerome fast.

"Can I get your last name?"

"Fuck no. Why are you really nosing around?"

"Said why. Trying to figure out why Martha was killed. Starting to wonder if drugs were involved."

"Why you think that?" Jerome casually pulled out a knife, the kind you brought to a knife fight to scare all the other knives, and balanced the point on the plastic coffee table.

"Abigail's an addict. That's obvious. She looks enough like her sister." Abigail's right hand went to the crook of her left arm, but she stayed quiet. The fight was out of her. Jerome was in charge. "Drugs are money and money attracts murder. Something like that could have happened out in the hall."

"Best be careful with your could-haves."

"Any chance you're in the pharmaceuticals trade? If there were a supply and money in the apartment, that'd make for an even bigger target."

Taylor already knew no one had broken into the apartment the night of the killing. He wanted to figure out what Jerome was about. Was it more than the lease?

Jerome rose smoothly, the knife at this side. Mission accomplished, but Taylor now needed to get out of there with what he knew.

Taylor eased off the stool and took a step back toward the door.

Judo in a real fight? Not ready for this.

"Take it easy. More violence gets into this case—that makes things worse for you. The detectives around here are busy, but it'll get their attention."

"Never met a reporter before. Not much impressed. You're bothering me with some serious impertinence. I want that to go away."

The knife, still down by Jerome's side, had been an invitation to keep backing toward the door.

Jerome brought the weapon up and settled into a fighting stance.

Shit.

First, a distraction.

Taylor hurled his reporter's notebook at Jerome's face. Taylor's instructor wouldn't have been impressed—notebooks weren't part of the judo tradition—but improvisation had gotten him out of worse jams.

Jerome batted away the flapping paper like a big annoying moth.

He thrust with the knife in a modified roundhouse even as Taylor stepped the other way.

Taylor moved his left arm up to the vertical, hand in a fist, and blocked Jerome's swinging arm in the middle. Taylor's right hand grabbed the knife arm higher up.

Now isn't the time to review steps. Do.

He snuck his left arm under the man's elbow and grabbed his wrist.

Twisted hard.

Harder.

The knife dropped to the rug. He increased the pressure, forcing Jerome facedown into the shag carpet.

He snatched up the knife and the notebook with his free hand.

From the floor, Jerome grunted, "I'm going to fuck with you."

Taylor slipped to the door.

"Your knife will be at the One-One-Two. Along with my full report to Detective McCauley, the narcs, the desk sergeant, and the janitor. The cops will know who to look in on if something happens to me. I'm writing Martha Gibson's story. If you're not a part of it, good for you. Stay out of it."

"Why do you give a shit?"

"The usual reason. No one else does."

CHAPTER 7

———◆———

THE KNIFE DROPPED with a pleasing *thunk* on Detective McCauley's desk.

The *thunk* didn't please McCauley. "What the fuck?"

Taylor laughed.

McCauley scowled. "Oh, so the reporter who's interested in *other* murders is a comedian too."

"I liberated that from a guy named Jerome, boyfriend to Martha Gibson's sister. The sister, Abigail, is a smack addict. Jerome looks good for a sales agent in that booming New York trade. Reacted like it, at least."

"How'd you get the knife off the guy?"

"Been studying a little judo at the insistence of my girlfriend."

"That's so nice. She worried about you? She ought to be."

"She's an ex-cop. Said the academy didn't give much hand-to-hand training to the women."

"As it should be. What's a five-foot meter maid going to do when the shit hits the fan?"

"I'll let her know your views. Help you up off the ground afterwards."

McCauley frowned, seemingly unsure how his machismo

should react to a threat from a female ex-cop delivered by her boyfriend.

In the end, he moved back to the knife, and said, "What do you want me to do with this?"

"Whatever you want. I don't want to get stabbed with it."

"Uh-huh. The guy's already got another by now."

"No doubt. Now we'll all know who stuck one in me if something unkind happens at a future date. I also thought you might be interested in the angle. Murder and drugs go together nicely."

"Did you look around this room when you came in?"

He had. The squad bustled like Union Square subway station at rush hour. Since Taylor had been here a week ago, bulletin boards had been put up. Pictures and documents were tacked everywhere, all certainly related to the murders committed with a single Charter Arms Bulldog .44. More detectives had arrived.

"Yes, I'm impressed. This many cops still in the precinct, and it's St. Patrick's Day. Probably a record. You must be serious about this guy."

McCauley had to smile at that. "There are some guys here. This is their first March Seventeenth on the job since they've been on the job, even counting years they were scheduled to work."

"Okay, got it. Lots going on in the big case. What about the narcotics angle?"

"Narcotics isn't murder."

"If Martha Gibson had the temerity to get ambushed in her apartment building with the wrong gun, she's shit out of luck?"

"You're like the other newspaper shooflies. No respect for the guys on the job. We're working on the Gibson case. Doesn't mean I have to like your theories."

"I respect the cops who respect the facts. Can't seem to find enough of them. I'll talk to the narcs. Maybe they know something."

"They can't do anything about the murder."

"Yeah, *riiiight*. There's five a day in this town. Somebody better start working on the rest of them."

"Asswipe."

"I'll stop by if I get more on this."

The narcotics detectives would normally be in some corner of the same squad room, but most everyone had been moved out to accommodate the Omega Group Task Force, as the detail of detectives looking for the .44-caliber murderer were called. Taylor shook his head at the police department's grasp of language—or lack of it. Omega was the last letter in the Greek alphabet. Did they expect this was the last time they'd be going after some nut with a big gun? New York's last terrible killer? Or were they that pessimistic about how long it would take? Either way or any other way he thought of it, it didn't make sense. He'd ask his grandfather, an immigrant from Greece who owned a coffee shop on Madison, if there was some other meaning he wasn't getting. He didn't hold out much hope.

Taylor found narcotics in the basement. He chose the least junkie-looking of the junkies in the room and guessed right. Detective Caputo was a Serpico knockoff. Same beard, same shaggy hair. The Serpico look *would* be good news if it meant the guy was straight as Serpico—six years after Frank Serpico's revelations, narcs were still the most corrupt cops on the force. Too much cash in the drug game. Too many drugs in the drug game.

The detective greeted Taylor with actual interest, not something he was used to.

"You sure you're not lost?" Caputo said. "The Omega guys are upstairs."

"I'm working on an alpha."

Caputo leaned his head forward like he was being told something important, but couldn't work it out.

"Just a bad joke. I'm doing a story on another woman killed last week. Martha Gibson. Richmond Hill area. Apartment at

155-99 on Eighty-Ninth Avenue. Her sister's an addict, and I'm thinking the sister's boyfriend may deal. Trying to confirm it."

"What's this joker's name?"

"Jerome. Didn't get a last."

"Hispanic?"

"No, Black."

"That's interesting in itself. The neighborhood's pretty Hispanic, and the Hispanics have a tight lock on the business."

"Much violence between dealers?"

"What do you think? There's enough competition, there's enough killing." He opened a gray-metal index card box and flipped through it. "I cross-reference by name and address the guys we see moving around. A Jerome McGill, a seller, seen going to that address several times in the last week. We're not sure if he deals from there."

"He may have just showed up. The sister, Abigail, claims Martha wouldn't let him come over when she was alive. You get a lot of this—sales from apartments, rather than street dealing?"

"Yeah. Too easy to get busted on the street. With an apartment, you get a peek at the customer. Lot of them make you call on a payphone nearby. Then there's usually some kind of code at the door. Being in an apartment, you're a lot safer from cops. And robbers."

"Didn't help Martha Gibson."

"What's your theory?"

"Maybe someone took her out thinking it was Abigail to get at Jerome. Some sort of retribution. They could have followed Abigail from Jerome's place. She stayed there several nights a week."

"Hitman thinks he's getting Jerome's girl. It's happened before. You should share it with homicide."

"Tried to get McCauley to listen. Apparently, they're too busy planning the capture of the last murderer in all New York. What's the best way to figure out if McGill is shifting his business to the apartment? He was pretty concerned that Abigail hold onto it. Probably rent-controlled. Seems small beans in a heroin business."

"Smart businessman keeps his costs down." Caputo laughed at his own joke. "Does the building have an intercom?"

"Yes."

"If it were me, I'd look for traffic from a payphone into the building. You know already—junkies have that look. Then again, some don't. Look like you and me. New York's one big party, and everybody's in on it as the city spins down the toilet."

Upstairs, Taylor used the phone booth—three sides covered with stickers from bail bondsmen—to call the City News Bureau. On his way back through the squad room, he had grabbed a couple of quotes from the captain in charge of Omega—yes, lots of calls from the public, yes, lots of leads, no, no breakthroughs—and gave them to Cramly with a description of the busy squad room and its bulletin boards and ringing phones. You'd have thought Taylor had phoned in the next Pulitzer winner, so he felt compelled to add, "That's what they're going to tell me every time I ask, so I'm going to leave it alone for a while. Clear?"

"What, wait until someone else is shot?"

"The read I'm getting here is they don't have anything. That may be what happens next."

Cramly sputtered, "But, but—"

"You got your forty-four-caliber-killer story. One I wasn't even planning on doing. Now let me get back to work on news. You know, something that's new. Any messages?"

"An Edmond DeVries asked that you call at your earliest convenience. Said it like that. Real uptown."

The DeVries phone rang as Taylor scanned the slogans from the bail bondsmen. "Let us help when the rest have given up." *Uplifting.* "You're innocent until proven guilty. And we don't even care." *Nicely blasé.* "Ever shower at Rikers?" *Direct.*

The butler, or maybe someone exclusively assigned to

phone duties, answered and offered to see if Mr. DeVries was available. He was.

"Thank you for getting back to me. I was wondering if the police have gotten anywhere on Martha's case?"

"No, not anywhere, really. I'm not sure they plan to. Right now, it's little old me."

"Because of the serial killer?"

"Probably some of that. Right now, all I have is possible drug dealing. Angela Gibson's boyfriend is likely a pusher. I'd like to talk with you again about Martha. I'm trying to get a fuller picture of her life."

"I don't know that I have anything more to add, but I'm happy to talk."

"May I stop by tomorrow?"

May I? My brain is moving uptown.

"We're heading out for the weekend." *Which begins on Thursday. Nice.* "How would three twenty on Monday be?"

"See you then."

CHAPTER 8

———— ◆ ————

GRANDPOP BROUGHT OVER two pieces of baklava, each with a candle it. In a booming voice, he started singing "Happy Birthday." Everyone in the place sang along—the cabbies, office workers, deliverymen, rich old ladies who could afford better but preferred the Oddity. The booths with red vinyl seats, the stools, the counter, all of this was the Odysseus Coffee Shop on Madison Avenue at 75th Street, his grandfather's place, known as the Oddity to everyone but those stumbling in for the first time.

Grandpop set the plates down at the front booth, one before each of them. He'd insisted they not use the family table at the back. "Thank you for starting your joint birthday celebration at Odysseus. Happy birthday, Samantha, who makes my grandson so happy."

"Thank you, Stamitos."

"Happy thirty-seventh birthday—"

"Hey," Taylor said, "how come you have to mention my age?"

"Because we are polite. As I was saying, happy birthday, also, to my grandson, whose first name I'm forbidden from speaking."

"What'd I say about the singing part?" Taylor said.

"Always I will sing."

"I know." Taylor smiled as he sunk his fork into the honey-soaked flaky pastry of the baklava. "I need to say something to make sure next year you don't have a brass band."

Grandpop stroked his chin. "A band, you say? Now that would be the good way to honor a woman as wonderful as our Samantha. Even you too, perhaps."

"Did you get all the charm in this family?" Samantha said, smiling at Taylor at the same time.

"My charm," Taylor said, "is you don't have to worry about being BS'd by my charm."

"No, your charm is you're all about the facts. You can't move far from the truth with facts as your obsession—"

"It's not an obsession."

"Okay, let's say 'focus' then. I'm a big fan of hearing the truth from those I keep close to me."

"Thank you, I believe I should say."

Grandpop turned to get the coffees and the ouzo. The diner didn't have a liquor license, but it always had ouzo. With a full head of white hair and a barrel chest, he wore a white apron over a gray t-shirt and dungaree overalls.

"I'm glad we decided to do it this way." She slid a bite of the dessert off her fork and into her mouth, smiling even bigger as it hit her tongue.

Samantha's birthday had really been two days earlier, on March 15, while Taylor's was April 1. Last year, their first birthdays together, they went all out on each other with the restaurants, presents, and surprises. The whole new couple thing. After that exhausting exercise, the proximity and odd calendar dates of their birthdays—the Ides of March and April Fool's—gave them an idea. Well, gave Taylor the idea, since he'd never much liked celebrating his birthday on the holiday for practical jokes. He'd suggested they honor both on hers. She'd said no; it should be on a date in between—but never

March 17. They both loathed being out on St. Patrick's Day, amateur night for drinking in NYC. That led to this little joint party on Friday, March 18, at the Oddity.

Grandpop poured the ouzo.

"Sit down with us, Stamitos," Samantha said.

"He never sits in his own place."

At which, Grandpop promptly sat next to Samantha, who slid in laughing.

"Good God," Taylor lifted his glass, "you're Ilsa in *Casablanca*. You got Rick to join a guest." Taylor tipped the glass and swallowed fast. Ouzo might be a part of his heritage, but he didn't love it. The taste was a clove, coriander, and cleaning-fluid shock every time.

"Ingrid Bergman is a wonderful actress." Grandpop emptied his. "She's no Samantha. That is why I sit down. Samantha is here with us." The old man's eyes, brown irises green-ringed at the edges, focused on Taylor. "We want her to stay with us."

"Charm, charm, charm." More laughter. "I'm not going anywhere. How could I, now that you've actually sat down to have a drink?"

Grandpop started pouring again, and Taylor said, "No, not a second."

Taylor's Third Rule of Drinking required avoiding the hard stuff whenever possible—tough for a man who often found himself in cop bars. And bad-guy bars. Rule two was no booze for breakfast. That was the one he found easiest not to break. He'd evolved the rules over a period of years, yet never talked about them, not even with Samantha.

"Two birthdays." Grandpop pushed Taylor's hand away from over the glass. "Two toasts." He filled the glasses to the brim.

"All right, fine. Question for you. For a story I'm working on. Omega means the last, right?"

"It is the last letter in the Greek alphabet. People use it to refer to a last thing. Or the first and last. Like the Alpha and the Omega in religion."

"Any other meanings?"

"None that I know of." Grandpop's face grew serious. "We also can drink one to your father, if you wish."

"I don't wish."

"Don't worry about how this old man feels. I reconciled myself to him years ago. I won't speak ill of the dead. So I won't speak."

"None of us will. None of us needs to. We're not drinking to him."

"I want to speak," Samantha said. "We didn't have to do any of this birthday stuff so soon. We don't have to go out to Chumley's tonight. We can go home." She turned to his grandfather. "I told Taylor we could wait."

"I don't want to wait. I want our celebration. The one we talked about. He's not taking that away from either of us."

The old man stood up. "You two work it out. With what that man did to my grandson here and Billy and my daughter ... well, enough. Not speaking ill of the dead, if only so my own dear late wife won't haunt me. It's a thing she wouldn't allow."

Samantha took Taylor's hand, and he squeezed it to affirm this was what he wanted. Some great wave of guilt should have ruined his dessert with her because he wanted the man to be so gone and his life to go on. It didn't. Instead, as he continued to do, he found Billy again, a fifth grader, smiling, swinging a stickball bat, calling for Taylor to come pitch. Then a teenage Billy, winking, like he agreed with Taylor. He was able to let go of the Professor, but it was bringing back memories of Billy—which would be good, except it was like tearing off four-year-old scar tissue. Maybe he hadn't healed at all; he'd buried the pain under constant work.

Taylor and Samantha left the Oddity and took the subway, ending up at Chumley's in Greenwich Village half an hour later. The bar was empty as a tomb for a Friday night. St. Pat's hangovers were being nursed all over New York. Or had already been put to bed.

As luck would have it, the booth where Samantha and Taylor had had their first ever drinks was open. Then she'd been a police officer under investigation for abandoning her partner during a chase that ended in the officer's death. At first, she'd been deeply suspicious as to whether Taylor could help her in any way. He did, and she'd helped him. They'd identified the killer in a double murder and a ring of corrupt cops. That was the good news, if you could call it that. The bad news was Samantha's father, an NYPD sergeant, had been one of the cops running the gang. He'd been killed by his partner before Taylor or Samantha could stop it. Afterwards, Samantha had decided she couldn't go back to work in the NYPD. She was seen as corrupt by some, a source for Internal Affairs by others.

For Taylor, there had been another hard lesson in that catastrophe. Once he set things rolling, a story didn't always end with those 20 column inches in the paper. Events could get way out of control. Lives changed. Destroyed. Tough as it had been, he wouldn't change things. He'd met Samantha. He'd fallen in love with her.

Taylor sipped his Rolling Rock. "How goes the divorce case?"

Samantha handled mainly divorce work and shoplifting investigations for Raymond & Associates, Investigators. Taylor knew she could do much more. He was sure she'd have gotten a gold shield if she could have stayed and the NYPD ever started treating women fairly.

"A mountain of paperwork. I'm trying to figure out where this guy hid *her* money."

"You're working for the wife."

"The husband took off with a Braniff stewardess."

"Literally took off?"

"Living in Jersey City."

"I thought it was a joke. Or a joke on a stereotype. The guy running off with a stewardess."

"This guy did it. He's more an asshole than a joke."

"Because he skipped out on his wife?"

Samantha's eyes narrowed. "He'd be an asshole if he stayed with her or fell in love with a sanitation worker. She had assets—cash, securities, and jewelry—inherited from her parents. They were supposed to be tied up by a trust. Gone. Missing. The paperwork's not helping, which is pretty much what he intended. Only thing I've found so far is he purchased a small parcel in the Adirondacks. No house or buildings on it."

Taylor flagged for two more beers.

"Keep your pants on, buddy," said the waiter, which was how the staff sounded when they were being polite at Chumley's, a former speakeasy that still acted like one, up to and including a front door you wouldn't know was the door to a bar unless you already did.

He finished his first beer. "Maybe he hid everything up there?"

"Like buried treasure."

"Make it hard to find. The land only in his name?"

"Definitely."

"Why don't you go to the cops? It's larceny."

"They hear divorce, they run the other way unless I have something really solid. You think I'm going to have to dig up two acres of upstate land?"

"Unless there's a treasure map." He picked up the second beer and smiled.

"*That* would be a story." Her eyes, the blue of gunmetal, which belied the warmth inside her, smiled back.

"I'd write it."

"I bet you would. You're really going to keep away from the forty-four killer?"

"What's there to get near? I read the papers every day. They've got nothing. Speculation. Theories. No evidence but the bullets. Took the police six months to connect those. Not a decent witness. The papers are rewriting the same thing, turning it inside out and upside down and sideways."

"People are scared."

" 'Course they are. Hearing the same drumbeat every day with nothing happening. The waiting game. That'll scare the shit out of you."

She took a drink from her bottle of Schmidt's. "I talked to a guy I know on the force—one of the few who will still speak with me."

"What'd he say?"

"They're going through every Charter Arms Bulldog revolver registered in New York. They're chasing tips based on the police artists' drawings. Interviewing anyone who says a neighbor or a coworker is a weirdo, then interviewing the weirdo."

Taylor shook his head. "That will take months. I got enough to do without rehashing the same facts every day. No one cares Martha Gibson was gunned down in her hallway. So I do."

"Another of Taylor's strays."

"Lots of loose ends on this one. The late Martha has a druggie sister with a pusher for a boyfriend. Martha worked for this DeVries family on Park Avenue. May be big family secrets there. Maybe not. Maybe she heard something. Maybe not. There's got to be other people I can talk to, find out why this woman's life was taken, ten feet from her front door. Beats the hell out of interviewing the man or woman on the street about how scared he or she is of Mr. Forty-Four—the interview only frightening them more."

"You know your business."

"Nah, I'm probably making a colossal career mistake. Gotta go with the stories that got me here."

"You had me check out that Manning Corp where the victim worked for four months." Samantha pulled out her notebook, the type issued to a police officer. A little habit she couldn't—or didn't want to—let go of. "Importer of shoes from Europe with a three-thousand-square-foot office in that famous building. Been there twenty-three years. Ricky MacDonald's the president. He's got one conviction for solicitation and was arrested for sexual assault. Got off on that one."

Taylor nodded. "Helpful, as always. Maybe there's something in this story about sex, rather than drugs or a rich family. Or maybe I haven't found the right connection—"

"It's all about connections."

That was his line.

"Yes it is. I still need to talk to Martha's parents. Get another perspective on Abigail and Jerome. See if they know of anyone else who was a threat. I'll go door to door in her building if I have to."

THEY TUMBLED INTO the bed of their tiny bedroom in the Murray Hill apartment. It had started with more beers in the living room and making out on the couch. Mason leapt up on the bed with them, knocking Taylor's face with manic tail wagging. Samantha fell over, giggling.

"No, Mason!" Taylor pulled at his collar. "It's living room time for you." He pulled the dog into the next room and turned up the Blondie song while he was at it.

Samantha kept laughing. "This is *so* sexy. We need to settle in one place—one place with more space."

"I don't know if my mother's god, the universe, your mother's god, or fate wants that—for me at least. Thieving carpenters. Temporary use of a dry-docked houseboat in the Bronx. An apartment in Brooklyn Heights destined for the owner's brother-in-law. All in two years."

"I miss Brooklyn."

"I miss you."

"I'm right here."

"I miss more of you."

He kissed her as she unbuttoned her shirt and pulled off her bra. He was still fiddling with his belt as he kissed her.

"I'll do that," she said.

The belt came off with a whisper.

They made birthday love drunk and slow, and for the moment, happy.

CHAPTER 9

———— ◆ ————

TAYLOR STEPPED OUT of the elevator onto the DeVries floor. Their floor, their whole floor. With so little space for most people in New York, it was a concept he still had a hard time getting his head around.

Instead of the butler, a young Black woman greeted him. This surprised Taylor only because he figured a household like this ran on rules that dated from the last century.

"Mr. DeVries will meet you in the library," said the woman, who looked to be in her early to mid twenties and was dressed in a maid's uniform. White apron over a black dress. She had a plain, flat face and hard-to-miss dark-green eyes.

She started walking and Taylor stayed even with her, rather than following.

"You're a maid? Like Martha was?"

A sharp look. "You're the reporter?"

"Doing a story on her. On what happened to her."

Intensity came into her eyes. She checked behind them, spoke in a low tone. "Have you been told anything yet about a conversation Martha overheard here at the apartment?"

"By her sister," he replied. "No details. Martha got a phone call. She told the caller she didn't want to meet. Denied hearing whatever the caller asked about or knowing who was involved. That the one?"

"She went home really upset the night it happened. It was a week before she was …" Carol left the sentence unfinished. She didn't want to pick any of the words for murdered.

"What did she hear?"

"There isn't time now."

"Have you told anyone? The cops?"

"No." A near whisper. "They haven't even come. They talked to Mr. DeVries once on the phone. I don't want anything public. Like Martha, I need this job."

"You understand what 'off the record' means?"

"You think I'm stupid because I wear this?" She tugged at the apron.

"No, I … I'm sorry. If you know something, I need to hear it. I'll keep you out of it. It might keep the police away if I'm the one pushing the lead."

"I'm not a coward. I liked Martha. She was good to me when I got here."

They approached the library. Taylor wrote his phone number on a sheet of notebook paper, tore it out, and handed it over. She stuffed it in a pocket like it would burst into flames if it stayed out in the light.

"What's your name?"

"Carol Wheelwright."

"Call me."

Inside the library, DeVries already had a cocktail. Taylor figured a lot of hours were the cocktail hour around this place—or maybe DeVries had his own problem with the stuff. Smiling, the gray-haired man rose from his chair to stand a good head above Taylor, and offered his hand.

"Pleasure. What can I get you?"

"Another Rheingold is fine."

Maybe I have a problem.

"You really are a committed beer drinker." DeVries signaled to Carol, who turned on her heels and was gone somewhere else on the Eighth Floor.

"You don't like beer?"

"At a picnic, down by the ocean. Sure. Of an afternoon, nothing really beats a well mixed drink."

"What're you having?"

"A Tom Collins. My favorite. Well, my favorite cocktail with gin. A one-hundred-year-old classic."

"Do you have a favorite for each of the spirits?"

"Never much liked vodka. Or the damn Ruskies." Taylor's eyebrows lifted too quickly. "Don't get me wrong. I'm not one of those Goldwater-Reagan types. Liberal for a Republican. A long family tradition. Rocky and Lindsay. That sort."

"Lindsay didn't leave the city in very good shape."

"Think you'll find the problems go back to Wagner—even further than that. Lots of budgeting magic, with a few of my dear old friends in banking skimming off a bit all along the way. Never trusted quick money. They kept telling me about the easy, easy profits in municipal finance in those years. How could a city with so many hard-working people, so much business, and so much money get in such deep trouble? Criminal behavior."

"Not the kind you go to jail for."

"No, and it's a damn shame. How can I help you with your reporting on Martha? I haven't thought of anything else related to her work here."

That's okay. Goal Number One, connecting with a staffer, already accomplished. Now wander the conversation around and see if I hook something else.

"Did Martha ever have any problems with vendors or suppliers?"

"No. That would be cook's area to take care of anyway."

"Or building staff?"

"Hardly. They're well vetted."

"Let me tell you what I've learned." Taylor reported in detail what he knew about the drug connection, including that Jerome McGill had an inordinate interest in the rent-controlled apartment. "I admit, I haven't gotten as far as I'd like. Other stories have come along. We're a small wire service. Have to feed the beast."

"I imagine it's some beast." DeVries turned his eyes, which were the gray of a heavy mist, to the ceiling. "Journalism is going in the wrong direction."

"*I'm* not going in the right direction, I'll say that. Back at the *Messenger-Telegram,* I'd have the time I needed to go after this story. The beast could stand to let me do some reporting."

"The Garfields really messed things up. I don't say it because I lost a packet when your paper closed. I've recorded bigger losses. The city needed a newspaper that wasn't trying to be the *Times* yet wasn't engaged in this awful tabloid war. New York City news as a priority, straight and tightly edited. That's what the *MT* did."

Taylor wanted to ask a question to keep the conversation about Martha going, but his mind wandered for a moment as memories of the paper flooded in, almost overwhelmed him. The newsroom, his desk, the cop shop, faces of colleagues, the *MT* for sale on newsstands, the presses running, sharp black headlines standing out from gray newsprint. His mood blackened and sunk under the weight of what he recalled. He'd kept the darkness away during the past several months by staying true to this commitment to make it work at City News. DeVries didn't mean to cause him pain, but he had.

Didn't help that DeVries picked then to ask the obvious. "Do you miss it?"

"Every single day." The blackness swirled. He was sweating in this cool room. Stuck forever at the City News Bureau. That was something to raise a real fear. Yet it was a reaction few would understand and many would think a joke—afraid of having a job, of sitting in an office typing for decent pay when decent was hard to come by now.

Time to quit fishing while he was ahead. He needed to hear from Carol before pushing harder. He finished the beer.

"I'm sorry to take up your time. In murder, you look at home first, then you look at work. After that, the field gets a whole lot bigger."

"You sound like a cop."

Some police-beat reporters would take that as a compliment. Not Taylor.

"I tell stories. I don't arrest anyone. Cops have the power—to arrest, interrogate, search. I can only ask questions of those who will talk to me and ask more based on the answers I get."

From outside came an attention-getting clearing of a throat like you only heard on TV. A rotund man in a three-piece pinstripe suit stood next to Charlie DeVries.

"Ah," DeVries rose from his seat, "Taylor, this Nicholas Fourier, my accountant." He stopped, paused a second, and turned to Taylor. "Martha was loved in this household. If you find out more, please come see me."

Taylor briefly considered and discarded the idea of asking to interview all the staff. He wanted to pursue Carol's approach first. Asking to talk to everyone could alert the very person who was involved.

"I'm sorry, Nicholas. The time flew by."

"It always does if I'm out here trying to fix things." Fourier had a round, angry red face.

"Let's take this into the office." For the first time, DeVries sounded put off, maybe embarrassed.

"Why did you sell those munis? I told you—"

DeVries put his hand on Fourier's back to turn him in the direction of wherever the office was. "In the office, please, Nicholas. I have a guest."

Guest. There was a change. Usually, it went, *not in front of the reporter.* More and more, Taylor liked DeVries, no matter they came from opposite ends of the New York social solar system.

Taylor wasn't sure of the way out. He'd been too busy taking in the rooms and their fixtures as he'd been led through the maze on his two visits.

Charlie DeVries remained. An office *and* a library. Taylor's brother had the line for it: *Nice work if you can get it.* Billy didn't get work. Or an office or a library. He got dead.

"Can you show me where the elevator is?"

"You think I'm the help?"

"Never that."

"Follow."

A command, not a request. Charlie walked with a bit of a weave. *Early happy hour for at least half the family?*

"You're still working on Martha's murder?"

"Yes. Your father is concerned about what happened to her."

"Give him that. He cares about people. That's the good side of him." He handed Taylor a business card. "Martha was a nice lady. Not sure how what happened all the way out in Queens connects to us." He might have been talking about Montana. "Call if I can help. That's my service. They'll find me anytime."

The card contained Charlie's name and a phone number set in a typeface invented around the time of Gutenberg. No job, no company. The business card of the wealthy.

On the elevator ride down, Taylor thought about Carol Wheelwright's hint that she knew something. Whether she called him or not, he'd find a way to talk to her.

THEY HELPED THE short fat man onto a table. His name was Jerry something, the managing editor of the *Long Island Press.* His paper had died today, Friday, March 25. This was the paper's wake, held in a bar and grill called the Lamplighter Inn in Jamaica, Queens, where the paper had been headquartered on 168th Street. Taylor was here out of respect, as were reporters and editors from the other New York papers and newswires. Despite its name, the *Press* was a bona fide New York paper, based in one of the outer boroughs, and in recent years, particularly strong with its coverage of local government corruption. Jimmy Breslin, the top *Daily News* columnist, got his start at the *Press*.

Once every borough but the Bronx had its own daily. The *Brooklyn Eagle* had finally given up the ghost in 1963. The *Staten Island Advance* still published, owned by the same company that just killed off the *Press,* which had fought the big New York papers and Long Island's *Newsday* for stories and readers until it had been crushed between.

Jerry Something wobbled, and hands reached to steady him.

He raised his glass. "The paper started as the *Long Island Farmer* back in 1821. One hundred fifty-six years later, we're burying it as the *Long Island Press*. We keep burying newspapers in this town. This keeps up and we're not … we're not …." A wobble and a misstep and Jerry Something fell over into the arms of his unemployed staff.

Taylor couldn't blame Jerry. He'd seen people drunker back in 1975, on Nov. 6, at the wake for the *Messenger-Telegram.* He would have liked to hear what Jerry was going to predict would happen if New York kept losing its papers. For everyone here, it was personal. Jobs. In 1975, it'd been a job for Taylor, too. There was something more, yet like everything else New York was losing, no one talked about it.

"Saw a lot of papers go under during my career." The skinny old man offered his hand. "Ted Prager. Worked for one that died, *The Morning Sun*, among others."

"I know your name. You were an assistant city editor at the *News*. Taylor with City News Bureau."

"At the end, yeah, in the fifties. I was a police reporter for decades before I sat down at that desk."

"Same beat."

"You working on the serial killer?"

"Leaving that for others."

"Surprises me no one's brought up the Three X murders."

Taylor's look must have told Prager there was good reason

no one had brought it up—or at least Taylor hadn't. He'd never heard of a Three-X anything.

"Time heals, I guess. People forget. We don't learn from these stories. In the early summer of 1930, Joseph Mozynski was enjoying an extramarital tryst with Catherine May on a quiet street in Whitestone, Queens. The car door flew open and a deafening roar followed. Mozynski slumped dead in May's arms. The killer calmed down May and assured her he meant her no harm. After helping her clean herself up, he rode with her on a bus and then a trolley to near where she lived, at which point he handed her a slip of paper with the victim's name stamped with the killer's signature, a circled Three X."

Taylor took out his notebook. He wasn't much for historical stories. He wanted the *new* in news. However, he hadn't seen a sidebar on the 3X killer published anywhere. Be easy enough to write up Prager's interview. Would keep Novak happy and Cramly off his back for a good ten minutes.

"Five days later, one Noel Sowley was shot to death at another Queens lovers' lane. Now the cops and the press knew a maniac was on the loose. People were scared to death to use any of the dark byways of this borough. Believe me, they were much darker and quieter back then. Cops sat in cars in pairs with one wearing a wig so they'd look like a couple."

Taylor looked up from writing. He'd heard cops were setting up as decoys now.

"That's right," said Prager with a satisfied smile. "Same sort of thing the detectives are doing with the forty-four killer. My city desk assigned me to do the same with a colleague, Rosaleen. It was no fun being a sitting duck for a murderer, let me tell you. I didn't let my wife know, not because anything was going on, but so she wouldn't worry. We spent the tense nights smoking and coming up with theories about when, where, and how Three X would attack again. Instead of a murder, letters started coming in to one of the evening papers. Almost daily. Three X said his work was nowhere near done. He was going to kill fourteen more men—members of a secret Polish-White Russian society who had not lived up to their commitments. He named the society the Red Diamond—a group that only existed in this nut's mind, as it turned out. Made damn good copy, though.

"One night, as Rosaleen and I were sitting in the car in Queens, trying to draw his fire, a man was shot in his car in Brooklyn right in front of his wife and daughter. Luckily, he recovered, but witnesses immediately identified the assailant as Three X. After that, only letters. At one point, the psycho announced seven of his fourteen victims had redeemed themselves but the rest must die.

"The watch continued night after night with false alarm after false alarm. The public demanded the cops get the killer. Cranks flooded the police with letters and phone calls claiming to be Three X or one of his agents. Pretty soon, fake letters were arriving in cities across the country. With no more killings, police and public interest slowly dropped off. Still, it was more than a year later when the last real letter came, saying only three more victims remained to be killed."

Prager took a sip from whatever was in the brandy glass he held.

"Nothing more was ever heard. The Three X murders remain unsolved to this day."

"I can't believe I've never been told about that case."

"People forget so fast. You know how quickly papers move on. One thing doesn't change."

"What's that?"

"The hysteria."

CHAPTER 10

———•———

TAYLOR STRAIGHTENED HIS tie for the third—or thirtieth—time as the elevator climbed to the DeVries apartment.

"You look fine," said Samantha. She was wearing a simple black dress that looked better than fine. A string of pearls lay stark white on the pale skin of her upper chest. She'd borrowed them from an old schoolmate who'd married well—they'd grown up together in the Bronx.

"When he called, the butler actually 'recommended' a tie. Very nicely, but like he was inviting over the Beverly Hillbillies. I wear ties."

"Maybe he saw you on one of those days where you'd taken it off and stuffed it in your jacket pocket." She grinned and kissed him. "You know, like right after lunch."

"A tie is like hands around my throat. How is this useful clothing?"

"Or perhaps you came wearing one of those knit, squared-off types you like so much. Not very Park Avenue."

The elevator operator, who hadn't said a word on Taylor's previous visits either, stopped the machine and slid open the gate and the door. Elevator men who worked in office buildings and stores, you couldn't get them to shut up. Different rules for Park Avenue, apparently.

At the door, they were greeted by the butler, now dressed in white tie and tails. He led them to the biggest room Taylor had passed through on previous visits. It was crowded, with people squeezed everywhere around pieces of furniture so ornate they looked like *New Yorker* cartoons of ornate furniture.

Carol Wheelwright approached them with a tray of champagne glasses. Recognition crossed her face and was chased away briefly by fear before her countenance returned to the mask of the servant.

"Champagne, or would you like something from the bar?"

Samantha took a flute. Taylor broke his Third Rule of Drinking and ordered a Manhattan. He couldn't imagine standing in this crowd with a Rheingold, even in a glass.

Carol left to get his drink. She probably didn't want to come back. She hadn't called Taylor in the five days following their brief, cryptic conversation. How could he get to her? The middle of a giant dinner party was hardly the place to do an interview. Aside from last night's wake for the *Press,* he'd spent much of the past two days watching Martha Gibson's apartment building, then got so impatient he'd gone up to the floor to watch the door. Nothing. Nothing at all. He couldn't keep up the stakeout. He had other leads to follow, and his regular duties at City News. He needed something solid. Carol had sounded like she might have just that.

Samantha sipped the champagne while giving the room the sort of slow, easy scan practiced by someone paid to watch other people. "That's good champagne. Money, money, mo—"

"Taylor," said Charlie DeVries. He'd come up right behind Samantha as she was speaking. He held a glass filled with rocks and something clear. With him was a taller, handsomer man. Blond hair parted at the side. Straight WASP nose. Real Park Avenue looks. "Dad invited his reporter friend. This is—"

"Samantha Callahan," Taylor said.

Charlie introduced his friend as Bobby Livingston.

Samantha's cream-white cheeks reddened. "I apologize. I didn't mean—"

"Oh, please." Charlie jingled his ice at both of them. "The biggest lie on the avenue is that people *don't* talk about money. They do, all the time. The biggest joke? We don't have nearly as much as people talk about. What do you do, Miss Callahan?"

"I'm a private investigator," she said, in a demure tone. Charlie really had caught her off guard.

"Well, you're both probably more intriguing than ninety percent of the other guests. You may scare some of them, though. Me, I'm interested."

"Your father called and invited us on Thursday," Taylor said. "He didn't give a reason."

A stunning young woman in a purple silk dress joined them. "Is Charlie saying all the wrong things? It's his special way on social occasions." Somewhere in her twenties, she wore her black hair cut short and had full lips painted with red lipstick and little other makeup. "I'm Audrey DeVries." She extended her hand, and Taylor and Samantha introduced themselves. "He's convinced himself sarcasm offers some dark insight into all our lives."

"I was *not* being sarcastic. A reporter. A private eye. They're a breath of fresh air at a stuffy do like this." A wave of his free hand.

"You agree with Papa on the guest list? Now that *is* a breath of fresh air."

Audrey was her own breath of fresh of air. She was so pretty, she glittered. Something like art, Taylor observed rather than felt. Samantha was his kind of gorgeous, and to this day, he was amazed she'd been interested in him. Was still interested. Audrey was for another kind of human being and another kind of world—*this* world, one in which he'd only be an observer for a brief time.

"I got my master's in journalism at Columbia," Audrey said.

"Excellent school." Unlike most of the grad program's alumni, she hadn't stated it like a claim on the world. Audrey's open, smiling face loosened him up enough—that and the Manhattan—to let him talk about the start of his own career, which he usually was too insecure about to bring up around the journalism-school grads invading newsrooms everywhere. "I came up the old-fashioned way—hired out of high school as a copy boy. Back when papers did that sort thing. Those days are over. A lot of those papers are over."

"Oh my goodness, when we had seven daily newspapers in this city."

"I was working then."

"You know what's also gone?" Charlie said. "The days when you could make money investing in newspapers. Papa won't listen to me. He won't even listen to Mother. He refuses to see how bad things are. He still thinks we've a seat on the board at the *New York Sun*."

"Don't exaggerate. He does not. There hasn't been a *New York Sun* for decades. Papa's exploring options."

"By inviting that gross Australian?"

"Rupert Murdoch's here?" Taylor said.

"No, one of his top executives. From his U.S. company, News America. Rupert couldn't make it." Charlie's usual smirk turned downward into a false frown.

Audrey touched her glass to Taylor's. "I work at the *New Yorker*. Fact checker. I really want to get on a newspaper."

Taylor worried what Samantha might think of this glass tapping, so he squeezed her hand. "Good magazine."

That sounded obvious. Or stupid. Or both. Don't read it. Don't know anyone who works there. Don't know anyone who takes out the garbage there.

"Bad job for a DeVries," Charlie said. "You should be carefully manipulating the suitors you've had since your coming out."

"Ease off, Charlie," said Bobby, who'd listened to the conversation impassively. "These aren't the ancient times you're imagining. Even Park Avenue changes."

Charlie laughed. "Every year that passes in the real world takes a decade on the avenue. We're kind of like Brigadoon. We have a lot of catching up to do. Hippie, what's a hippie? Though Audrey was ahead of us there. She did have her little phase."

"I'm so glad you've met Bobby," said Audrey, ignoring her brother. "We've all been friends forever. Our families have known each other a long, long time."

"Even I know Livingston's an old New York name," said Taylor.

"Yes, well we're a small twig at the end of a small branch of that family tree," Bobby said.

Taylor's tie seemed to tighten itself. His clothes started to itch. The talk of family trees and suitors fired up an acute sense of not belonging he'd held at bay. He took a good gulp of the Manhattan, the medicine for such discomfort.

"I work for the City News Bureau."

"The local wire service?" Audrey said. "I read about it in *Editor & Publisher*. I go through the magazine every week, cover to cover. Looking for that newspaper job."

An older woman with a resemblance to Audrey stepped between her and Charlie. She wore the sort of sequin dress Taylor had expected to see lots of at the party.

Audrey turned. "Ah, Mother, this is Taylor and Samantha."

"Taylor's a reporter," said Charlie, with glee in his voice. Taylor got the feeling trouble-making was Charlie's number one occupation. "Samantha's a private eye."

Samantha was probably having the same reaction. Enjoyment of the party fell off her face. She didn't like being a punch line.

"Oh God," Mrs. DeVries said to Taylor, "are you with that Australian?"

"No. I work for the City News Bureau."

She shook her head sadly. "I have *real* friends I could have invited. Not that he cares. He must think he's running the New York Press Club." She took a big swallow from a highball class. "I'm sorry, I don't mean to be insulting."

"Well, at least you don't *mean* to be," Audrey said. She smiled, and Charlie coughed on his vodka or gin.

Mrs. DeVries didn't think it was funny. "Why *did* my Edmond invite you?"

"He didn't say. I'm looking into the death of Martha Gibson."

"Wonderful. The dunderhead is going to have us talking about the murder of our Negro maid during dinner. Why bother even hosting?"

"Mother!"

Before Audrey could say more, the butler rang an actual gong for actual dinner.

Taylor found himself one person from DeVries at one end and sitting directly across from a man with an oval bald head. The man was wearing a gray suit with wide pinstripes that seemed to jump off the fabric. He was looking for something—on Taylor's jacket, through him, somewhere in the room, somewhere else. His brown eyes kept searching.

At times during his career, Taylor had been stuck covering big dinners when a political reporter couldn't go, but those rubber-chicken affairs were nothing like this. He'd never sat down to a meal with so many courses, half of them unidentifiable, all delicious.

DeVries sipped red wine, set his glass down and turned to the oval-headed man across from Taylor. "Carter, Taylor is in your business."

"Oh, is that right? What do you own?" The stretched vowels of an Australian accent.

"A notebook. I'm a reporter."

"Who for?"

"City News Bureau."

"That's that little newswire."

"May be little, but we get what you miss."

"We own a New York paper now. We don't miss anything we don't want to miss."

"I've beaten the *Post*."

"That was the old *Post,* mate."

"New and old. Beat them both."

DeVries laughed, warm and liquid, and tapped the table. "Love the competitive energy in newspapers. It's different from any other industry." Charlie was near enough across the table for Taylor to catch his eyes rolling hard to the right. "Taylor's had some good ones. Back with the *Messenger-Telegram* too. You know we were investors in that paper?"

"Should have talked to us first," said Carter. Those vowels kept stretching. They made a Brooklyn accent sound cultured. "You lost your shirt there."

DeVries' friendly smile, if anything, grew. It seemed no matter how hard people poked at him, he took it like it was a part of the friendship.

"Carter, I invited you here to meet some of the people in town—"

"Who *run* the town."

"Run, in, whichever. You're also getting to meet one of our journalists."

"We already employ a quarter of the city's journalists. Had to fire some deadbeats at the *Post*, of course. Don't know what you Yanks are thinking when you train reporters."

DeVries eyed Taylor, friendly, but also like a prize. "Tell him a couple of stories."

Taylor didn't want to, and at the same time, he did. He recounted the story of the drug gang murders during the Bicentennial a year ago. In March, he'd reported on a huge marijuana farm out on Long Island.

"Read that one the *next* day in the *Post*. I guess someone's hearing about what's on our wire even if you don't subscribe."

"Well then, if you're that damn good, come see one of our editors."

Carter turned his gaze on the woman next to him—those eyes that kept searching for things—leaving Taylor and dropping to settle on her cleavage.

The offer, a single simple sentence, hit him like a live charge. The possibility of a job with a newspaper, a New York City paper with a circulation of half a million. *The Messenger-Telegram* had been down around 350,000 when it died.

I'll have to eat everything I've said about the Post's *fear-mongering—chasing fact into the land of fiction.*

Before he could fully consider that dilemma, Carol Wheelwright finished pouring coffee and headed out of the long dining room. Taylor excused himself for the bathroom.

He caught Wheelwright before she could duck into the kitchen.

"We need to talk."

"Are you trying to get me in trouble?"

"I'm trying to figure out why Martha was killed. *Why* gets me to a *who*."

"I can't help you."

"What's happened since Monday? Did someone get to you?"

"A cop came around. Didn't talk to staff. Lucky we're invisible. I don't know what I'd do if he did. I'm scared. If Martha got killed for what she heard, I might get the same if someone thought I knew the same."

"I'll keep you totally out of it. Even if it means no story. I said I would. Someone's got to do something for Martha."

Wheelwright lowered her eyes. "I'll call that number you gave me."

"Uh-huh. That didn't work. It's been a week. No phone calls. What are your days off?"

"Tuesday and Sundays."

"Meet me at the Odysseus Coffee Shop, Seventy-Fifth and Madison, at three on Tuesday."

"I live in Harlem. I'm not coming downtown on my day off."

"Carol!" It was a yell from the kitchen.

"Fine. Name the place."

"One Thirty-Five West One Twenty-Eighth Street. Apartment Seven H. It's off—"

"Lennox. I know. I'll see you at three on Tuesday."

Taylor returned to a cheese course and coffee. He listened now. Some politics, some gossip, some new play about which he was clueless. Martha Gibson didn't come up. The .44-caliber killer didn't either. The warm, comfortable insulation of the room. The way the guests seemed to feel separated from what the city could do to them. Taylor thought the opposite, like their money and old traditions and attitudes would draw the bad right to them and they'd never see it coming. His throat was dry. He'd been slow with the wine. He wanted to squirm. Or yell.

As a test, to give himself something to do, he asked those around him what they thought of the murderer in the headlines.

"Just some nut who's killed a couple of kids in the outer boroughs," said a jowly man. "They'll get him."

"What do you expect if you sit in a car in the Bronx at two in the morning?" said a woman almost as fat in the face.

Carter perked up at the talk. "He's a psycho, mate. We're selling a lot of copies of the *Post*. We're going to sell a whole lot more because of him."

Taylor set down his coffee. "Mr. DeVries' maid was murdered the same night as the last victim of this killer. No one's doing anything about that tragedy."

"Not every tragedy's a story."

Mrs. DeVries, anger obvious on her face, walked the length of the dining room, bent down, and spoke in her husband's ear with a hissing noise like a pissed-off snake.

"My wife reminds me," DeVries said, "cordials are being served in the living room."

Mrs. DeVries turned slowly and smiled, though without enthusiasm, at Taylor and Carter, and only with her mouth. Her eyes held on to the anger, and her hands were balled into fists.

CHAPTER 11

———◆———

THE WINTER OF 1976-1977, the second coldest on record, had finally let go of New York by mid-April. It was still the big city, and that meant the signs of spring were mostly human. Light jackets and sweaters. Faces less grim, under sunshine that actually warmed them. No more strange long strides to avoid the slush, which by the end had looked like a mix of dirt and poisoned ice cream.

Taylor walked to the Dublin Castle Pub on Eighth, which, with its neon-on-stainless-steel sign and blacked glass, looked about as much like Dublin Castle as New York looked like York. Jersey Stein had agreed to meet him there, pretty much out of pity.

Taylor hadn't made headway on the Martha Gibson story in three weeks. Blame the job. Unfortunately, blame didn't reduce his frustration. He had to turn three or four stories for the wire service most days; that was three or four more than the one he cared about. Most people thought reporters worked on one story at a time. Not unless you were Woodward or Bernstein. Any good reporter had five balls in the air. Any good reporter had one ball he cared about most—the story he wanted. Or needed.

Three different weeks Taylor had planned to go over to the Gibson apartment to see if drug dealing was going on and who the customers might be. He wanted to get another interview with Abigail Gibson if he could be sure boyfriend Jerome McGill was away. He'd been yanked back by all sorts of breaking news. Four-alarm fire in a posh building on the Eastside. Running gunfight after a bank robbery in the north Bronx. One rumor of big news coming on the .44-caliber murderer that was so strong, he'd had to check it out. Turned out to be nothing. Less than nothing. Plus dozens of lesser stories that were read on the radio once and disappeared into the ether.

The Gibson story was getting old. Old was the enemy of news. He might have given up, except for the certain conviction no one else was doing anything on Martha Gibson's homicide. McCauley and anyone else he called at the 112th Precinct all said the same thing. "Waiting for a break."

Waiting's the key word. Who the hell is going to make that break?

Most frustrating of all, he'd gone up to Carol Wheelwright's apartment on two of the last three Tuesdays—her day off. She wasn't there. He'd waited as long as he could. He had a bad feeling she was dodging him.

With a few minutes to spare one day, he'd called Martha's high school in Bed-Stuy, the name remembered from her diploma framed and hung in the apartment. Teachers there still remembered her. Good quotes about a smart young woman who had done everything right to get out of a tough neighborhood and into City College. The quotes from the college folks were the same, grades better.

Taylor liked Martha Gibson, strange as it might sound, since he'd never met her and never would. The more he got into any victim's life, the closer he thought he was getting. Then he'd pull himself up short. It was a mirage. The sum total of all his facts couldn't let him in on who the person had really been. He was building his own portrait, and it was one he liked. That was okay by him. The dead were as far away as anyone could get. This was the best he could do. If he liked what he saw, he liked what he saw.

Jersey Stein sat on a stool with a Tab in front of him. The investigator for the Manhattan DA's office never drank. Taylor ordered a seven-ounce pony.

"You're the only reporter in New York not asking me about the nut job."

Stein's hazel eyes over prominent cheekbones gave Taylor the up and down like he was deciding whether Taylor was a new witness worth interviewing.

"There are homicides enough to go around," Taylor said.

"This Martha Gibson out in Queens. I've got nothing."

"That's from asking?"

"Because your weird hunts entertain me—sometimes—I got an investigator for the Queens DA to call the precinct. Took them half a day to find the file."

"Is a lot of that going on now? Files sitting in stacks because of the forty-four-caliber killer manhunt?"

"C'mon, Taylor. No conspiracies. Every case has to be investigated. They've got nothing on Gibson so it sinks to the bottom of the stack."

"They're not chasing this one. I can tell. I'm talking to people before they are. Besides, look at the numbers. Sixteen men moved onto the Omega Task Force. Five murders a day in New York. Who fills the gaps?"

"Guys are doing overtime to cover."

"Everyone wants in on the manhunt. The monster hunt. Young, White girls. The victims could be the kids of detectives. Real emotional connection there. It's a pretty powerful pull."

"Did you hear that one detective's daughter came close to being a victim?"

"Who?"

Stein laughed. "At least you tried. That stays protected."

"How about case referrals to the DA?"

Stein pushed his hand through his thinning hair. "Down a little in this borough. *Not* enough to say something's going on."

"Hope not. Big town. Lot of bad guys. Gibson worked for this Park Avenue family, DeVries."

"You mentioned on the phone. I've heard of them. Hard not to. Gave a lot in my boss's re-election campaign. You probably need to be more careful of them than a lot of those bad guys. They have pull little guys like us can't do anything about."

"Edmond DeVries seems like a decent enough a guy. Not so sure about the son. The father says he's a liberal Republican."

"All New York Republicans have to say that."

Taylor waved at the bartender for another round. He decided to make Novak happy with a question, while satisfying his own curiosity.

"You think the psycho is going to attack in Manhattan? Only Queens and the Bronx so far. There are direct highway connections between those boroughs."

"I don't know where he's going to hit next. Nobody does. There's still nothing solid on this guy. One cop told me they're going to need him to strike again to catch him."

"That's a fucking frightening strategy."

"They've got guys driving around lovers' lanes and discos, all concentrated in the Bronx and Queens. Some detectives are parked with mannequins next to them in their cars."

"I'd heard that."

"I've got one other thing for you on Gibson. I looked into Jerome McGill, the sister's boyfriend. He's a transplant from Harlem. Name rang a bell with me. His main game on this island wasn't dealing. Specialty was contract killings."

"A hitman?" Taylor pictured the knife he'd used his junior judo to free from Jerome's grip.

"Drug trade always has a need for janitors. He sets up the

hits and hires extra help from a regular pool of gunmen. That's from two confidential sources. Never been able to pin a killing on the man."

"Which gang?"

"Independent. Like I said, killing's his main business. Theory is his drug dealing is mainly to take care of himself and the guys he hires. The benefits package. He needs to be careful, though. Contract work means he can't be in conflict with the drug gangs that hire him."

"Both lines of work are so ethical."

"Maybe Queens is more laid-back. Or maybe he's quit the murder game."

"Not clear what he's doing," Taylor said. "I haven't seen him actually sell yet. Know he's sometimes at the apartment. On the other hand, this lead is more proof that the guys at the One-One-Two aren't even trying with Gibson."

"Wouldn't say that. Movement of intelligence between the boroughs is terrible. Never been good. What they knew in Manhattan they didn't in Queens. I passed it along. I mean look at this forty-four psycho. First killing was in July. Took until March to make the connection to the other shootings."

"Shouldn't that be fixed?"

"Oh sure. But at least we put a man on the moon."

.44-CAL. SLAYER
KILLS GIRL, BEAU
Gun Linked to 3 Other Deaths

—*Daily News*, page 1, April 18, 1977

Fourth Woman Slain by Same Gun

—*New York Times*, page 1, April 18, 1977

Chapter 12

———◆———

EIGHTEEN-YEAR-OLD VALENTINA SURIANI and Alexander Esau, 20, were shot at three in morning sitting in a car parked in the Bronx near the Hutchinson River Parkway. Taylor spent that Sunday running to the press conference and chasing police sources and anyone else he could think of and rewrote everything everybody else was rewriting. The Associated Press and United Press International had more and had it earlier. The whole process depressed him. He couldn't add anything to the story, and two more young people were gone, killed by a crazy man who hunted lovers' lanes in a city where small apartments didn't leave room for romance.

Depressed, listless, and helpless.

He knew how to get stories. He'd reported on the murders of young people in the past. With this one, the cops complained to him about the impossible task of tracking down one psychopath in a metropolitan area with a population of 15 million people. They needed the killer to make a mistake, which, so far, he hadn't. Taylor didn't know how he could help, except sit in a car with Samantha somewhere in the Bronx late at night like old Ted Prager had in Queens, playing target for the Three X

Killer. He wasn't putting her at risk with a strategy that would likely produce no leads. He knew one thing. Reporters chasing reporters wouldn't save any lives.

The next day, he flipped through the *Post,* imagining the mad scramble at the paper to find the deepest fear in the story, stretched vowels stretching across the newsroom from Murdoch's office. The coverage went almost to the sports pages. The *Times* finally put the murders on page one, though with only a two-column, single-deck headline buried beneath President Carter proposing amnesty to illegal aliens, Albany boosting pay to state workers (what happened to that financial crisis?) and of course, the opening of the Yale Center for British Art. Taylor most certainly didn't believe in exploiting the story, but the *Times* didn't need to make an extra effort to show how its home city wasn't its highest priority—or even in the top three.

The next day, Chief of Detectives John Keenan held a City Hall presser—speaking carefully like Taylor had never seen, a Chief of Ds walking on eggshells—to name Deputy Inspector Timothy Dowd to head the Omega Group. The task force would move to the 109th Precinct in Flushing and more detectives were being added to the effort.

More crimes are going to get lost in the shuffle.

Like he'd told Jersey Stein, it was a numbers game. The NYPD had taken huge cuts during the budget crisis. More than a hundred detectives were going to be shifted to Omega. There couldn't be enough overtime to close the gaps left in other investigations.

Taylor knew only one way to fight his helplessness—go after the story he *could* get, chase the murder of Martha Gibson, and after that, those of the others snuffed out in the daily destruction of life on the city's streets. He had to get one of his leads—Abigail Gibson, Carol Wheelwright, a DeVries, or Ricky MacDonald—to connect him to a reason for Martha Gibson's death. Or it would soon go in the books as one of New

York's senseless unsolved killings. Too many got that label.

For a third time, he arrived at Carol Wheelwright's apartment, a walk-up in a classic Harlem brownstone, a beautiful building somehow untouched by the urban decay that had attacked the buildings around it like a virus.

The door opened fast on his second knock. It wasn't Carol. A muscular man north of six feet grabbed Taylor's jacket, yanked him inside, slammed him against the wall for good measure—enough measure to jar his teeth and start his head aching—spun him, and shoved him into a chair.

"Careful of the furniture," said Carol Wheelwright. "I worked my job to buy this set."

The man stepped several feet away and picked up one of those new aluminum baseball bats.

Sunk deep in the chair, Taylor decided on not moving as the best strategy. The bat would hit him before he could get out of the seat. Anyway, this may be one of the formalities of doing an interview in this corner of New York. Taylor had gotten through worse to find out what he needed.

"Put the bat down, Robert," Carol said. "You're not going to need to hit him."

"Thank you."

"Yet." Carol turned to face Taylor. "I told my brother you'd given up. You were simply digging around rich people business and got bored. Here you are."

"I stopped by twice, looking for you."

"It's my day off. I don't sit around all day waiting for you."

Robert slapped his hand with the bat he was obviously reluctant to put down despite his sister's instructions. A rough, smudged-looking tattoo on his arm shifted as his muscle flexed. Still, Taylor knew the type.

"You served?"

"You got an opinion on the war like every-fucking-body else?"

"My younger brother was killed. Called MIA in 1972."

Now he propped the bat against the wall. "Sorry to hear that. Who was he with?"

"Tenth Mountain. They said he went after some NVA taking potshots. Didn't come back."

"Marines. I enlisted. It's important people remember."

"Yes, it is." His stomach squeezed into a cold ball to remind him he'd been doing the opposite the past two years. "Because everyone's trying to forget."

"Not trying. Succeeding."

Robert sat next to his sister and sunk deep into the navy-blue cushion of a squared-off modern couch, lifting her a little. Taylor could see why Carol was proud. The living room was furnished in the new Scandinavian style, a striking yet interesting contrast to the century-or-more-old moldings and trim of the interior of the brownstone. The narrow-planked floor was polished to a mirror shine. Framed prints, some produced in an intentionally distorted style, hung on the wall. Famous Blacks like Martin Luther King Jr. and Malcolm X. Others Taylor didn't know.

"A White man is doing a story on a Black woman from Queens by coming up to Harlem?"

"You go where the story takes you. Carol said something was going on in the house. Martha might have been involved," Taylor looked straight at Carol, "or she knew something. I'm not going to get you in trouble. Your job is safe."

"How do I know I can trust you?"

"You can trust him," Robert said. "You don't do it the way he's doing it unless you want to do it right. Plus, he's got the memory for what happened. That's important."

This caught Taylor off guard, but he'd take it—the benefit of the brotherhood of 'Nam by extension.

"It's not a lot, but it sounded serious. Martha was taking flowers for the tables outside the sitting room. The family uses that room when it's just them. She heard a man talking clearly."

"Who?"

"No one she knew. Voice was deep, sort of. She said it definitely wasn't Charlie or Mr. DeVries. He never yells anyway. The man was saying—"

"Is this word for word?"

"Best as I can remember it. He said, 'We can't wait any longer. The money's going to be *completely* gone. All of it.' "

"Who else was in the room?"

"She couldn't tell."

"Mother, Audrey, Charlie, guest?"

"Martha had no idea. Charlie's girlfriend of the moment was over for lunch that day. I didn't see her leave. If people are talking, Charlie's going to be heard. So I guess that would rule him out. The second person was speaking low, Martha said, maybe sitting on the other side of the room by the windows. She couldn't tell if they were male or female. Couldn't tell anything. This other person said something, and the male voice got angrier, louder. 'I don't care. He might as well be throwing the money out the window. The crazy things he's investing in. Still writing the same checks to charities when you're going to be the charity. He has to be stopped.' The other voice went on for a while. 'Fine,' said the loud one. 'As long as we take care of him by then. Final and done with. No frittering away what's left.' Martha heard steps come toward the double door. She left the flowers half arranged and hurried back down the hall. The doors opened."

"Was she seen?"

"She didn't turn to check. She kept going until she was in the kitchen. She never knew."

"When did this happen?"

"A week before she died."

"Who else did she repeat the story to?"

"Just me."

"You're sure?"

"She was scared."

"What about Mr. DeVries?"

"She liked him. We all do. He's a kind man."

"Would she tell him because she liked him?"

A pause that meant Martha might have.

"What would he do if she did?"

Taylor could guess, but he wanted to hear it.

"He'd ask the family about who was in the room. He's always trying to solve problems. He thinks he can every time. He's too nice to some of them."

"If he did do that, whoever it was would know Martha overheard the conversation. Except for the highly unlikely situation that those in the sitting room weren't family *or* staff."

"That's not possible."

"Then someone would know she overheard a conversation that could be the planning of a murder. Or, they'd know because she'd been seen retreating down the hallway. 'Handle it by then' might mean something else. 'Final and done with' doesn't mean many other things."

Carol sighed.

"How do Mr. and Mrs. DeVries get along?"

"Oh, she's prickly, but she's always been prickly. It's the way of the ladies down there." She smoothed her dress across her thighs. "Those two always make up when they fight."

Taylor rose from the chair.

"I still haven't spoken to Martha's parents. Do you know the address in Bed-Stuy?"

"I'll write it down."

She handed him the address and walked down to the stoop with him. The afternoon offered that comfortable warmth of spring that made it easy to not notice the temperature at all. Above, between the brownstones on both sides of the street, ran a stripe of light-blue sky with two thin clouds crossing the stripe, possibly the two slowest moving objects in the city that day.

"I guess I have to trust you," Carol said.

"You *can* trust me."

"You know something else was going on with Martha. She had a job before the DeVrieses."

"Yeah, Manning. Her boss was coming on to her. She quit. He's been out of town. I want to talk to him when he gets back."

"Quitting wasn't enough to get rid of that guy. He followed her around. Sent dirty notes. He attacked her."

"What did he do?"

She stared over his shoulder, avoiding his eyes. "He caught her in the courtyard behind the Park Avenue apartment building. Was probably waiting there. He pushed her up into the corner of the fence and was tearing at her clothes. Luckily for her, one of the building's janitors—Freddie Maxwell—came out and chased him off. He'd hit her a couple of times before, but this was the worst."

"Did she go to the cops?"

"You kidding? Black woman, White man. Black witness. Besides, she was scared about the attention it would bring to the building—"

"And the DeVries family."

She nodded yes.

CHAPTER 13

———◆———

TAYLOR RODE THE subway out to Bed-Stuy and found the Gibson's building, which was in poor condition. Some windows boarded up. Others broken.

A middle-aged woman, thin and quick on her feet, invited him in as soon as she heard Martha's name. The apartment was in much better shape than the building. Furniture of dark wood. Porcelain knickknacks took up space that framed pictures didn't. Some of the photos looked antique.

Mr. Gibson rose from the couch and folded a newspaper—*The Daily News,* with another .44-caliber shooter story on page one. There were reminders every day, every hour that the killer was out there.

Gibson shook Taylor's hand.

"I'm very sorry about what happened to Martha," Taylor said.

"Please have a seat." He pointed to an easy chair upholstered in a complicated pattern featuring antique cars—Model Ts, Model As, Duesenbergs, Packards, Bearcats, Hudsons.

Taylor sat and couldn't help but continue observing the furniture and fixtures all around him.

"You're wondering why we're in this awful building?" Before Taylor could find a polite way to answer his way out of the question, Mr. Gibson continued, "We've lived here almost thirty years. Moved over from Harlem when it was a good neighborhood. Now, the landlords are giving up. Our landlord is giving up. We like this apartment. 'Course, wouldn't matter if we didn't. We can't afford the rent anywhere else. So we're going to hold on. How can we help?"

His voice was matter-of-fact, though his eyes looked sad and tired.

"I'm writing a story about your daughter. I want to learn as much as I can about her life."

"Her life was in her apartment. We've been to it once since she was killed." He let the paper drop into his lap like a dead thing. "We saw our junkie of a daughter and that thug McGill she's living with. They ... *he* threw us out after five minutes. We only wanted some of Martha's things. Pictures. The diplomas. Mementos of her life."

"Be careful of McGill," Taylor said. "He's a contract killer. Seems attached to the apartment."

"Oh goodness." Mrs. Gibson perched on the edge of the same couch her husband was sitting on. "We've got to get Abigail out of there."

"Do what with her?" Mr. Gibson said. "She'll steal from us to buy dope."

"She's still our daughter. Our only daughter now." She turned to Taylor. "We were so at a loss during the funeral .... We thought we'd deal with other things—with Abigail and the apartment—once things settled down. Suddenly, he's living there full-time."

Taylor took out his notebook and opened it. "I'd like to ask some questions about Martha."

The wife nodded.

"Did she like working for the DeVries family?"

"I think she was adapting. I mean, she was disappointed at

leaving the job at Manning. The family treated her well. They were all at the funeral."

"Do you know why she left Manning?"

"Bastard," said Mr. Gibson.

Taylor paused to let the one word sum it up. "She was brave. I've only learned today he continued harassing her after she left. Did she mention that to you?"

The Gibsons looked at each other. Mr. Gibson shook his head. Finally, Mrs. Gibson said, "She didn't say anything. We thought it was because she'd had such a big setback. She started doing odd things. Peeking through the curtains when visiting us. Pacing. Looking out the window of her own apartment all the time. If you asked her why, she would go quiet. Wouldn't talk about it."

"He do anything to her?" Mr. Gibson asked in a near whisper.

"My source says he tried to attack her and was stopped by a janitor outside the building where she worked. He'd hit her a couple of times before that. That's all that I know."

"Poor Martha." The father brought both hands to his face and rubbed his fingers deep into his forehead. "She worked so hard. First college degree in the family. Took in her sister when she knew what kind of mess that would be. Was certain she could help Abigail. And the worst happened to Martha instead. The very worst."

Mrs. Gibson left the room and came back after a couple of minutes clutching a handful of tissues.

"Why are you visiting us now?" Mr. Gibson asked.

"As I said, I want to tell her story."

"She's been dead a month."

"Some stories take a while. I'm going to talk to her boss MacDonald at Manning. Did she ever say anything about problems in the DeVries household? A family member who didn't like her?"

"That seemed like the part of her life that was improving—if slowly, as the job was an adjustment. She was calmest when talking about her work. She mentioned Mr. DeVries often. He sounded liked a good employer and a good man. Sent her on a couple job interviews."

"What about the staff?"

"She liked them all."

"Talk about the rest of the family?"

"Didn't say much. Martha was the type who only talked about people if she had something good to say."

CHAPTER 14

———◆———

Ten or 15 years ago, Taylor used to be able to read the graffiti on subway cars. "Tony loves Mary." That sort of thing. As the spray-painted messages multiplied to the point where they covered everything—windows, walls, seats, ads, subway system maps—the graffiti went from readable to cryptic. It seemed that the more of it there was, the more the vandals (or artists, depending on your view) needed their own symbols and styles to stand out. He couldn't make out anything in this scrawl-covered car. He'd done a story on the graffiti explosion a couple of years ago and had had to pay a kid to translate for him. The kid had this wry smile as he did it, leaving Taylor to wonder if he was getting an accurate report. Tough to fact-check except hire another wry-smiling teen. It was their language.

He took his notebook out of the Army field jacket. He'd removed the winter liner from the coat two weeks ago. He'd wear the outer shell until summer heat made it impossible. Out of habit, as a salve to a mind twitching to know what sort of story he really had, he read each page of his notes on the ride, then flipped back and forth comparing quotes and facts.

There was no guarantee the murderer of Martha Gibson was in the notebook yet, but as was also his habit, he made a list of possible killers based on what he knew.

First, she could have been killed by some unknown player in the drug game because of Abigail Gibson's heroin habit. Add in the fact that Jerome McGill was into drugs, and according to Jersey Stein, contract killing, and Martha could easily have died because someone mistook her for Abigail. Next on the list came whoever had the conversation in the DeVries' sitting room. For certain, it was a threat against Edmond DeVries. Not certain: did the speaker see Martha retreating to the kitchen? Taylor had called this morning to get the information about that threatening talk to DeVries—and to find out if Martha had already told him about it—only to learn the family had left on a three-week European vacation. The butler had said he had strict instructions not to put anyone in touch. Taylor insisted he take a message and pass it on to Mr. DeVries. Even the words *life or death* didn't seem to impress the butler. Three weeks was a long time. City News Bureau's budget didn't extend to sending him searching for them around Europe.

At the 112th, Detective McCauley, on hearing the story about the conversation, had told Taylor he was pedaling hearsay of hearsay.

Finally, Martha's ex-boss Ricky McDonald made Taylor's list for harassment and attempted rape. Taylor had three ways to go, though two involved unknown attackers. All the possibilities on his list could send him in the wrong direction. It *could* be some person and motive he hadn't uncovered yet. This is what happened when he dug into the life of a victim. The dead left behind histories that were complex, and not even those closest to them knew everything.

Instead of going back to Manhattan from Bed-Stuy in Brooklyn, he changed trains for Queens. He decided he'd give the McGill stakeout a bit more time. Whatever McGill got up to, it could lead to a story, even if that wasn't what brought a killer into Martha Gibson's life. He hoped to score both. There was chance in every direction he might pick.

He walked past the red-brick apartment building, crossed the street so he was cattycorner from the main entrance, and found a bench with a good view of the front door. The minutes, then hours, ticked by. He watched three men and one woman, all of them scruffy and dirty enough to be addicts and too much of both to live in the building, use the payphone halfway down the block, get buzzed in and come out no more than five minutes later, hurrying away with that telltale junkie shuffle. Why hadn't he seen this on his previous stakeouts? Maybe Jerome had waited a few weeks before he started selling from the apartment, had supply issues, had waited a decent period of mourning …. He chuckled darkly at that thought.

He witnessed six possible sales. *Yeah, maybe.* Could be any apartment. He had no proof. He planned to follow the next probable addict all the way in to confirm they were going to the Gibson flat.

Before he could, McGill came out of the building carrying a slate-gray duffle bag. He checked up and down the street, the wary move someone out for a stroll wouldn't make, and started walking. Once McGill reached the far corner, Taylor got up and followed on the other side of the street. Short of Hillside Avenue on 182nd Street, McGill unlocked a red Granada. Taylor sped past him to Hillside, flagged a cab, and got in.

"A red Ford Granada is going to come out of that side street. Follow it."

"C'mon, pal, I ain't got time for crazy movie horseshit."

Taylor dropped $10 onto the front seat. "For anything under seven bucks on the meter. Goes higher, it gets better for you."

Taylor couldn't lose McGill.

The cabbie stayed with the Granada, which made a fast stop at the Jamaica subway station to pick up two more men, both Black, one medium height, one tall. They drove east through Queens, mainly using Brinkerhoff and 109th Avenues.

On the radio, WNBC-AM segued from ABBA'S "Dancing Queen" to "Southern Nights" by Glen Campbell. Taylor decided he'd be pushing it to ask the driver to change the station.

He leaned over the front seat for the best view into McGill's car. At a stoplight, McGill handed the duffle over to the man in the back, and that man opened it and took out several objects. A hitman and his gang … what else could he be removing but weapons?

After a 20-minute drive, McGill pulled to the curb on Rockaway Boulevard in front of a row of shops several blocks from Aqueduct Raceway. All three men got out. Taylor threw another $10 over the seat and exited the cab, telling the cabbie to get out of there quick and report a shooting at that address. The cabbie took off so fast Taylor worried the driver would forget the other thing he was supposed to do.

The three men came together in front of Philby's Pawn Shop. They all held guns down at their sides. The display windows were so empty of merchandise, it was a dead giveaway this place did some other sort of business.

McGill and one of the other men started for the door, while the third held his position as lookout.

Whatever was going to happen, it wasn't going to be good and it was going down now.

Waiting for the cops was no plan. If the cab driver did bother to call it in, they'd get here far too late to stop the crime.

McGill and his accomplice were halfway to the front door.

The back entrance.

Taylor ran down a narrow alley between the pawnshop and an adjacent Chinese restaurant. He pulled open a metal door covered in chipped red paint.

"There's guys coming in the front with guns …."

Four men rose quickly from folding chairs, one knocking his to the floor with a crash. All four pointed their own semiautomatics at Taylor's face. On the table was piled white bricks, stamp bags used to hold heroin for sale to junkies, and cash in a stack half as high as the drugs.

"I don't know who you think you are," said a small Hispanic man, "but you just ended your life."

"I'd really worry about the guys coming in the front."

At that instant, gunfire erupted from the front of the shop. The men turned, with the little guy signaling two to go down a short hallway in the direction of the firing. Seconds after they disappeared, the noise of weapons doubled, tripled. A cacophony.

Taylor dropped to the floor.

I tipped off one set of villains that they were getting hit by another set. I'm way too close to this.

Taylor crawled back to the door and slipped out, while the remaining two men were focused on the gunfire. Once he was in the alley, two bullet impacts puckered the door. This was definitely as much of this story as he needed to see up close and personal. He sprinted along the back of the shops, ran next to a fence and into a parking lot. He could stay lost in here until the police arrived.

Three squad cars pulled up seven minutes later. McGill was a dead tangle of limbs outside the front door, his life over and his mission a failure because Taylor had informed the other bad guys. Two were dead inside. Everyone else was gone.

Emptiness, something hollow in his chest. He hadn't pulled a single trigger. He hadn't made a plan to come here. Some of those seven men were bound to die no matter what he'd done. But the outcome changed when he'd gone in that back door. He wouldn't have done things differently. He couldn't know it was bad guys in back as well as front. Maybe that was what the emptiness was about. At some point in these brutal situations, he had to make a choice—and that choice couldn't help everyone, or even only the good guys.

He phoned in a quickie on the gunfight to Cramly.

Back at the office, he called Mr. and Mrs. Gibson and told them they'd have no problem visiting their daughter and getting Martha's things.

Next he called the 106th Precinct, where the man on the desk was surprised Taylor was asking about the shooting.

"Detectives just got in the house."

"Why the attack?" He wanted hard numbers.

"Pawn shop had about seventy-five thousand dollars worth of heroin and half that in cash money."

"A robbery?"

"No, a hit. Detectives think someone stepped on someone's territory. Couldn't tell you who. They're still working on it."

McGill died doing what he loved.

Taylor filed an update. Cramly asked how he had such a detailed description of the gunfight.

"Good reporting."

"How CAN I help you?" A cigarette in a black holder bounced between the fuchsia lips of the blue-haired woman sitting inside the office door of Manning Corp.

"I'm here to see Ricky MacDonald."

"Do you have an appointment?"

Boxes were scattered everywhere around the office on the 55th Floor of the Empire State Building. Folding chairs served as furniture. The walls were painted a faded peach. The place, in New York's most prestigious address, looked like a warehouse. Who would invite anyone here for an appointment?

"I don't. I'm reporter doing a story about a former employee."

"Who's that?" Almost accusatory.

"The late Martha Gibson."

"She's dead?" The cigarette holder stuck straight out, clamped in her teeth. "I'll take you to my son."

Taylor was led through a doorway, around more stacks of boxes, until the woman held up her hand for him to stop and disappeared. She returned and showed him to a desk partitioned off by additional walls of cartons.

Like any good salesman, Ricky MacDonald rose and grabbed Taylor's hand like he planned to take it away. He had a pumpkin-shaped head and wore a leisure suit a deeper fuchsia than his mother's lipstick. The huge collar of his bright yellow shirt covered the jacket's lapel. The shirt was open three buttons down.

Taylor sat down in the one guest chair, which was metal and folding.

"Martha's dead?"

"You hadn't heard?"

"She only worked here a few months."

"Why'd she leave?"

He answered quickly, like he didn't need to think. "I fired her for insubordination."

"Not because she refused your sexual advances?"

A salesman's smile. "Is that the story she was telling? I'm sorry she had to stoop so slow."

Taylor didn't feel like dancing around with this one, who'd lied from the beginning and oozed sleaze. "You harassed her. You continued to do so after she left. Attacked her outside the Park Avenue apartment house where she was working. You've got history. Conviction for solicitation and arrested for sexual assault. Makes you a good candidate for her murder."

"The assault charge was dropped. The police haven't even talked to me about this."

"This is my lead. So far. I've got witnesses who say you attempted to rape her. Martha may be dead, but they'll tell her story. Cops read that, they'll want to know if you went after her again. Maybe this time to kill her."

Blue hair stepped around the corner of the box-wall. "You can leave now. Ricky's *much* smarter brother Harry is a lawyer. I called him. This discussion is over. That nig ... Negro girl wasn't worth hiring in the first place. Ricky should have known that. She's not worth wasting any more of this company's time. A news story about her?" She laughed. "They can't even read."

"Martha could read. Had a college degree, as I'm sure is noted in a file somewhere in this mess." Taylor stood. "Keep brother Harry at the ready. I'll get more on the attack from the janitor who chased you away. The cops will come calling when I write a story."

"Do you know who you're dealing with?" she asked.

"Mother, please. He's leaving."

"I know exactly *what* I'm dealing with. Maybe your son didn't kill Martha. I'll find out exactly what he did do."

"That's a threat," she said. "I'm telling Harry. That was a threat."

"Throwing me out makes your son look guiltier. Tell me what went on, and we can leave it there."

"Get. Out."

"Harry better be a good lawyer." He addressed the old woman. "If you're connected to any of this, that's conspiracy." Taylor tossed his card on the desk. "Tell the lawyer to call me. Remind him I'm looking for facts. I get enough threats from the two-bits and mob boys."

As he rode the elevator down, Taylor exhaled at getting that over with. He'd never planned on the light touch with MacDonald's interview. More like a hammer blow. Even if Ricky MacDonald hadn't done Martha's murder, he'd made her life miserable. Karma said someone should return the favor. A side benefit of Taylor's job.

THOUSANDS STOOD ON the Park Avenue automobile ramp that ran around the south side of Grand Central Terminal. That was the problem. Jacqueline Onassis, Mayor Beame, former Mayor Robert Wagner, and several actors and singers were up on a dais for this April 21 lunchtime rally to save Grand Central. The only real interview here was Onassis, and lacking that, at least one of the other *names* up in there in their seats. Who sits at a demonstration? That, among other questions, he wasn't getting answered because he wasn't getting any closer to those people.

Grand Central was seriously old New York and had

somehow survived in a city that tore things down without a second thought. Its survivor status was highlighted by the 59-story Pan Am Building, a symbol of the modern metropolis that towered behind the 64-year-old train station.

This fight was about air rights, all those floors that could exist above GCT if it were shoved into the basement of an office tower.

Penn Central Transportation Corp knew that and wanted to rip down the station to replace it with a—surprise—59-story skyscraper. Pretty much the same thing had happened to old Penn Station, an exquisite glass-and-steel classic that had resembled one of the great railway terminals of Europe. The new Penn Station looked like a dirty bus terminal and had been, in fact, shoved in the basement under an office tower and Madison Square Garden. The destruction of Penn Station was what had mobilized Onassis and all the other somebodies to save GCT.

In this battle, the city's countermove was to declare Grand Central a landmark. Penn Central was fighting that through the courts and today's rally was to bring attention to the case.

Taylor reconciled himself to man-on-the-street interviews.

"It's a symbol of New York, *true* New York," said Carl Miller, who worked on Lexington. "We've got enough skyscrapers."

A passerby stopped to listen. "You know what I think?" Which in New York meant Taylor didn't have a choice. "It's a dump. Full of the homeless. A homeless hotel. Look at the windows." He pointed to the huge windows, nearly blackened by dirt and cigarette smoke. "They haven't cleaned those in decades. Let them put the ball through it."

The rally-goer started to argue. Taylor left them to it.

CHAPTER 15

———◆———

TAYLOR FELL ONTO his back and slapped the mat hard. The crack was loud and his hand hurt with that belly-flop sting.

The second thing Taylor hated about judo was falling practice. The first twenty minutes of every session were dedicated to different ways of landing on the mat. Backwards, forward roll, sideways. When Taylor and Samantha started, their instructor had said they couldn't learn how to throw until they knew how to fall because there was no guarantee they'd be doing the throwing. It wasn't just learning, he said, but ridding oneself of the fear of falling. Taylor wasn't sure if *fear* was the right word. Sure, he didn't enjoy it. At the same time, he was a kid from Queens. Falling was a bad plan in any street encounter. What he wanted was no encounters—just good stories. To that, Samantha said he should switch to sports or the City Hall beat.

The first thing Taylor hated about judo was being the worst of all the students. Matched up against a guy who had joined about when he did but was already one belt higher, he got lots of practice in falling when he was supposed to be throwing.

Smack, his hand hit the mat. Again. No matter how hard Taylor tried, he could only drop the guy or leverage him into a flip a third of the time at best. So far judo had only worked for him when he'd surprised someone—Jerome McGill. Had that been beginner's luck?

The floor came up again fast, and he landed poorly.

"You've got to roll," said the instructor. "Roll. That's why we practice at the beginning."

Across the way, Samantha toppled a man bigger than her. Bigger than Taylor.

Before reengaging, he rehearsed in his mind the ways to hit the ground correctly, but that pissed him off. That was retreating. He put his opponent on the mat three times in a row.

Taylor met Samantha outside the locker room.

"You sure you want to do this?" she said.

"Yes." *No.*

"We could try something else. Boxing?" An excited smile.

"Not paying to get hit in the head."

He'd stick with judo because it was something they did together. Then there was how much she'd worry if he ran around after crime stories without any means of defense.

"Let's have dinner at the Oddity. Grandpop will be happy to see you."

"I think it's his grandson who'll make his night."

"Wouldn't bet on that. We can continue our discussion of self-defense there. Ask Grandpop about ancient Greek wrestling."

"They did that naked."

"You never know when I'm going to have a good idea."

She hit him in the arm.

"THERE WERE SEVERED arms and legs lying on the landing pad." The fireman looked at the top of the skyscraper.

Just over three weeks after the rally, Taylor was back on the same city block, but on the other side of Grand Central at the foot of the Pam Am Building. In the midst of chaos. When he'd arrived, he'd seen two firemen come out of the building and throw up. That alone he couldn't remember seeing before. He'd finally found a firefighter who'd done his work and could talk.

"We got a call—trouble with New York Airways Flight 572 from JFK."

"On approach?"

"No, after it landed on the pad." He pointed up to the flattop of the Pan Am Building.

Flights from area airports to the skyscraper had resumed in February after a nine-year suspension.

"What happened?"

"The big Sikorsky S-61 landed and let everyone off. Passengers were waiting to board. Suddenly, one of those huge blades snaps off and goes flying. Killed four people standing there. Chopped them into pieces. The blade went over the side and must have smashed into at least one window." He pointed at the glass all over Vanderbilt Avenue. "People on Madison hit by it too."

"Four dead, then?"

"Five. Part of the blade killed a woman at Madison and Forty-Third. Awful."

Firemen didn't call many things *awful*.

"That's probably the end of flights for good."

"No doubt."

Taylor ran for a phone.

TAYLOR SNATCHED THE pink message slip taped to his phone. It said *DeVries* and the home number. He hoped against hope this might be the first break in weeks on the Martha Gibson story—okay, not *break*, but at least live contact. The DeVrieses had extended their trip to Europe by an additional two weeks. *What's it like to go on a five-week anything?* Two personal trips by Taylor to 827 Park to get messages through hadn't done any good. The butler, if anything, followed orders.

He'd been cut off from reporting on any connection Jerome McGill might have had with the murder because the hitman had the misfortune of dying from gunshots wounds in front of the pawnshop. Were his activities tied to Martha Gibson's death? Taylor had no way of knowing. The detectives had closed the pawnshop shooting case about as soon as they'd opened it; he was getting nothing there. Abigail Gibson remained on his list, but she'd disappeared from the apartment.

DeVries sounded like Taylor's oldest friend. "Would you like to go for a ride?"

Taylor had to suppress a laugh at hearing the movie mobster cliché uttered with DeVries' Upper Eastside accent, which didn't so much sound like New York as formal and a little old-fashioned and from nowhere in particular.

Taylor, expecting a limo of some sorts, didn't notice the blue Thunderbird until the horn honked. DeVries waved at him out the rear window. It might not be a limo, but there was still a chauffeur in uniform and hat at the wheel. Taylor noted someone in the backseat, so he got in up front.

"Taylor, this is Joe."

"Pleased to meet you," Joe said with a nod.

"You met my wife at the dinner."

Mrs. DeVries was the other passenger in the back.

"Of course."

"Why is it your goal to embarrass me?" she said to her husband. "We could have taken the big car, you could have dropped me off, and our guest wouldn't need to sit up front."

"I don't mind, Mrs. DeVries—"

"Thank you for being kind. There are ways to do things and ways not."

"I'm going for a drive in the country, honey," DeVries said. "I didn't want the Town Car."

"Use the brains God gave you. If he did. In that case, you

should have dropped me off and gone back for this little sports thing."

Joe gave Taylor a sideways look that was hard to translate. Could mean, *Don't say anything more … Good luck … Run away* or all those things at once.

They dropped Mrs. DeVries at a well-kept brownstone in Greenwich Village right off Fifth Avenue. Taylor switched to the backseat.

"One of my wife's favorite designers. I think she keeps her in that nice house. Or I do, I guess."

Taylor nodded. He couldn't think of some friendly, we're-all-in-this-together thing to say to that. Samantha looked good in nice clothes. The kind she could afford. She also appeared mighty fine in jeans and a t-shirt—often one of his—on weekends. Weekdays, a skirt or slacks and blouse and jacket hid her curves some so she could blend in on stakeouts for shoplifters and wayward husbands. Still, she looked beautiful then too. Mrs. DeVries and her friends at that dinner party had been going for something more like an exotic plant—or out of a picture in a museum. All of them except the daughter, Audrey, who'd kept it simple and so looked better than the rest.

"Let's go up the Henry Hudson to the Taconic," DeVries said.

"Yessir." Joe clicked on the right blinker and turned to head for the West Side Highway.

"We are going for *a ride*."

"I wanted to talk—and to show you something. You know where, Joe?"

"Yessir."

DeVries picked up a silver bottle from a miniature bar sitting on the transmission hump. "I tried to convince Joe to call me Teddy. Won't even use Mr. DeVries. His father drove my father. Right, Joe?"

"Yessir."

"So I'm *yessir*." He shook the bottle and poured whatever was in it into two metal mugs in the bar on the hump. "I'd love to make that change at the house. First names for everyone. Enter the modern world. It would make my wife too unhappy." Taylor imagined unhappy could be quite a show. "Traditions must be upheld."

DeVries handed Taylor the mug.

"Thank you. It's a—"

"Moscow Mule. A nice little nip. Had to plan ahead, though. The Thunderbird doesn't have a full bar like the Town Car."

I hang around DeVries, I'm going to have every nice little nip available. Break every rule I've got too.

The cocktail went down easy. The West Side Highway became the Henry Hudson Parkway.

"Imagine Henry Hudson and his crew sailing up this mighty river," DeVries said. "Palisades. Shoreline heavy with trees on both sides. The first Europeans to see all this, all that would become Manhattan and the rest of New York and New Jersey. They could have no idea what they were looking at."

"Sometimes I don't think people know what they're looking at today."

"Very good point." DeVries clinked their cups. He took a good swallow. Taylor's head was already fuzzy and buzzy. This was not a seven-ounce beer. This was barely *not* drinking his breakfast. "I've always enjoyed talking with reporters."

"When I was at the *Messenger-Telegram,* Park Avenue only spoke to the Society Page editor and only on certain topics."

"Garfield would invite me down to your paper. I'd get a private briefing from a City Hall reporter or the business editor or one of the Washington correspondents. There are things reporters notice that others miss because they look deep and fast. They have to see an event or study an issue quickly and still get the story right."

No one else talked about the *Messenger-Telegram* anymore, not outside Taylor's head. The paper was another ghost haunting him. He never would have imagined how fast a newspaper could disappear—be forgotten. Not until he'd seen it happen. When he'd first started in the business, he'd thought papers were forever. He'd learned that was wrong pretty quickly, but still …. They weren't special to people, normal people, not like they were to Taylor—and, he presumed, other journalists, though he'd never asked. He was afraid the answer would make him the only weird, haunted one. Ghosts. There had been a time when he worked for the paper and had a mother and a brother not yet rigged up for war. They were all gone. His father was gone too, but he refused to let the man haunt him. The Professor had had his shot at that when he was alive. He imagined Mom and Billy around the kitchen table with the *MT* spread across it on some average day he should have enjoyed far more than he did.

"You can only go with what you've got by deadline. If you don't have it, you can't go with it."

"That's it! Great speed and great care. Using only what you're sure of. Sitting in the newsroom, reporters will tell you what they haven't confirmed yet, but the job trains them to separate the facts from the guesses. Most people mix all of it together so you're not sure what happened and what's guess and what's opinion."

"We never met when you visited. Did you ever speak to the cop shop?"

"Cop shop?"

"Nickname for the police reporters."

"I should have taken as much interest in crime as the political and foreign scene. Foolish snobbery. Like crime could never enter my world." A long swallow. "I miss Martha. To die that way. It so saddens me. That's not the only crime in my life."

"What's happened?"

"We'll talk when we get there. I want you to see the good first. I want to watch the forests along the Taconic in their full spring splendor. So much green, it's like everything wants to live as much and as fast as it can."

I can wait. We'll also talk about what Martha heard before we're done.

DeVries finished his drink while looking out the window. His head bobbed a couple of times and he was asleep, leaning into the corner of the seat.

Several miles later, Joe pulled off to get gas. Taylor got out, stretched, and moved into the front seat.

CHAPTER 16

———◆———

THE BIG CAR swung back onto the parkway. Joe didn't say anything. Taylor replied with silence. Sometimes the best approach was not to ask questions, to wait it out. They slipped by trees either side of the narrow roadway, rising through the Hudson Highlands—Henry Hudson sure got enough things named after him for his efforts—and the parkway had the look of an alpine highway. Long drops on one side. Stone walls on the other. A big curve and the drop and the walls switched sides. A car flew by them on the left, passing within the thickness of a layer of paint.

"Asshole," said Joe, "in that piece of junk. I could take him. Don't want to wake up sir."

Taylor nodded, releasing his tight grip on the hand rest.

The miles passed. Taylor took out the paper that was ever present in his jacket pocket. Slow day, as far as he was concerned. Before a crowd, Governor Byrne waved the signed bill allowing gambling in Atlantic City. The U.S. and Cuba were ready for a limited exchange of diplomats. That was the best of it. Governor Carey on rent control. *Skip*. The House considering creating a Department of Energy. *Skip*. The international energy conference in Paris ending in failure. *Double skip*. He turned the page.

Inside the paper, the U.S. and Vietnam resumed "gloomy" talks on normalizing relations. The U.S. expressed concern the Soviets planned to try Jewish dissident Anatoly Shcharansky for treason. And a thousand migrating sharks drove swimmers from the waters off Corpus Christi. After the movie *Jaws* two years ago, any shark story made it into the paper, though Taylor had to admit a thousand of them had the makings of a pretty good monster movie.

Deeper in the paper, he read through a juicy report on how doctors running Medicaid mills in the Bronx had agreed to cut in racketeers as secret partners after being threatened with death. Every time he thought he'd heard of all the ways to commit crime in New York....

The best police story: a 55-year-old Queens woman had contracted to kill her dentist son-in-law. However, that one was done and dusted. Nothing to track down, nothing the DA wasn't already announcing.

"You know, he likes you," Joe said.

"He's a nice guy. I like him."

"Yeah, but he's too trusting."

"Of me?"

"Of everyone. Used to be, you could do business with a handshake. You took care of people, they took care of you. Sir still works that way. No one else does. It's hurting him. I'm trusting you now because maybe you can help him out." He glanced into the rearview mirror. Light snoring from the back. "I don't know what exactly he's going to tell you. He's been embarrassed. Badly. The wife, she likes to spend. Running the DeVries household has never been cheap. The money's not there the way it used to be." He pulled out a pack of Winstons and offered. Taylor waved him off. Joe lit up. "You really think Miss Gibson's death is connected to the family? Because that's the last thing he needs."

"Don't know. I plan to ask about that today."

"The way she was killed. That didn't sound very Upper Eastside."

"You're right about that. Could be someone she met *through* work. One man connected to her in Queens was the type to do it, but he's dead so I can't ask him." Joe glanced over through the cigarette smoke. "Unrelated shooting. Bottom line, the detectives aren't much focused on Martha's case."

"Because of that psycho job?"

"Maybe. I'm trying to make my own headway."

Taylor had written off making progress on the McGill connection, but as always happened when he pursued one angle, another pushed into his mind, a sort of double-check backed by his internal editor—doubt. What if Abigail and McGill were the reason for Martha's death, rather than these high-society folks he was messing with? Messing with in part because their world fascinated him. One of McGill's accomplices was in Rikers. Abigail was still around somewhere. He had to find her or talk to the accomplice to really take that cause for the murder off the list.

"You know, my seventy-year-old mother's calling me every day telling me to be careful where I park," Joe said. "I'm saying, 'Mom, this nut's shooting young girls with long dark hair and their unlucky boyfriends when they go spooning in parking spots. How is that me?' Still, she's calling me daily. Everybody's going crazy."

Crazy.

Joe eased off into a scenic overlook and continued smoking.

Down bellow, green leaf covered a narrow valley so thickly Taylor couldn't tell where the bottom lay. In less than forty minutes, you could get away from everything that looked liked New York City and experience this.

"You should get in the back before he wakes," Joe said.

Taylor did, and they eased back on the parkway.

About fifteen minutes later, DeVries stretched. "You two get along?"

"Yessir. You know me. I get along with everyone." Joe ground out the third Winston.

"That you do."

The car left the Taconic and wound along back roads in a generally easterly direction, through curves, turning onto side roads and side roads of side roads. Cows, black with white patches, chewed in that strange circular motion. A horse galloped fast behind white fencing while another watched and grazed. For Taylor, who considered a four-block park the natural world, this was deep country, bordering on wilderness. These animals weren't in zoos. They had real jobs. A kind of reverse claustrophobia—or whatever the right shrink word for it was—made him anxious about so much open space. Agoraphobia, yeah—except the kind when there weren't big buildings rising to the sky next to crowded sidewalks.

At a mailbox with a newspaper tube below reading *Amenia Times*, Joe turned onto a dirt driveway that ran between two fenced fields, more cows on one side, more horses on the other.

"Clock the driveway," DeVries said, and Joe nodded.

Even running at a crawl, the car bounced down the drive. At one point, Taylor shouldered into DeVries and apologized. The T-bird pulled up to a green, close-cut lawn and three large trees in front of a white farmhouse with brown shutters.

"Just under a mile." Joe turned off the engine.

DeVries opened the door and arched his long frame. "A one-mile driveway. Now *that's* privacy."

Taylor gazed at all the emptiness, because that's what the country was to him. Without people, there was no crime, and without that, what would he ever do? A tree never mugged anybody.

"You'd definitely be left alone up here," Taylor said with little enthusiasm, "unless the cows and horses start talking."

Joe laughed, and smoke from his latest cigarette came out his nose.

"I want to buy this place."

"Oh, for a …" Taylor had to think a minute for the correct word, "for a country house?"

"No, to move—lock, stock, and barrel. Sell the Park Avenue apartment. Sell it all."

Now, Taylor *was* bewildered. Why was he on this trip? Did DeVries expect him to file a real estate story?

"Walk with me." They went around the back of the house, where there was a barn, red paint peeling, with a silo right out of a child's picture book. "About one hundred fifty acres. Dairy cattle. A few horses. They're field hunters. The place makes money, which is more than I can say about some of my recent investments. They say the recession is over, but you wouldn't know it from where I sit. Trading a recession for inflation seems like swapping poison for a gun."

The more DeVries talked, the more Taylor thought he was wasting his time on a trip with an old man eager for company. He knew nothing of farms or the economy.

DeVries' eyes narrowed as he considered Taylor's face. "I have to get this done. I'm tired of the game, the chase, and the ugliness. New York is so, so ugly now, and it's reached right into my home. New York money is ugly. All of it. I want to do a little good. Live more simply."

Is this what happens when a rich guy decides to become a hippie—a decade late?

DeVries walked toward the back porch and unlocked the brown-painted door.

"Finally, there's this."

DeVries, already inside, turned so fast as Taylor came through the doorway that Taylor jumped back into Joe, only to find a stack of newspapers pointed at him.

"The *Amenia Times*?"

"The local paper."

"Yeah, I saw the tube at the end the driveway."

"I want to buy it." DeVries watched Taylor's face. "You think it's crazy?"

"No, I, well …. You clearly love newspapers. You're intelligent. Which is good. Too many stupid men have owned papers. I can't imagine a weekly would cost a lot. Cost *you* a lot."

"Look these over. Tell me what you think."

"I don't know the business side. I didn't know my own paper was dying the day it did."

"Give me your view of the editorial. All the top gentlemen in publishing—Murdoch, Sulzberger—would laugh at me if I asked them. Probably already laugh at me now."

Taylor took the papers.

"My plan *was* to run the paper and a foundation. The farm already has a manager."

"Was? Is your family opposed?"

"No, they're not the issue. My wife supports me." Taylor's eyebrows rose against his will. "I know how Evangeline comes off. She understands what's happening. She agrees the city is a lost cause. Audrey's fine. She has her job at the *New Yorker*."

"Charlie?"

"Yes, he's angry. Thinks I'm giving away his birthright. He needs to get to work. All that time in night clubs. Chasing around show business people. He had me invest in a film. A total bust."

DeVries signaled for them to head outside and locked the door.

"My big problem is not pressure from the family. This is hard to say. Embarrassing. Twenty-five million dollars has been stolen from me. Cash and securities. It disappeared at the same time as my investment advisor, Denny Connell."

"He embezzled you?"

"I believe that to be the case."

"When?"

"He was gone March fourteenth."

"A week after Martha's murder."

"You see a connection?"

"Not yet."

"I kept it from the family for month, but I had to tell them. That's why we went to Europe. We had to. We had to talk. Figure out what to do next—away from everything else."

'The rich are different from you and me.' Long vacation to Europe is not the first thing I'm doing when 25 of my millions disappear.

"Have the cops gotten anywhere with it?"

"Nowhere, even though the thief is obvious. Everything I've set up—buying the farm and paper, the foundation—hinges on that money. I've some left in personal accounts that weren't touched, but we can't do these projects. We can't stay where we are either. If I get the money back, maybe I can save my name, as old-fashioned and silly as that sounds."

"Doesn't sound silly to me. I like my name. Goes on top of all my stories."

"I've been impressed with your work. With the stories you've written." A look from Taylor. "Oh, I've read many, going back a ways. I want you to track down Connell and the money. Once we have Connell and I close my deals, the story's yours. Exclusive."

Taylor didn't need to think about that deal. He nodded.

Back in the car, he pulled out his notebook.

Time to lower another boom.

"I've been waiting weeks to ask you about this. I tried to reach you in Europe."

"James is scrupulous in following instructions."

"Yes, well, you went traveling right after I learned about something Martha overheard while at work. She was outside the sitting room and the doors were closed. A man with a deep voice was speaking. She couldn't ID him. At least one other person was in the sitting room, but she couldn't make out what they said or who they were. What she *heard* may have gotten her killed because the unknown man made threats against your life. The man said ..." Taylor took out his notes so he could get the wording right, " 'We can't wait any longer. The money's going to be all gone. All of it. I don't care. He might as well be throwing the money out the window. The crazy things he's investing in. Still writing the same checks to charities when you're going to be the charity. He has to be stopped.' The other voice went on for a while and then the man picked up again. 'All right. As long as we take care of him by then. Final and done with. No frittering away what's left.' Martha heard steps coming toward the door. She rushed down the hall to the kitchen. She wasn't sure if she was seen. If she was, that man could be her murderer. Do you know who might have been speaking?"

"I don't. I will handle it."

"You could be in—"

"I can handle it."

Taylor had to try one last time.

"He knows what's going on in the family and he's angry. The other person must be someone *in* your family."

"I said I'll take care of it." Though his voice stayed controlled, DeVries' ruddy face had gone pale. "People get upset. Say what they don't mean. Please find Connell. I'll take care of this."

They rode in silence.

NEW NOTE: CAN'T STOP KILLING

—*Daily News*, page 1, June 3, 1977

.44 KILLER: I AM NOT ASLEEP

—*Daily News*, page 1, June 4, 1977

Breslin to .44 Killer:

GIVE UP! IT'S ONLY WAY OUT

—*Daily News*, page 1, June 5, 1977

CHAPTER 17

———◆———

"**W**HAT WERE YOU doing clapping at the end of that?" Samantha said as Taylor held the door for the movie theater on Union Square. "You liked *Star Wars* that much?"

"Why are you so surprised?"

"Not much in the way of facts in that movie. The last flick you really liked was in April—*The Late Show*, that grungy murder mystery with Art Carney and Lily Tomlin. You said it felt sort of almost real. A big compliment from you."

"I actually wasn't born with a notebook in my hand, running after crime stories." He smiled. "I loved sci-fi movies, monster movies when I was a kid. *Forbidden Plant. The Day the Earth Stood Still.* 'Creature Feature' in the afternoon. Never saw any of them in the theater. My father didn't believe in going to movies. I watched them all on TV. *Star Wars* felt like those did. Ships rocketing through space, blasters, robots."

"This one was different. Sleek. Those fifties movies were clunky."

"*2001* was sleek."

"And pretentious."

"You're right there. We're living in the future. So the future's got to look sleeker."

"Future? That movie was supposed to be a long time ago and far away or whatever it said at the beginning."

"Just a once upon a time thing."

"That's your cinematic analysis?"

"It is."

"Two years, and I'm still learning things about you, Taylor."

"Let's get coffees before we go to the newsstand."

At a little after ten in the evening, Taylor and Samantha walked up to a line snaking along the sidewalk to a newsstand at Lexington and 32nd Street, both holding coffees in blue and white cups decorated to look like Grecian earns. Most Greek coffee shops used the cups, and many non-Greek ones. Grandpop refused; he didn't like stereotypes and insisted on white cups with a thick red stripe. But his shop and his coffee were forty-some blocks north of Taylor and Samantha's neighborhood.

The .44-caliber killer, who had identified himself as Son of Sam, had without a doubt realized there was a three-ring media circus set up to cover his spree. This week, he'd declared himself the ringmaster. The killer had mailed a letter to star *New York Daily News* columnist Jimmy Breslin. The *News*, in a brilliant demonstration of its own showbiz promotion, had stretched the release of the letter and Breslin's reaction out over three days.

Two days ago, one reporter wrote a teaser with a few excerpts from the letter and an analysis of a symbol at the bottom. Taylor's favorite line from that story was the murderer telling Breslin he could "forget about writing about the Son of Sam because the killer doesn't want any publicity."

No way. The guy's a PR master.

On Saturday, a filler piece reminded readers they *had* to buy the Sunday paper to get the full letter and the full Breslin treatment. The story didn't mention Sunday was the most profitable edition of the week for any publisher. The Saturday story offered one more quote from the letter and confirmation from the cops that the letter matched the one sent to NYPD Captain Joseph Borrelli after the April 17 killings. The full text of the Borrelli letter still hadn't been published, only excerpts, most particularly the "Son of Sam" name the killer gave to himself.

Samantha blew into the white plastic lid, making a whistling noise. She sipped the coffee. "When was the last time you saw this many people lined up to buy a newspaper?"

"Maybe the day the printers strike ended last decade. Men landing on the moon and Nixon resigning were big. Still, they were different. The news had already been on television. People were buying those to collect. It's been a long time since a newspaper had something first that was this big. Give them credit, the *News* has done a masterful job ginning up attention."

The big brown delivery truck rumbled up. Two men in the back—union crew—dropped the heavy bundles to the sidewalk next to the newsstand. Everyone stayed in line, calm, polite. Surprising in New York these days. Maybe people needed to hear about a maniac and mayhem to decide to be civil. The newsstand operator snapped through the twine around the bundles with his knife and started selling the Night Owl edition of the *Sunday Daily News*. These copies didn't even have the comics, magazine, or other color sections.

Taylor bought one, and he and Samantha walked a half block away from the newsstand to stop next to a phone booth. The Breslin column started with a paragraph of the Son of Sam letter, then a bit of background, then Breslin putting himself in the center ring for some few paragraphs and finally the rest of the nut's correspondence. Taylor read Son of Sam's letter as one piece, with Samantha looking over his arm.

Hello from the gutters of N.Y.C. which are filled with dog manure, vomit, stale wine, urine, and blood. Hello from the sewers which swallow up these delicacies when they are washed away by the sweeper trucks. Hello from the cracks in the sidewalks of N.Y.C. and from the ants that dwell in these cracks and feed on the dried blood of the dead that has settled into the cracks.

J.B., I'm just dropping you a line to let you know that I appreciate your interest in those recent and horrendous .44 killings. I also want to tell you that I read your column daily and find it quite informative.

Tell me, Jim, what will you have for July Twenty-Ninth? You can forget about me if you like because I don't care for publicity. However, you must not forget Donna Lauria and you cannot let the people forget her, either. She was a very sweet girl but Sam's a thirsty lad and he won't let me stop killing until he gets his fill of blood.

Mr. Breslin, sir, don't think that because you haven't heard from [me] for a while that I went to sleep. No, rather, I am still here. Like a spirit roaming the night. Thirsty, hungry, seldom stopping to rest; anxious to please Sam. I love my work. Now, the void has been filled.

Perhaps we shall meet face to face someday or perhaps I will be blown away by the cops with smoking .38s. Whatever, if I shall be fortunate enough to meet you I will tell you all about Sam if you like and I will introduce you to him. His name is "Sam the Terrible."

Not knowing what the future holds I shall say farewell and I will see you at the next job. Or, should I say you will see my handiwork at the next job? Remember Ms. Lauria. Thank you.

In their blood
and
From the Gutter.
"Sam's Creation" .44

P.S.: J.B., please inform all the detectives working on the slayings to remain.

P.S.: J.B., please inform all the detectives working the case that I wish them the best of luck. "Keep Em digging, drive on, think positive, get off your butts, knock on coffins, etc."

Upon my capture I promise to buy all the guys working on the case a new pair of shoes if I can get up the money.

Son of Sam

"So sets racing one thousand psychiatric theories and two thousand more newspaper stories," Taylor said, "including mine."

He pulled out a notebook to write a few intro lines so he could phone the text of the letter in to the City News Bureau to go out to clients. It was a necessary formality, even though the big wires would do the same.

"I like his smoking thirty-eight idea," Samantha said. "I hope they get him, and they *get* him."

"Hard to argue with that. Breslin's not wrong when he says the guy's a good writer. Knows how to use a comma."

"You're focusing on commas?" She looked at him like *he* was the psycho.

"It's the little things. Shows the guy's smart, probably well educated. Listen to that second line." Taylor read aloud. " 'Hello from the cracks in the sidewalks of N.Y.C. and from the ants that dwell in these cracks and feed on the dried blood of the dead that has settled into the cracks.' It's good. Or good bad. Like a horror movie. 'Creature Feature.'"

"He's a complete horror movie. What's with '*Ms.* Lauria'? He's a feminist too?"

"Interesting touch of the modern there. One shrink will probably spend chapters on that alone."

Most of Breslin's own writing in the column featured interviews with the parents of Donna Lauria, Son of Sam's first victim. The murder had taken place almost a year ago on July 29, though it took six months for anyone to figure out she'd been targeted by a serial killer.

Breslin did spend a fair few column inches playing ace crime fighter. "The only way for the killer to leave this special torment is to give himself up to me, if he trusts me, to the police, and receive both help and safety," the columnist wrote. "If he wants any further contact, all he has to do is call or write me at the *Daily News*."

Taylor pointed to the words. "So there is another way for Son of Sam to end things."

He phoned in his stitched-together piece on the *News'* big scoop, what was called in the news business *a follow*. It was never fun to follow.

Cramly, in on Sunday duty, finished typing the dictated story. "How are we going to get anything if he's writing directly to Breslin?"

"Good question. Make sure you ask Novak."

Taylor and Samantha started the walk to their apartment.

A psychopath with his own brand name/nickname/ sobriquet/whatever-you-wanted-to-call-it hunting young people and writing letters to cops and famous newspaper columnists. A year ago, during the Bicentennial, with the city seemingly bailed out, Taylor had thought New York was making a comeback. Maybe he'd been wrong. Maybe they weren't in the middle of a three-ring circus, but banished to an outer circle of Dante's hell, with New York moving ever inward.

Dante was the sort of reference his father would have made. He couldn't escape the man, hard as he tried.

Existential crisis was another of the Professor's references. Taylor wasn't having one of those; he was suffering a deep-in-the-center-of-his-chest panic, like a lump of black lead squeezed his heart. He knew none of his skill, experience, or ability could be brought to bear on the Son of Sam story. He could interview scared citizens or bankrupt disco owners driven out of business because kids were staying home. That would get him jack shit on the real story here. Logic said he'd taken the right path. Nights like this—with that lump of lead, doubt—plagued him miserably.

If he sat in the office all day and wrote up whatever little scraps of Son of Sam info he could get, no one would blame him. Novak and Cramly would probably cheer him on.

He couldn't do it.

The Gibson story was his to chase. Now he had the lead on the DeVries investment advisor Denny Connell. He didn't know if it would lead to Martha Gibson's killer, but it could get him a story no one else had.

Taylor and Samantha turned onto their street.

Work wasn't the only thing dragging on him. Memories of Billy ghosted into his mind at least once a day now, as if they were his price for refusing to attend to the death of his father. He wasn't sure what kind of crisis to call this, but images, scenes, and bits of conversations he hadn't thought about for years had come back to him. He was fatigued. Missing things. Cramly had to yell at him twice to answer a phone in the office Friday. He should welcome memories he thought were lost. He couldn't. They were pushing him down a dark hole, with the weight of his job anxieties making it hard to resist the drop.

They were halfway down the block, and Samantha checked behind them for the third time since they left Lex. She had one hand on Taylor's arm, the other held to her side, most assuredly on the grip of her Colt Detective.

"He hasn't attacked in Manhattan," Taylor said.

"You read the note. He's a nut. Who knows what he'll do? I've got long hair and it looks dark enough at night."

"Yet I know judo."

An exasperated laugh. "I'm scared. Don't you think this is how the whole city feels?"

"Probably everyone under thirty. Anyone with a daughter or son under thirty. Probably everyone else, including seventy-year-old mothers of chauffeurs. Same time, we're far more likely to get murdered by one of thousands of other killers, none of whom will send a Boris Karloff note."

The temperature had cooled off from the humid eighties of midday—hot for early June. The weather forecasters, scaremongers by trade, had been warning that the record cold winter didn't mean a mild summer. The way things were going, Taylor wouldn't bet against the meteorologists. Not this time.

Inside the apartment, Mason—still unaware, always unaware he should be nervous—said hello to both of them. He'd already had his evening walk, though this wasn't something he believed until Taylor sat on the couch.

Samantha brought in a Rolling Rock and a glass of red wine.

Taylor turned on the TV, flipped between the local news to hear their take on the Son of Sam letter. Somehow, they made it sound more frightening than when he'd read it to himself. After *Eyewitless News* anchor Bill Beutel finished the story and co-anchor Roger Grimsby made a joke, the station cut to a commercial. An angler in a rushing river, with a serious New England accent, spoke to the camera, "I live in New Hampshire, but I love New York."

"Not seen this before," Taylor said.

A song started up, first low in the background, a chorus singing, "I Love New York." A woman came on next, holding a horse by the bridle. She spoke with a Southern accent. "I live in North Carolina, but I love New York." An announcer offered an 800 number for a 100-page New York vacation guide. The spot finished with a line on the screen: I, a red heart, and New York.

"I heart New York?" Samantha said.

"Think it means, I love New York."

"I know, but what the hell is that about? The song? Who's

going to love New York? Homicidal maniac. Bankrupt. Frightening murder rate. Who are they trying to fool?"

"Most of the pictures were of upstate."

"So they're giving up on the city?"

"Who knows? It won't last. The money won't last."

He turned off the TV and put side B of *Born to Run* in the cassette player of the all-in-one stereo. He wanted the last two songs. "Meeting Across the River" and "Jungleland." Especially "Jungleland."

She curled into his side. "Crime I can take. I wanted to put bad guys away. This madness is … evil."

Taylor sent seven ounces of lager toward the black lead weight. The pressure eased a little.

"Yeah, it is."

CHAPTER 18

———◆———

TAYLOR MIXED UP two Bloody Marys. His second rule of drinking—not imbibing breakfast—didn't count with brunch, since brunch wasn't breakfast, it being later. Sunday was traditionally the brunch day, but Taylor liked it better on Saturdays, coming so nicely as it did after a perhaps rough Friday night.

Mason watched Taylor stir the drinks. The dog assumed anything being prepared in the kitchen was either for him or might result in a spill that was for him. It was in these moments the dog attained his highest level of focus—his *only* level of focus, Taylor claimed.

Today's Bloody was a corrective for far too many little beers last night. He'd worked his ass off the past two weeks since he'd seen DeVries and needed it. Or wanted it. Or both.

He'd come up with some details on Denny Connell, but nothing on where he or the DeVries money had disappeared. The bunco boys weren't any help, of course. This wasn't their kind of con. They were used to street-level stuff, Three-Card Monte and wallet switches, along with home repair rip-offs and the collection of other swindles used on the aged.

Connell's office in a Lexington Avenue midrise had been turned over in such a way that Taylor thought someone wanted it to look thoroughly searched. Papers everywhere, sure. But why flip the desk upside down? DeVries was Connell's only client; he acted like the head of finance for the family, so there were no other victims for Taylor to interview. The landlord was properly pissed off he'd been stiffed on the rent, but had no info that would point where Connell had gone. Taylor had collected all the papers scattered on the floor and gone through them with DeVries. He'd said the documents reflected the accounts as they were before the theft. Probably left intentionally.

The obvious move for Connell would have been to flee the country, assuming he was able to transfer the money somewhere he could get at it. Taylor would need the FBI or INS to help with that, which was about as easy as finding a dentist who could do a painless root canal.

Abigail Gibson was still missing. This was no surprise. Junkies often moved when their supplier moved (or, in this case, was shot dead). He had hoped the rent-controlled apartment might bring her back. It wasn't free, but cheap as she would get aside from a shooting gallery. Instead, the need for smack had sent Abigail wandering, and she hadn't been at the apartment the times Taylor had checked. The last and only time her parents had seen her, they had given her cash to help with the rent, which probably only helped her buy more heroin. She could be dead, an overdose, by now. The loose end was like an itch at the back of Taylor's neck. He wanted conclusive proof the junkie and the hitman weren't the reason Martha was murdered.

He'd visited Chris Jones, Jerome McGill's surviving accomplice, at Rikers, but the gunman wouldn't talk. Taylor had tried to sell him on the idea that a news profile might help Jones' case, but Jones politely told Taylor to go the fuck away.

He delivered the Bloody Marys to the living room. Samantha was reading the Saturday *Daily News*.

The horseradish sent a spicy tingle up his nose. The sting of a Bloody Mary was almost as important as the vodka. Almost. He flipped the *Times* to a story on the Emergency Financial Control Board approving New York City's budget and the formal request for a $750 million seasonal loan from the U.S. Treasury. He'd committed to reading this dull financial stuff because it was his city and he ought to know if and why it was going over the edge—something he'd never expected until it almost happened in 1975. New York's near bankruptcy was tied in tangentially to the double murder that brought Samantha and him together—into collision first—in the fall of that year.

The phone rang as he tossed the thin Saturday paper on a side table.

"It's him. All a mess. Everywhere."

"Who's this?"

"Carol Wheelwright. Mr. DeVries. He's badly hurt. Here at the house. Shot."

"Did you call the police?"

"Yes."

Taylor hung up and told Samantha. They were downstairs in five minutes, hailing a cab in light Saturday traffic.

"Nothing like this in this building before," said the elevator operator, speaking for the first time in Taylor's presence. "Nothing. The nicest man. He never deserved anything like this."

No one met them at the elevator. Taylor followed the sound of voices in the direction he was used to going—toward the library. Two uniformed patrolmen stood on either side of the body. Taylor showed his press pass, which these days had a 50-50 chance of keeping him at a crime scene. Press-police relations had slid from collegial to adversarial, starting in the late sixties. These cops seemed more concerned about when the detectives would get there … because DeVries wasn't badly hurt. He was badly dead.

He'd been shot sitting in his favorite chair, a book on his

stomach, *The 1900 Atlas of Dutchess County, New York.* Taylor
counted three bullet holes, including one in the cheek and one
through the book, which leaked blood from the hole like the
tome itself had been injured, plus four others in the wall and
a table. A broken vase and smashed lamp probably bumped
up the total. Someone walked in and sprayed weapon fire at
DeVries. A quick hit? An angry hit? Both?

Taylor backed out of the room, scanning the entire area for
anything out of place. He knew nothing of forensics. The cops
would toss him if he touched a thing. This visit was only worth
what he could see and write down—*and* any interviews he
could get.

In the next room, Carol sat slumped in an ornate wood chair
with a gold brocade cushion.

He stepped closer, stood over her, and waited.

She lifted her head, tears streaming down her face, her nose
running. "Is he—"

"Yes. The cops didn't tell you?"

"They haven't said anything to us. They look at us like we all
might be murderers."

"Who heard the shots?"

"No one. He was alone."

"In this place? How is that possible?"

"Several staff have Saturdays off. Cook went to shop after
she made breakfast. Mrs. DeVries went down to her mother's."

"Down?"

"Three blocks. She goes every Saturday morning. Charlie
hasn't come home yet from being out last night. Some
weekends, it's not until Sunday afternoon. Audrey is staying
with a friend. There's a group of them, friends since childhood."

"Is she close by, too?"

"Fifth Avenue. About ten blocks."

Samantha went down on one knee in front of Carol. "There
was a window when he was alone. Who would know this?"

"The whole family, I guess. No one ever said it outright, but he's usually alone for a couple of hours on Saturday morning reading. I think it was one of his favorite times. Oh God ...." The tears started again. They waited. "Sorry. It was longer today because I got here late. The subway."

"Careful what you say to the detectives. You gave the killer more time."

"I would never .... I don't."

"I know. Be careful."

"Careful of what?" A short, bald man approached in the kind of trench coat Taylor associated with a peeping tom. The man held out his gold detective's badge as if it might have some magical power over them.

"We're being careful around the whole apartment," Taylor said. "It's a crime scene."

"You are ...?"

"Taylor of the City News Bureau." He showed his credentials.

"One thing I like my crime scenes clean of is reporters. Out."

"It's okay. We're finished. Your name, Detective?"

"You'll hear it when I make an arrest."

"I can call the squad and find out."

"Knock yourself out."

The detective's partner, a younger, taller man who slouched in a dark blue coat, laughed at the empty toughness.

Taylor called the elevator. When the door slid open, he asked, "When did you start today?"

"Six. Saw no one strange my whole shift."

"Other ways into the building?"

"There's the utility elevator just inside that door." He pointed at a corner of the foyer where the wood paneling had seams—a doorway. "The hallway also leads to the fire stairs. The door out of the building downstairs is locked on the outside. Doormen, janitors, and elevator men have keys."

"What's outside?"

"Dumpsters. Loading area. Little courtyard-like space. But not nice. Used for the business of the building."

"Thanks, man."

"You going to write up the old man's death."

"That's only the start."

A gray metal elevator door—nothing like the ornate brass and wood of the guest elevator—was recessed into the wall on the other side of the doorway made to look like it wasn't there.

Wouldn't want anyone to know there's a backstage. Or garbage.

Samantha pressed the button and the lift arrived quickly. The inside walls were covered with the padded canvas used in all of New York's best service elevators. On the ride down, they both looked around for anything interesting, really anything at all. Samantha knew more about evidence, but the descending box was empty.

Out in the hallway, laundry bins, a couple bags of concrete powder, and five appliance-sized boxes lined a breezeblock wall painted the same gray as the elevator door. As was the floor, though shinier. Taylor went left and slowly eased open the door to confirm what he'd guessed: this was the backstage entry into the lobby. They walked the other way to a rust-colored steel door that stood out from all the gray like a golden portal. It was open about two inches. Taylor pushed.

"This is the one the staff has the key to, right?" Samantha asked.

"To get in from the outside." He stepped down. "The lock's smashed off. So … not an inside job."

"Or someone wants people to *think* not an inside job."

"You're smart detective."

"Yet only a private one."

"Bet ya brunch you'll figure any of this out quicker than those two upstairs."

"A man who compliments with a bet. What more could I want?"

"I could want something obvious down here. That's not my luck on this damn story. Nothing obvious about any of it."

Taylor and Samantha went back to the lobby and questioned

the doorman at the desk, who was more broken up than the elevator operator. The forensics and medical examiner staffers showed, along with the pointless yet obligatory ambulance. The doorman confirmed nobody but residents and staff had come through all morning—three in, five out. He showed Taylor the book.

The last two people to show up with an interest in the murder were a reporter from the *News* and his trailing photographer. Taylor checked his watch. It had been an hour and a half since Carol had called him at home. Must have gone out on the police radio minutes earlier. Major name on Park Avenue shot in his Park Avenue apartment, and it merited one reporter and one photographer.

Son of Sam.

The reporter, an old-timer named Coogan, asked Taylor what was going on. Taylor gave the guy all the obvious stuff, everything the police would know. He warned Coogan the detective wasn't much for visits, but Coogan moved toward the elevator. "I'm tight with this precinct. That's why they sent me. I handle all the Uptown stuff."

"Lucky you."

Taylor and Samantha stood to the side in the lobby. The body came out. Coogan came out. The detective came out and smirked. His partner followed, still slouching like he was trying not to look taller than his boss.

"Let's go to the Oddity."

"You're hungry?"

"Not really." Murder didn't generally put him off food, but he'd liked DeVries. "I need to think. My complex story got turned upside down."

"Why'd you help Coogan?"

"DeVries deserves to appear in the paper. I'm surprised the *Times* didn't make it. They don't miss Park Avenue murders. Not ever. The only murders they really care about."

"Didn't you tell me Saturday's a bad day to die because of thin staffing at the papers?"

"Yeah, there's that."

And Son of Sam.

'.44-Caliber Killer' Wounds Two
In Car Parked on Queens Street

—*New York Times*, page 1, June 27, 1977

.44 KILLER HITS
AGAIN, WOUNDS 2

**Jimmy Breslin's Exclusive
Interview With Victim**

—*Daily News*, page 1, June 27, 1977

CHAPTER 19

———— ◆ ————

THE WHOLE PRESS conference was a handful of familiar facts and too many unanswerable questions. Taylor listened and wrote mechanically.

"Judy Placido, seventeen, and Salvatore Lupo, twenty."

"Why can't you find this guy?"

"Any identifying evidence at the scene?"

"How do the parents feel?"

"Why did these victims escape death?"

"How long can this go on?"

"Do you need more cops?"

"Better cops?"

"What about the FBI?"

"Describe the exact wounds."

"More detail than that."

"How close was the nearest unit?"

"Were any cops nearby acting as decoys?"

The answers were what he'd expect. All the specifics were rehashed from the previous shootings. When the questions got really stupid, Taylor got up and phoned in his piece.

What the hell is wrong with me? There are victims in all these attacks. They count.

Yeah, but the circus didn't count them, except as good for the sidebar. The circus wanted the horror show. The fear. The monster. Son of Sam.

He left the 109th Precinct and stopped off at the 112th on the way back to Manhattan. McCauley was at his desk.

"Anything on the Gibson murder?" Taylor said.

"Will you tell me why you still care? Nigger maid with drug dealing going on in the apartment."

"You're not investigating because you're a bigot? You're not even on Omega."

"Listen to the lefty reporter." McCauley kept reading a typed report. "We've got daughters and sons murdered and wounded. They could be, any of them, my kids. My partner's kids."

"Martha Gibson has parents. I've met them. Very nice people. Very sad people now. So let's ignore your racist views for the moment. It remains the responsibility of the NYPD to investigate her murder. Every murder. To get as many killers convicted as possible. Not focus on one single case because the victims look like your family."

"Oh, fuck off."

"Handful of young White people. Big deal. Black woman who works as maid. No deal."

"Say it any way you want."

"I'm going to *write* it anyway I want. Anything you'd like to add to my story, *Detective McCauley*? I've already got the spelling."

"You motherfucker."

McCauley jumped from his chair, grabbed Taylor by the sport coat and ran him into a filing cabinet. He hit hard. The noise was loud.

"Shoving me around," Taylor said as McCauley's fists closed together on his chin, threatening to tear one or more seams in Taylor's jacket. "Nice color for the story. That's color in its proper usage."

McCauley slammed Taylor into the steel cabinet, jarring his shoulders and rattling his teeth.

The detective was pulled off by two others. Another walked Taylor to a chair, where he sat like he was waiting to see the principal. The principal turned out to be Lieutenant Mark Garrison, the officer in charge of the homicide squad.

"What's your problem with McCauley?" Garrison said.

"Besides the fact he slammed me into your furniture?"

"Yeah, besides that."

"He's a racist, for one."

"Noted. Is that your story? Because you could go 'round all the precincts for that one." Garrison, with a young face made to look older by a nearly bald head, held out his hands like Taylor was welcome to take on that project.

"I'm working a story on Martha Gibson's murder."

"I've got the file right here."

"Looks to me like not much is being done. As in nothing. Racism? Because of Son of Sam? You tell me. I'm getting the feeling cases aren't getting investigated because of the circus out there." He waved in the direction of Flushing and the 109th, though Garrison could have no idea.

"You've got a feeling? Huh. Is that what you base your stories on. Feelings? Not that I should give a shit. I catch villains, not headlines. You do the opposite."

Discomfiting warmth spread across Taylor's chest and up to his face as he realized he'd let what he thought was going on—and the fact McCauley was an asshole—run well ahead of what he actually could prove. The facts. What else did he have, aside from McCauley?

Garrison didn't wait for his answer. "Granted, there are a lot of men on Omega. The public demanded it. They didn't demand we stop doing our jobs. We're getting all the overtime we need for this squad and the other squads to chase perpetrators. After that, guys are going off the clock. On the regular squads. On Omega. Volunteering." He plopped a file in the middle of his desk. "Indicted this one for second-degree murder. Husband-wife beef." Another file. "Drug shooting." He kept dropping files. "Conviction, manslaughter. Indictment, man killed his twelve-year-old son." The litany of death and court action left a six-inch pile. "Martha Gibson's been tough. I'm gonna admit that. No witnesses. Hit and run shooter. We don't have a motive. Maybe it was tied up with the sister and her late boyfriend. Boyfriend's dead. Yeah, McCauley's got a bad attitude. He's also overworked, and I'll admit, like some guys, obsessed with the psycho. There are guys walking around here like zombies. At all the squads. Because we want to grab up all the villains who do murder." He rolled his chair back. "We'd have lost everything if we let this crazy man not only scare people, but stop us from doing the job. *The* job. Not on my fucking watch. If there's a homicide in my zone, I want it solved. I help any squad anywhere else in the city. So if you know something, tell me."

"Maybe you're right. The case may have died with Jerome McGill. At the same time, Martha Gibson worked for the DeVries family in Manhattan. She knew things she shouldn't. She definitely heard people talking about what sounds like criminal activity, perhaps murder. *Probably* murder." Taylor recounted the conversation Martha had overheard in the sitting room. "Edmond DeVries got shot to death last Saturday."

Garrison flipped through a file. "We visited the family after Martha's murder. Didn't hear anything like that then."

"I gave it all to McCauley in April. He wasn't impressed."

Garrison looked up, returned to writing on his steno pad. "We'll go back. I'll talk to McCauley. I'll give the lead to his partner. He'll get on it. Still, this overheard conversation of yours, that's secondhand. Martha's gone. You're not giving me the source."

"No, I'm not. I can't. Still reason to wonder. DeVries is dead. That's firsthand."

"We'll call over to Manhattan."

"You're right. Stories *aren't* based on feelings," Taylor stood and offered his hand, "or ought not to be. I shouldn't have gone with an assumption. I'm sorry."

"A reporter who apologizes?"

"There are a few of us. You'd think there'd be more, since it's the only job I know of where you've got to publish your corrections right out there for the whole world to read."

TAYLOR WALKED TO the subway at about half his normal pace. He'd apologized before. That didn't bother him. It was what got him to the apology, the headlong charge to not only get the Martha Gibson story, but somehow show the case was part of some bigger problem. If he wanted *that* story, he should have done the reporting. He rubbed dry hands together. He remembered what his first city editor had told him: "I don't give a shit what you think. Tell me what you got."

He boarded the train. What did he have? By any measure, he'd given the story more time than he should, had, or could afford. The Gibson murder and the DeVries murder, and filling City News Bureau's bucket tugged his mind in different directions every day, almost stretching his thoughts out of shape. Was that why he'd made the mistake back at the precinct? He couldn't do it all, and he had no real proof—or, at least, not a single person—connecting the two murders. He almost needed to drop the Gibson story to pursue the DeVries murder and keep Novak happy. He couldn't, not yet. He'd stretch himself as far as he could. Saturdays, usually half days at the office or out interviewing, would now have him working full-time. Sundays, too, if need be. Samantha wasn't going to be thrilled. He owed it to DeVries. He liked the guy. Martha Gibson, a stranger, was even more important. There was only one reporter in town on her story.

On the ride into Manhattan, multiple versions of the same *New York Post* headline formed a wall across from him as riders read the story he already knew. The train car was steamy, all the windows open, the thunderous noise of the speeding train drowning out everything—everything but his thoughts. His mind couldn't stop moving. Touching one idea. Moving. Considering a theory. Not for the first time in the past three months, he came back to Carter, Rupert Murdoch's protégé from the DeVries dinner party. He hadn't forgotten the offer of a job interview. Like any bargain with the devil, it was hard to let go of because it offered something he wanted so badly. He'd picked up the phone more than once to make an appointment and hung up without dialing. Taylor wanted badly to work at a newspaper, but now all newspapers weren't *newspapers*. Was he being a snob? Couldn't he carve out a place for his stories like he had at the *Messenger-Telegram?* Yeah, that had taken ten years, and Murdoch, by all accounts, was a hands-on manager who thought news was another form of entertainment. He rewrote heads. Assigned reporters. Killed stories. Taylor might end up doing the same work he saw filling the new *Post*.

City News was a small wire, not a big paper, but things had gotten better. He had his choice of stories, because Novak trusted him as long as he filled the bucket every day. The company was doing well. Novak had doubled the service's subscribers—New York and suburban FM stations, one TV newsroom, and some newspapers in New Jersey and farther upstate. He couldn't say his stories weren't getting out there.

Just not in a New York paper.

It always had been more than a goal for Taylor; it had been a need. If the *Post* wasn't for him and the *Times* didn't want him, that meant the *Daily News*. He'd wait a long time, given the guys in their cop shop. Or he could move to another city.

Never.

"I WAS WRONG today."

"Shock, horror," said Samantha, on her third beer. He'd noticed she was drinking more.

"You should write headlines. You okay?"

"Why?"

He nodded at the beer. "You can have as many as you like, but it seems like more lately."

"Everything's so screwed up. It's not that I'm afraid. That I see myself being attacked by the nut. Those fantasies always end with me taking him out." She smiled, all confidence at that thought. "It's like the city is wrapped so tight and scared about him, and at the same time, the old fears are here. New York is still going bust. Crime and arson. They say we're out of the recession, but homeless people are everywhere. The poor too, crammed into bad housing. Things were supposed to be better by now. They're not."

"Not by a long shot."

"Son of Sam equals chaos. The whole city is on the edge of his chaos and some bigger chaos." She slapped the couch to tell Mason he could jump up on it. "After they catch or kill this guy, what gets better?"

He'd not heard her talk like this. His thoughts were usually the darker ones.

"There's us."

He took her hand and led her to the bedroom, leaving Mason on the couch.

Samantha pulled off her blue smiley t-shirt. Taylor stepped close to her. The smell of warm skin and Prell. She kept everything simple. He couldn't get enough of it. He kissed her, squeezing her rear gently. She pushed him back on the bed.

"I don't want to go slow tonight," she said.

He pulled off his pants and underwear fast. She didn't bother to wait for him to get his shirt off. She left her bra on. She straddled him.

"Couldn't wait for naked for this escape."

She slowly rose and fell.

She kept going. He started moaning. She joined in.

TAYLOR WOKE UP at two a.m., and a half hour later was still

awake. He went out to the living room, put on the headphones that made him look like an air traffic controller and slipped in the self-titled cassette *Ramones*, which the band had finally put out last year after playing live almost constantly since their formation—usually at CBGB. He followed it with the band's second album, *Leave Home*, which had come out in January. Next, a bootleg of the Sex Pistols, who had yet to produce an album, and then Patti Smith. The music raged and rattled him. That was okay. He wanted, needed, sought to be rattled. Rattled was different from chaos. Rattling and raging, you were the one in charge. Not with chaos. That happened to you. He worried about Samantha. What she'd said. She was the steady one.

He came out of a dream that was as realistic as a film of his first Ramones-Patti Smith show, seen with his previous girlfriend. Samantha was shaking his shoulder. The wall clock said 4:20. He went back to bed, finally ready for sleep, and for some reason, guilty like a little kid for letting Laura Wheeler into his dream, though she'd been out of his life for two years.

CHAPTER 20

———•———

TAYLOR'S T-SHIRT STUCK to his skin and the damp soaked through his dark-blue short-sleeved dress shirt. The temperature was going to top the 86 degrees forecast. He was sure of that. The humidity would be about the same, making his walk along Booth Street that much stickier. On one of Taylor's check-ins, Detective Caputo of narcotics in the 112th had told him Abigail Gibson had been seen hanging around Myrtle Avenue and Park Lane South at the edge of Forest Park. Made sense; it was 12 blocks north from Martha Gibson's apartment. Abigail hadn't wandered too far.

"It's a popular intersection for street sales," Caputo had said. "I know she's been there because she got frisked a couple of times. She was lucky. Not holding."

"Why don't you shut the corner down?" Taylor asked. It was an obligation of the job, even though he knew the answer.

"We do. They come right back. Or jamokes who look just like them."

There isn't just one kind of racism in the NYPD. There are all sorts of flavors.

Taylor took a seat in a window of Bubbie's Corner Spot and

ordered a cup of coffee as rent for the table. He took off his sport coat, hoping the single rattling fan would cool him.

He didn't have to wait long. Abigail appeared across the intersection. She stood by herself, her arms wrapped around her body like the steamy air was somehow cold. Her head turned one way, then the other. Pretty easy to guess she was looking to fix. He'd wait for her to buy, then follow. After ten minutes, she did the unexpected—turned and walked into the park.

Shit.

Forest Park was big, and big parks were dangerous any hour of the day.

He left a quarter tip, hustled through gaps in the traffic and entered at the same gate. His shoulders dropped in relief when he found she hadn't gone far; instead she was sitting on a bench next to an elliptical walkway that had other benches spaced out around it. To Taylor's immediate right was a playground, all its pieces rusting. The slide had a hole through it, with crusty black metal around the edges.

Three or four homeless people—at least judging by the amount of stuff they had—had created an encampment inside a triangle of three large trees on the other side of the ellipse. If Taylor went farther into the park, he'd find more homeless— and likely folks looking to give him trouble. You wouldn't know it from the kids laughing on the swings and an old couple sitting on a bench to the left. They were still on the edge of civilization. Taylor walked the long way around the ellipse to a seat cattycorner from Abigail. She could see him if she looked over, but he doubted he was in any way on her mind this minute.

The junkie continued her unceasing search for someone. Someone with something, no doubt. She started rocking as she squeezed herself, a sign of worsening withdrawal.

A White teenager came down the path, walking in that slouched shamble street operators taught themselves. He wore a leather jacket, which threw Taylor back to the toughs of his teenage years in his Queens neighborhood. Petty criminals, they'd shoplifted, bullied, and drank beer. Heroin was a ways off in the future. This teen circled slowly, passing close enough to the old couple that the man was forced to pull in his feet. For good measure, the kid smacked the newspaper out of the old man's hands. The man started to lean on his cane to stand up, but his wife pulled at him. From his seat, he picked up the paper and opened it again with a look of angry resignation.

Abigail straightened up as the teenager approached. She watched him with intensity, still squeezing herself like her own body would escape her grip if she didn't.

The boy stopped, held the slouch as he stood in front of her. They were conversing, but Taylor only got the impression of voices. Abigail leaned forward, concern pushing the pain off her face. She reached for the boy's jeans, gripped them at the sides and tried to pull him closer.

The slap came with the speed of a snake. A screech of pain. Blood leaked out of Abigail's mouth as she moved her hand to it. One wasn't enough. He hit her again. He was probably the type who enjoyed it.

That was more street theater than Taylor needed. He jumped from the bench, sprinted around the walkway and grabbed the old man's cane. Improv felt better than judo in this scenario. That didn't mean he would play fair. He swung the walking stick hard at the teen's head, delivering a blow that sent the kid staggering sideways. Taylor hooked the kid's ankle with the cane, pulled him to the ground and shoved the hook onto the boy's throat.

"We do not hit girls. Don't they teach that in Queens schools anymore?"

Angry choking, which Taylor figured was hard to pull off.

He frisked the teen, found a switchblade, and dropped it in his pocket.

He pushed the cane harder. The kid coughed, grasping at this throat, didn't sound so angry.

"We're walking out of here. See this?" Taylor held up his police credentials. "That's an NYPD press card. Soon as I hit the avenue, I'm going to send every sort of cop I see in here looking for you. I'm going to tell them you're carrying a Charter Arms Bulldog Forty-Four."

Taylor took Abigail's arm and backed away slowly. He needn't have worried. This pusher was in the bully-girls-coward class. The boy ran, still holding his throat, deeper into the woods.

Taylor handed the old man his cane. "I can pay for any damages."

"Never mind about that. My privilege. There was a time I could stand up to little shits like him."

"Language, Malcolm!" The wife grabbed her husband's arm again.

Back in Bubbie's, Abigail refused food. She held a napkin to her split lip. A bruise was rising on her cheek. The waitress offered ice. She refused.

She turned to Taylor. "Just give me a couple of bucks."

Taylor ordered two coffees. He put two sugars and two half-and-halfs in his. Abigail put in even more.

"That kid your new dealer?"

"It's more like a sharing relationship."

"I can bet what you share." The comment didn't seem to bother her. "I need to clear up something with you."

"Gimme some money."

"Answers first. How often did Jerome come to the apartment before Martha was killed?"

"Never. I told you he didn't. She'd call the cops if he did. Or he'd kill her. I'm messed up, but I loved my sister. I wouldn't let that happen."

"Never has to mean never. This is serious as death."

"*Never*. Only after, when you were there."

"You ever buy dope in the building?"

"Shit no. I had a home there. Martha took care of me. Always trying to get me to kick." Her voice went wistful. She smiled wanly at her golden oldie days two months ago, when her sister was alive. "She got me clean for three months. I never scored anywhere near the building."

"Junkies lie."

"I had Jerome. He had the stuff. He liked having me around." She tried to smile, but her hand went to her lip. "Maybe you want me around some."

She put her hand on his leg. He lifted it off.

She started shaking.

"C'mon." He led her out of the coffee shop, hailed a cab and they got in. "I'm going to repeat myself. *This* is for your sister, who you say you loved."

"I did!"

"What you're telling me is absolutely true. I can rule out anyone shooting her because you were buying or Jerome was dealing. No one came gunning for you and got her instead?"

"How many times do I have to swear it?"

"I don't know. I'll probably case the damn building anyway to confirm. Ask what people saw and heard."

"Nothin' and nothin'."

Going door to door would be a royal pain in the ass. Still, it was about facts. Abigail Gibson didn't strike him as someone who worried too much about those. More about manipulation. This story needed facts bad. *Facts are stubborn things ....* The beginning of his favorite quote, from John Adams. Facts were a story's floor, roof, and walls—everything. If he could report enough facts, he could write what happened. To Martha Gibson. To Edmond DeVries.

She looked out the window. "Hey, the fuck, we're in Brooklyn." She said it like it was another country.

The cab pulled in front of the methadone clinic.

"Get out."

"I'm not doing that."

Nevertheless, she opened the door and stepped to the curb. Taylor had to pull the door closed.

"Then don't. Then die."

"You're a shit."

"That's been said before."

"You owe me cash."

"I owe you nothing. You owe your sister."

"You think you know everything!" she said. "You don't."

Taylor told the driver to hold up and spoke out the window. "I doubt I do. Junkies lie."

"Didn't lie." Out of nowhere, she wretched and threw up in front of the clinic. She coughed and somehow started talking again. "Left it out. It wasn't my fault."

"What wasn't?"

"Twenty bucks."

"I swear, Abigail—"

"Twenty bucks or I don't talk."

Taylor held a ten dollar bill out the window.

She walked over to the cab and took it. "My dealer, the one before Jerome, he followed me back to the apartment building one day."

"Name."

"Jimmy. Don't know last. They call him Jimmy the Cryptkeeper."

"Why'd he follow you?"

"Says he likes intelligence on his clients. Keeps the cops away."

"So your dealer *did* know where you lived."

"It's worse than that." Her face wasn't sad now, but rapt in the anticipation of getting a bag of heroin. "Ten dollars worse."

Taylor held up another bill but kept it inside the cab.

"Before your big revelation, where's this Jimmy deal?"

"Mt. Olivet."

"The cemetery?"

"Says it's safe unless there's a funeral around. Jimmy's real small and doesn't want to get busted, 'cause inside he gets busted up. He didn't work anywhere near the apartment. I didn't lie about that."

"You're a real saint."

"One day, Jerome came along with me to see Jimmy. He'd just gotten to the neighborhood. He didn't have his supply yet. Like I said, Jimmy isn't much. He's got this high, squeaky voice. Jerome hit him. Only a couple of times. Took some extra hits off him. Didn't want to really rob him, only get a treat out of the deal."

"You're telling me your boyfriend robbed your dealer and your dealer knew where you lived?"

She nodded slowly, her eyes on the portrait of Alexander Hamilton. "Jimmy was no threat. I swear."

"Maybe he knew threats. Maybe he paid for threats, like people paid McGill."

He handed her the money. She turned and looked at the front door of the clinic, turned back around, gave Taylor the finger, and walked off down the sidewalk.

So much for trying to help a stray. He failed more than he succeeded in that effort. Samantha said it made him a good man that he tried. Or a stupid one. Taylor took the cab to the nearest subway stop. A taxi from Brooklyn to Manhattan was for a splurge or emergencies.

CHAPTER 21

———◆———

During a call Thursday with Carol, the first time he'd reached her since the murder Saturday, she told him of something he should have guessed. Studio 54 was Charlie DeVries' favorite nightspot, though he made the rounds at most of the top clubs, restaurants, and after-hours joints that Taylor would expect of a man employed in spending his family's money. He needed to interview Charlie outside the apartment, the domain of the detectives.

Taylor hadn't been in Studio 54 since it exploded on the scene two months ago, whatever the *scene* was. He hated disco music. Add it to the cultural plague that made the seventies seem like the answer to the wrong question, a question he didn't remember anyone asking at the end of the sixties. Whether he wanted in or not, getting in was going to be a hurdle. Taylor was as likely to be invited to dinner at the governor's mansion as he was to find his way past the red velvet ropes of Studio 54.

"Is there anything else you need?"

Taylor had stopped asking Carol questions to puzzle on how to get past the bouncers.

"Ask around if anyone else on staff heard conversations.

Threatening conversations. Or knows who the stranger in the room might be."

"I don't want to spy."

"You liked Mr. DeVries, didn't you?"

"Of course I did. But the police."

"Then don't be obvious about it. Anything someone heard or saw could help. Had you heard that Mr. DeVries was planning some changes?" Taylor left out the specifics because he wanted to see who knew and how much. Even Carol.

"The family was meeting privately. A lot. They went on that long trip. We all were afraid it was bad. During one of those meetings, Charlie started yelling and stormed out."

"What'd he say?"

"I only heard one line, as he ran from the sitting room to the elevator. 'And you say *I* throw fucking money away.' He was gone for two days."

"How is Mrs. DeVries doing?"

"She's taken to her bed. The doctor's been by almost daily. Will only let in Mrs. Frist—"

"Who's that?"

"The housekeeper. You must not have met her. Mrs. Frist says she hasn't eaten anything but soup and not much of that."

"Who on the staff was Mr. DeVries closest to?"

"Oh, Joe, of course. He's so upset. He took a week off."

"Where's he live?"

"The Far Rockaways." Taylor took down the street address. They weren't called *far* for nothing. It would be a long-assed haul to that Queens seaside peninsula. Didn't matter. The chauffeur was someone else he needed to talk to away from the DeVries place.

He thanked Carol, hung up, and dialed a number that might be the one way a reporter could get into Studio 54. The owners cultivated both fame and exclusivity, a tough balancing act. An old friend from his newspaper days—the theater critic at the *Messenger-Telegram*—had landed a gig doing PR.

"You want in to Studio 54?" the friend asked.

"I'm doing a feature."

"That can't be true."

"Do you want the real reason?"

"I do *not*. Someone else put you on the list for Friday if you're *ever* asked."

THE FIRST DAY of July arrived with temperatures holding in the mid-eighties. The humidity had decided to hang around there too. Taylor worked late into the evening, mainly organizing his notes. He tried some calls but came up empty. He knew things wouldn't get going at the club until eleven at the earliest, at which point he'd walk the 11 blocks to Studio 54, simply named because the club had been installed in an old opera house turned TV studio on 54th Street west of Broadway, making it an exception, since most of the popular clubs were downtown. That hadn't gotten in the way of Studio 54 becoming the center of the disco universe, populated by movie and TV stars, politicians, rich folk, people famous for being famous, and the few plebs the bouncers let in based on how good the women looked. Men on their own were doomed.

Taylor approached the black marquee with its silver *54* set in a typeface of an art deco style from the twenties, the last period New York danced as the world was about to burn. Forget Studio 54, Taylor had somehow so far survived the disco era without actually entering *any* disco, province as they were of gossip chasers and star fuckers. Well, that wasn't exactly true. He had been in two—one in Queens, one downtown—but they had been transformed from dance halls into crime scenes. A romantic entanglement had left one dead in Queens—the under-aged girl in the middle—and some gang beef downtown had offed two and sent two to the hospital. Three of the victims were bystanders.

Studio 54 was its own ongoing crime scene, at least when it came to drug dealing. Any sort of drug available in whatever quantity. Busting the rich and famous didn't get a street narc anywhere. How would he even get on the list? Taylor walked up to the bouncer and told him his name was on the press list. He was sent to a side door—reporters rated the service entrance—followed a hallway, and came out into the former theater's cavernous space, the music throbbing but the dance floor nearly empty.

More waiting.

The bartender laughed at the idea of a Rolling Rock and was unimpressed with the idea of beer in general. Taylor slid an obscene seven bucks across the bar for a Heineken.

Prices like that will definitely keep me sober.

He positioned himself so he could watch people as they came in. Once the place got busy, it could take him all night to find Charlie DeVries. The flow slowly increased. The music, one bit of fluffy trash after another, played without a break, one track flowing into another, the DJ overlapping the beats to make it one unending awful song. The costumes—you couldn't call this clothing—made the arriving guests a peacock parade. *Look at me!* The men in tuxes and sparkly suits. The women dressed in less and less and less. Naked would arrive any minute.

Just when he thought his beer tab was going to hit $21 with no discernable buzz, Charlie walked in with a woman on each arm, each in a skimpy, blood-red dress that looked like the type of metallic paper you wrapped Christmas gifts in.

What is it about dressing identically with disco people?

As he watched, Taylor understood why Charlie, though a rough copy, wasn't as good-looking as his father. He had a pinched, perpetually sour face that became plain ugly when he smiled, which he did when he entered the big room. Following right behind Charlie was Bobby Livingston, chin raised high like he'd come out of the womb that way. He also had a woman on each arm, also in identical dresses.

Shown to a table right away, they popped a bottle of

champagne, danced some, and ordered another bottle. Taylor headed over. He didn't want Charlie too shitfaced. Drunks made awful sources. Tell you anything and everything, and you never knew what was fact.

"Evening, Charlie."

He looked up from the woman on his right.

"The reporter. How'd you get in here?"

"This place likes to show up in the papers."

"Chasing celebrities now? That's fine. *We're* celebrities."

The girls laughed. Bobby didn't.

"Trying to figure out who killed your father. Who ... and why."

"What, you think *I* did it?"

"No. Doesn't work like that. Interviewing everyone in the family to see where that leads me. *Do* you have an alibi?"

"That Saturday morning I was at an after-hours club with forty of my closest friends. The police already have the list." He finished his glass and refilled it. "Buy us a bottle, and I'll talk about anything else you like."

Taylor didn't have the cash for a bottle of champagne. He barely had enough for another beer, that and a Macy's charge card maxed out from furnishing the Manhattan apartment. He was embarrassed, and it pissed him off that Charlie could do that to him.

Some speech about not buying interviews would only get him laughed away from the table. Bobby frowned. At Taylor's delay? At having a reporter standing there?

"I'm afraid I don't—"

"I'll take care of it," said Bobby. "Have a seat." He pulled over an empty chair from the next table.

The bottle came. Everyone drank and Bobby took all four girls out on the dance floor. Maybe he was trying to help Taylor—that noblesse oblige thing—or maybe he liked dancing with four girls.

Taylor set down his glass and slipped out his notebook. "How'd you get along with your father?"

"We were up and down. Think you saw that. As I'm sure you heard, he wanted more focus in my life. Me, I think I'm pretty focused on what I do." He laughed. "I wanted him to do a better job managing the family money. I did not want him to get killed." More champagne went down Charlie's hatch. "I am crushed."

He actually looks it.

"What was wrong with how he managed his money?"

"Not his, *ours*. We're all supposed to inherit. He let twenty-five million go missing."

"Mr. DeVries said Denny Connell stole it. You blame your father for that?"

"He hired the guy. Fired the white-shoe firm we'd used for four generations to go with this crook."

"What about your father's new plans?"

"The farm, the foundation, all that? Craziness."

"How's it crazy to simplify your life?"

"Losing twenty-five million bucks certainly simplified *his* life. All our lives."

"Any idea who wanted him killed?"

"Of course not. Or the police would know already."

"There is one person, so far unidentified. Martha Gibson overheard a conversation before she died. In the sitting—"

"She was eavesdropping?"

"She was taking care of the fresh flowers outside. Her job, right? She heard two people, a man with a deep voice and another person whose voice she couldn't ID or hear distinctly. The doors were closed." Taylor flipped forward to a folded page in his notebook and went through the quotes again. He finished with, " 'All right. As long as we take care of him by then. Final and done.' "

"Well, that's shocking stuff." Whatever jokiness was in Charlie's voice left it. His tone was serious and low; Taylor leaned closer to talk over the thudding music.

"Yes, a threat, a threat that seems to have been carried out."

"Have you told the cops?"

"The detectives investigating Martha's death know. The one on your father's case won't return my calls."

"I'll make sure he does."

"Some of what the man said in the sitting room, some of it sounds a lot like your criticisms of your father."

"I didn't like what he was doing. I didn't make threats. Did Martha say it sounded like me?"

"No, in fact, she said it didn't. The person she could hear clearly, that is."

"No! It wasn't me. I'd never do that."

"I'd be careful what bits of that sitting room conversation you repeat. Hearing it may be what got Martha killed. The murders could be connected."

Charlie shifted in his seat, agitated. "You've heard all our secrets. The missing money. Papa's plans. I don't know who was in the sitting room. I don't even know anyone was there. This is coming third-hand from a dead woman."

"The fact she's dead is looking like proof enough."

"Or something else. She was mugged. Some senseless New York violence."

"Nobody's given me anything to counter the theory that that conversation was a threat, likely a murder threat, against your father. You haven't. Martha had no reason to make it up. You already said you were unhappy with your father's management of the money."

"Everyone liked my father—because of all the money he passed out. To everyone but his family."

Charlie waded into the heaving throng. Arms, legs, torsos moving, twisting. The tang of sweat oddly mellowed by cigarette smoke. Everybody was rubbing everything against everybody's everything else.

Taylor returned to the bar.

As he had nothing better to do, and planned never to come back to this place, he positioned himself so he could watch the night pass at Studio 54. Bits of garments came off men and women. Some didn't have much to take off. They were already in some form of underwear, negligee, or transparent clothing. He counted at least four drug deals. Two guys next to him at the bar did lines and went back to dance. The bartender sanguinely wiped up the little bit left. At different times, he saw Andy Warhol, Debbie Harry, Jack Haley Jr., the child actress Brooke Shields, and all those familiar faces that he was certain were someones but didn't know who because he didn't follow the someones columns in the papers. Warhol appeared in four different locations, like he was a ghost specially assigned to haunt the disco. Except for the shock of white hair, he looked something like normal in his traditional tux. A man in a thong sat on a motorcycle. Dancing, sort of. A gold-painted nude couple formed a frozen statue, his hands thrown in the air, her hand on his dick as she crouched as if about to start a blowjob. Tough position to hold, in so many ways.

Charlie and his friends returned to the table, left to dance, returned. Did that all night.

The one thing he didn't see in Studio 54 were leisure suits, the supposed uniform of the disco male. Studio 54 was a cut or four above those, he figured.

By four a.m., the place had only started to clear a little. Charlie's party got up and headed for the exit. Taylor followed. He didn't know what these people did afterwards, but it had to be something worth witnessing once.

CHAPTER 22

———◆———

THE SIX OF them climbed in a stretch that took off east on 54th Street and turned uptown on Broadway. There were no cabs around to "follow that car" with this time. Anyway, the money for the fare was inside Studio 54's cash register.

What was I thinking? Of course they have a car. Like they are going to walk to the subway like me?

The street was empty but for the trickle of people coming out of the club. Oddly, this was an almost safe time to be in Times Square. Since the nice pickings from the theater crowd were long gone home, the professional muggers were gone too, leaving the desperate sort—drug addicts who weren't well armed. In Times Square, that left the odds in your favor for keeping your money or your life. Even the hookers had thinned out, gone to rest before the next shift at the Crossroads of the World. The porn theaters that ran 24 hours a day lit the streets with bright white marquees framed in flashing colored bulbs.

Taylor hurried along at a good clip despite the quiet. There was a big difference between less dangerous and actually safe. As he went, he came up with an idea. He stopped at an all-night diner on 46th Street on the east side of Duffy Square and ordered a coffee. He got out the calling card Charlie DeVries had given him. After he took a few sips from the heavy white-porcelain mug, he went to the shop's payphone, dialed the number on the card, left his name and the payphone's number with the answering service and sat at the counter drinking more coffee, which he needed at this point. He'd dumped in a third packet of sugar, in case that might help.

The phone rang, sounding especially loud at 4:30 a.m. in a Duffy Square coffee shop. All heads—which meant four, counting the waitress and cook—turned.

Taylor raised his hand. "Got it."

"Who's looking for me?" said Charlie.

"It's Taylor."

"You want to talk more at four thirty in the morning?"

"Nah, I'm done with work. Looking to hang out."

Charlie repeated Taylor's words. "Okay. Conditions."

"To hang out?"

"This place appears in *no* story."

"Like I said, want some fun."

At a place I can never write about? What's the point?

He might get closer to Charlie. He was curious what these people did at this time of the morning, and his night was already blown. Might as well take a low-odds shot in the dark that he'd get a lead for later.

"Oh, it'll be fun. Everything here is absolutely illegal. Dangerous also," a drunken snort, "to the sort of fella who asks questions. I'm getting you in, but you're on your own after that."

Taylor hustled across Duffy Square and Times Square to the Paramount Building and City News Bureau's offices on the nineteenth floor. He took eighty bucks out of the emergency cash box in Novak's desk, leaving a five and a nickel. He wasn't sure if Novak would consider this an emergency, but he knew he couldn't go wherever he was going with a dollar and loose change. Check that. Novak would *not* consider it an emergency unless a really good story came out of the trip instantly—like tomorrow—a story Taylor had agreed not to write. He'd work it out with Novak later. He called Checker Cab on the office phone and waited in the lobby of the building.

The taxi made a right and another right to head up Tenth Avenue toward Washington Heights, Manhattan's secret northern neighborhood and the location of the address Charlie had given him. Maybe it wasn't so much secret as a neighborhood few visited unless they actually lived there. The Heights had good housing—apartment buildings and row houses—yet it was a long subway ride from midtown, with Harlem and Central Park in between.

As the cab traveled north, Taylor occupied himself by rolling through his geographic memory of the city, an internal map acquired through years of visiting crime scenes all over the five boroughs. Washington Heights wasn't even Manhattan's northernmost neighborhood. That was Inwood, if you meant *on* the island of Manhattan. It was a place so green, rocky, and hilly, it seemed to Taylor he'd already reached upstate when he visited Inwood. Finally, there was Manhattan's geographic asterisk, Marble Hill, which was the only part of the borough attached to the North American mainland (and the Bronx). This was because the Harlem River had been filled in on the north side of the neighborhood in 1914 after the Harlem Ship Canal had cut the neighborhood off from Manhattan on the south. Little geographic details always helped in stories, though some more than others. He couldn't think of a crime that had brought him to Marble Hill. It would happen someday. This was New York. Nowhere was safe.

The cab stopped at the address on St. Nicholas Avenue written in his notebook, a church. The front door was boarded up. Lights from inside flashed across the stained-glass window facing the street, illuminating reds, greens, blues, and whites.

"You must really need to pray," the cabbie said.

Or might want to start.

He paid, got out and headed toward the back, which was the only instruction Charlie had given him. Hadn't even told him the place was a church.

The walk along the side of the building grew darker as he moved away from the street. This side of the church had no windows because what looked like the rectory was attached. There were a lot of good places to get jumped in New York at 4:45 in the morning. This one would make the list, particularly if Charlie had it in for him. He ran his fingers along the gritty stone wall to guide him under a canopy of trees in total darkness.

A door sprung open steps away from him, throwing out blinding light and music that was more bass bump than anything else.

A big bouncer—more the enforcer type—grabbed Taylor and pushed him up against the church wall.

"Interesting way to greet your guests."

"I know who all my guests are. When they're coming. Buddy, none of them fucking looks like you."

He spun Taylor to face the wall, patted him down, turned him back again, looked at the cash in his wallet and laughed. "How long you think you're staying?" The only other thing he found was the reporter's notebook.

"What's this?"

"A notebook."

"It looks something like the kind cops use."

"No, not a cop."

"What the fuck are you doing here?"

"Charlie DeVries invited me."

The man yelled into the rectangle of light and noise. "Hey, Eddie. Charlie DV say someone was coming?" There was a wait, and a grunted "yes." The goon pulled Taylor off the wall and pushed him toward the light. "You're a guest tonight. Go find Charlie. Bother any of the regulars or break any of the rules and I'll break you on Broadway."

All the pews were gone, replaced by circular tables out by the walls and a gaming pit in the middle. Taylor counted two craps tables—the busiest—two roulette, and three for card games. The altar was still in place, with enough candles to pose a fire hazard around the edge of the nave, which was the dance floor. By Taylor's rough estimate, there was even more flesh on display here than at Studio 54—so much he was finding it hard to find a place to look and not end up staring at someone's private parts.

Jee-suz. If the Greek Orthodox God of my mother does start sending down lightning bolts, this place will top the target list.

He found Charlie and his gang in the front corner with a close-up view of the dance floor.

"The chronicler of our life and times," Charlie said. "Slide over here." He pulled on the arm of a black-haired woman and she slipped off a chair and onto Charlie's lap. "You like Our Little Chapel?"

"Novel use for a closed church."

"Yes." He laughed and started hiccupping. "Novel."

Bobby Livingston, who sat on the other side of Taylor, appeared to be more with it, his dark-blue eyes scanning the room like he was looking for a sin he wanted to try.

"Do you come here every night after the club?" Taylor said.

Bobby focused on Taylor. "No. This is but one option. Our Charlie likes to gamble when he can stand up. And see the dice. I like something a bit more physical."

Taylor wasn't sure what that meant, but it made him think of two legal sex clubs he'd heard opened recently.

Charlie got up, and the woman dropped to the floor with a squeal. Turning to Bobby, he slurred, "I'm gonna go back to the craps. Maybe they unfixed the dice."

"Take a bit of a break, partner."

"I did break. As the night is again no longer young. Why does that always happen? I'm playing. I'm down twenty."

Taylor knew he didn't mean twenty bucks, so he understood

even better the bouncer's reaction to the money in his wallet. Bobby poured Taylor a Jack Daniels and Tab without asking if wanted the drink, then joined Charlie at the table, where Charlie pushed stacks of cash across to place a bet. *Nope, not twenty bucks.*

The black-haired woman dumped on the floor struggled to get up—hampered by six-inch heels and booze and probably something else. He helped her. They half danced for a few seconds because she was so unsteady. He got her into her seat.

"Who runs the place?" Taylor said.

"Brave first question."

"Somebody must, right?"

"Somebody always must." She offered a lopsided smile. "Some things maybe you may not want to know. As you're asking … the Concierge is in charge of Our Little Chapel."

At this point Taylor didn't care how drunk she was. He needed basic info. A starting place.

"That's a title, not a name."

"No, he's called *The Concierge*. No one knows his real name. People—the right families—need things. He takes care of it."

"A casino?"

"Just a part of what he does. He delivers too. Drugs. Women, I hear. Think Bobby may avail himself of that service."

"What else?"

"A smart man wouldn't ask more questions. Didn't Charlie tell you no reporting? The Concierge plays an important role in high society. That's all I can say."

He looked into the bleary green eyes of her passably pretty face, though her mouth was too small. It didn't look like she meant *high* ironically. He wasn't asking.

Taylor gazed around what was, in essence, a major criminal enterprise—if the woman was to be believed—that provided illegal pleasure to the rich. He'd agreed to make this goddamn visit off the record. *What a story. I'm a fucking idiot. No, Charlie knew what he was doing.* Taylor would no more break his promise to drunk Charlie DeVries than he would to sober, pious President Jimmy Carter. You blow your credibility with sources, and you're done.

He couldn't write a story on the visit. Okay. Maybe there were connections in this room he could track down later?

He took a hit off the Jack and Tab, stood up and started a slow walk around the room, checking out the faces of the men and women at tables, then those gaming, looking for … he wasn't sure what, he wasn't sure who. A face he knew, in a place filled with people who rarely entered the world he covered? Probability was pretty low. Even if he was off the record, he could still look around.

Someone disagreed.

A new bouncer, normal height but muscular, slammed him into the inside wall.

"Enough slamming, man. We're in church."

"Bud told me to keep an eye on you."

"Why? Charlie invited me."

"Your first black mark. His judgment isn't very good most times, and he isn't really a favorite customer."

"Who *are* your favorite customers?"

The thug smashed him twice into the wall, sending jarring pain from the pack of his skull to his eyeballs and clearing his head of whatever expensive buzz he'd had. More raps like that would do real damage.

Taylor grabbed the thug's left shoulder with his right hand and spun from the wall. He levered the bouncer hard and fast over his hip, putting him on his back. The hip sweep he'd been perfecting in class for the past month.

Time to go.

He didn't even get a chance to turn. Another bouncer grabbed him from behind in a hammerlock. The joints from right wrist to elbow to shoulder screamed. The first thug rose to his feet and pulled a thick sap from his jacket pocket.

"Goddammit no!" Charlie yelled. "I'm tired of fixed."

He heaved over the craps table with a crash. Bills floated onto it like autumn leaves. The bouncers left Taylor for Charlie and to retrieve the house's money.

Police sirens wailed from outside, a few blocks away.

The thundering music died, and a woman's voice came from the sound system: "Please do not panic. This is our weekly clean-out, under arrangement with the relevant authorities. We have ten minutes to disperse. Walk quietly through the rectory. There will be cars for everyone, though some may have to share."

The last part of the announcement caused the only groan.

The two goons holding Charlie looked unsure what to do.

Taylor went over. "You don't want a customer caught in here. That would be bad for business."

They stayed frozen, one with the sap at the ready. Taylor was pretty sure these two had difficulty keeping more than one thought in their heads at a time. The table's staff picked up the bills and asked the other players how much they had down.

Bobby Livingston stepped up and handed the two enforcers big wads of cash. "Good man, good man. No one's complaining. The boss will be happy."

They let go of Charlie. The lead thug pointed at Taylor. "You in here again, you're a grease stain on the sidewalk. I don't care whose friend you are."

"Do you think up those lines ahead of time?" Taylor was already walking toward where the crowd exited.

"Talk to any of our customers about being customers—"

"I get it. Grease stain. Sidewalk."

"No. Then I fucking shoot you."

Taylor moved through the rectory, which was clearly the storage place for the booze, food, gambling paraphernalia, and—Taylor didn't doubt—drugs. When he came out the back, Charlie stumbled behind him, followed by Bobby.

"Be seeing you," said Bobby.

He and Charlie walked toward the street. Charlie puked.

"Damn, Charlie, my shoes."

The limos pulled away. In front of Taylor, the sun rose over the South Bronx, illuminating high in the sky a spiral of smoke from one of that night's fires, likely arson, likely destroying housing people needed. The sun tinted the roof of Our Little Chapel an orange that said sin rather than new beginning.

CHAPTER 23

———— ✦ ————

"I'M STILL PISSED off," Samantha said. "We talked about this before."

"I know you are." He said it without much enthusiasm—a mistake that made her angrier—because his head throbbed like the bass beat in the clubs last night. Purely lack of sleep. Never got the chance to drink enough booze to have a hangover. He should have spent this Saturday in bed, but he had work to do.

She scooted in front of him and walked backwards. "I am serious. I was a cop. I know how dangerous all this is. That club, or church, or whatever the hell it was. Everything illegal? By yourself?"

"What was I supposed to do?"

"Gambling. Drugs. Enforcers. There must have been guns. How good are you at disarming someone with a gun?"

"Not quite there on that one yet. Not so good with two against one, either." He offered an apologetic smile as she fell in alongside him.

"You can't go into that sort of place without some kind of backup. No cop would do it."

"I'm trying to get a story. I'm not a cop. I had to play things as they played. Anyway, two wouldn't have gotten in."

"Taylor," she took his arm, lowered her voice to a whisper, "you could disappear in a place like that. Never be found again. The richest people in town. Drug dealers. Cops on the pad. I can't have you disappearing on me. I won't."

"Pretty good story, though." A ploy to distract. "If I could write it. I need to track down this *Concierge*."

The ploy failed. She let go of his arm. Sounding disappointed, she said, "You aren't taking me seriously. You get this way when you really want a story and it's not happening. You get crazy obsessive."

"What do you want me to do? Two good people dead. The cops aren't getting anywhere. Both cases getting colder by the day. Which means the stories are getting even colder. This is what I do. There wasn't time to get you or anyone else near there."

"You can't die. I love you. I … I can't—"

"No plans for that."

"This is my bottom line. You call me. So someone knows what hole you're going down."

"I'll call."

"Promise?"

"If you promise not to argue with me. Or try to come along if that won't work."

"All that to get a phone call?"

"Yes."

"Fine. Agreed." She thought for minute. "You know, this Jimmy the Cryptkeeper's another example. Who tries to interview a drug dealer out on the street?"

"In a cemetery, actually. I have. A bunch of times. You know that. You're with me today. I'm covered. I promised last year not to do stakeouts on my own. I'm mending my ways."

If I ignore the days I spent watching Jerome McGill alone. How can I keep my promise? We both have jobs. I have to move when I can.

"You got kidnapped last year doing the same thing."

"You rescued me."

"Only because I had the sense to keep an eye on you."

"Every other time, I've managed to talk my way out of trouble."

She dropped into an unhappy silence. This was an ongoing stress in their relationship, had been for more than a year. Samantha wanted to control the risks he needed to take. She usually fell back on what she'd have done as a cop. Like he'd said, he didn't work like a cop. Couldn't. He had to find a way to make her happy, though. If this strain stayed between them, he might lose her. That was a risk he could not take.

At first, Taylor wasn't sure how to find Abigail Gibson's dealer. Mt. Olivet Cemetery was big enough by itself. It was one of five running east to west in eastern Queens. Lutheran All Faiths Cemetery was across the street, while on the other side of the Queens Midtown Expressway and the BQE were Mt. Zion, Cavalry, and First Cavalry. What if Jimmy switched among them?

From a distance, the tombstones of Mt. Olivet bristled out of the ground, appearing too close together, one on top of the other, as if even in their dying, New Yorkers couldn't escape the crowd.

After waiting forty minutes, Taylor saw the solution to his problem, as individuals who looked nothing like mourners headed into the Mt. Olivet gate across from where they stood. Taylor and Samantha watched a couple more, then followed a Hispanic-looking teen. He took a right and walked up a hill to a large mausoleum with pillars like the Parthenon. The teen disappeared around the back. He returned quickly, was startled by the sight of them, and trotted down the path past an open grave awaiting the arrival of a coffin and mourners.

Taylor signaled. Samantha pulled out her pistol and went around the other side.

Jimmy the Cryptkeeper—a tiny, caramel-colored man with

a big, floppy Afro—sat on the edge of the mausoleum. He was pulling hard on a joint. He turned warily when Taylor came into his field of vision.

"Who the fuck are you?"

"A reporter. I have a couple questions for you."

"No one comes up here that I haven't cleared. I don't answer questions from anyone. Fuck reporters."

"I could let the cops know about the unconventional location you're using."

A stiletto knife appeared in his hand and the blade popped out.

"I could get you ready for one of these graves and go use one of the other monuments in this lovely resting place."

"Uh-uh." Samantha was at the corner with the gun aimed at Jimmy's head. "Put the knife away, and I'll put this away."

Jimmy saw the sense in that. "A reporter with a redheaded lady who packs? This some kind of TV show?"

"No, just life, Jimmy. Do you remember a customer named Abigail Gibson?"

"I got lots of customers. Why should I remember one for you?"

"Abigail's sister was murdered. Could be drug-related. Abigail's boyfriend, a hitman named Jerome McGill. He knocked you around. Took some merchandise he didn't pay for."

"I did hear *that* McGill's not breathing anymore."

"That make you happy?"

Samantha eased her way around toward Taylor, her eyes on Jimmy the whole time.

"Didn't like what he did to me. I didn't off him."

"How about Abigail? Maybe you went after her and ended up shooting her sister by mistake. Or sent someone to do the job."

"Look around you, man. You know why I work up here. I want no fucking trouble from no fucking body. I want to move my stuff without getting robbed, or grabbed by the cops, or grabbed *and* robbed by the cops. I want things nice and quiet and easy. That's why the only dead I like are the ones who already are."

"You own a gun?"

"No. Don't do guns."

"You did follow Abigail home once."

Jimmy's head dropped. "Look, man, I check out all my customers first time. Another thing keeps me safe from the cops."

"You have an alibi for March eighth?"

"What is this, *Perry Mason*?"

"If it was, he'd say you already have motive."

"You going to put the cops on me?"

"The way it works is I write a story with everything I can find out. If that story has information in it the detectives find interesting, they'll come calling. If you have an alibi, you aren't part of my story."

"I'll jog my brains. I'll ask my old lady. I don't deserve to be in that story. McGill might have been rough with me, but if I started shooting every time somebody was rough, I'd be on the FBI's most-wanted."

"I'm checking back with you in a couple of days. Be here and give me something if you don't want to be news."

TAYLOR AND SAMANTHA caught the bus down Cross Bay Boulevard, named because it crossed Jamaica Bay via a bridge and an island to get to the Rockaway Peninsula. They got off in the neighborhood of Rockaway Park with the bay on the right and the Atlantic Ocean on the left. From the ocean beach to the bayside, the neighborhood was four blocks wide at this point. Beyond the neighborhood was Jacob Riis National Park and Breezy Point, the end of the peninsula.

The two of them walked to Joe Mulligan's house at Newport Avenue and Beach 130th Street. Air that had been hot and sticky in the middle of Queens was cooled by a sea breeze.

Mulligan bent over the hood of a black Town Car, polishing. He spied them through the windows of the car.

"Welcome to the Irish Riviera." He wore plaid Bermuda shorts, rubber thongs, and a golf shirt of an entirely different plaid. Though he'd previously used an approximation of the formal-sounding diction of his late boss, now he spoke like a man of Queens—with the harsh vowels of the Rockaways.

Taylor introduced Samantha.

"Callahan, now there's a good name." He set the polishing cloth on the front bumper. "Taylor, I'm not so sure of." He laughed a little at this, but was far more restrained than on their drive upstate.

He led them around to an emerald-green side yard set with aluminum folding chairs, the seats and backs made of woven red-and-white-plastic strips. Mulligan insisted he get them something, jogged into the house, came out with three bottles of Guinness beer, a yellow-plastic bowl of potato chips and a smaller one containing French onion dip.

"My granddad taught me to drink this. Makes me an oddball in this neighborhood of Murphys and," nodding to Samantha, "Callahans. They all like their Piels and Budweiser. Gotta remember the home place. One for sir." He lifted the bottle in salute.

Taylor sipped his Guinness. Sharp, heavy, the taste of chocolate gone bad. He'd never liked the stuff.

"How's the family doing?" Taylor asked.

"Pretty, pretty bad. Mrs. DeVries is still in her bed. The police had to interview her from there. Audrey, poor thing. Mother's no help. She's overcome. A good person, kind like her dad."

"Charlie?"

Fred lifted the bottle again. "Charlie's drinking his way through his grief."

"I was with him last night. He appears to be gambling and whoring his way through it, too."

"He's one of those kids … handed all the opportunity in the world and got more and more confused about what to do with it."

"That's a kind assessment."

"It's what sir would say."

"You were close to him."

The hint of a smile left his face. "Best I ever worked for."

"A lot of riding around. With him. The rest of the family. You ever hear anything that made you think someone was coming after him? Or anything that was off?"

"No, nothing. I mean, Charlie complained and whined and got more money. Same as the other families I worked for before my dad retired. If that was cause for murder, Park Avenue would be a warzone."

"He was going to get less with the changes DeVries planned. I mean, had to be."

"Sir was going to provide him with an income. Charlie was going to have to cut back on that lifestyle of his. Grow up and be the adult that matched his age."

"Yes, his *lifestyle*. I was at an after-hours club with him this morning. Drugs, gambling, prostitutes, God knows what else. A real criminal operation. Maybe he ran up a big debt. Or pissed someone off. They took it out on his father."

"Story land to me. Nothing I know anything about."

"You heard of someone called the Concierge?"

"Yeah." Mulligan shifted in his chair. Finished half the bottle of Guinness.

"What do you know?"

"Only a little, and that's probably too much. He's a guy who gets Park Avenue people what they need. Legal, illegal. Whenever fast is a priority. Former boss used him. Ordered drugs. I made a few pick-ups. Quit that job. I wasn't getting busted for his habit. Concierge makes deliveries now, so that problem's solved. Charlie's received 'em. Never talked about the Concierge with me. You're not supposed to. One of the

Concierge's rules. Which is why I don't know any more than that."

"Who was your former boss?"

"I like my job. I like my life."

Taylor asked him about the conversation Martha had overheard in the sitting room. Mulligan had already listened to Taylor recount it to DeVries on their drive back from Amenia. He'd kept his mouth shut then, probably because he was expected to.

"I was worried when you told him that. Sir thought he could solve every problem in the family. Couldn't tell you who the mystery man was who did all the talking. I'm rarely upstairs. There is one thing I haven't been able to get out of my head."

"What's that?"

"It can't be no accident. Sir was killed after he said he'd handle that conversation. He walked into some kind of buzz saw."

"Did you talk to Martha Gibson much?" Samantha said.

"To say hello. Like I said, not upstairs much."

"Did you tell anyone about the conversation Martha heard?"

"No! I never repeat anything I hear in the car. I am now because sir's dead. I want the sons of bitches caught."

Taylor drank more of the beer. He was almost getting used to it. Or maybe a light summer buzz improved anything. "What do you know about Denny Connell?"

"He was in the car a whole bunch. He and sir went to meetings together. A lot. They were always going over numbers. Connell was some fast talker. I don't know numbers and couldn't tell you what he was going on about, but sir often made him go back. Repeat things. I'd grab a look in the rearview, and sir had this look like he wasn't getting it."

"Connell was confusing DeVries?"

"Looked like it."

"On purpose."

"I didn't know his play then. That's what I saw happening. Like I said, don't know numbers. I picked Connell up at his office a bunch of times. Either got him first or went with the boss. Except for the one time I drove him alone. He came down from the DeVries apartment and gave me an address downtown. The boss hadn't given me instructions so I started to ask, and Connell ordered me to get moving in pretty spicy language. I figured it must be okay. The only person in that car more than sir himself was Connell. The destination was a strange place for a meeting—a warehouse in the Gansevoort Market. On Ninth Avenue."

"The meatpacking district?" Samantha said, surprised.

"Yeah."

"You're sure?" Taylor said.

"Remember all my runs."

"The address? When?"

"I can check my log book for specifics and call you."

"I could use that information. If you think of anything else ...."

"Sure, anything to help the family."

TAYLOR AND SAMANTHA walked back toward the bus, but Taylor veered hard left. In three blocks, they were on the beach carrying their shoes. Samantha strolled at the edge of the surf while Taylor stayed just out of reach of the waves.

"The water feels so good," Samantha said.

"Like the sand, where it's hard, wet, and cool. Where you leave a print."

"This makes up for coming all this way, doesn't it?"

"Oh, this trip was well worth it. Mulligan confirmed the Concierge exists. Now I can go after the story without breaking my word to Charlie about Our Little Chapel."

"He won't be happy."

"Happy, unhappy. That's not my worry. Long as I keep my commitment to a source. Who knows? That address Connell went to might be worth something, if only because it's the first lead I've got on him aside from his abandoned office.

The Gansevoort is a strange area for him to be going. There's nothing in that neighborhood but dead cows, mob-run unions, and places mobsters like to hang out."

Since it was the first day of the long July 4th weekend, they kept walking past houses, then several big apartment buildings, until they came to an old, weathered clam bar. Joe's. Were all clam bars named Joe's? They ate a dozen little necks raw and two-dozen top necks steamed, accompanied by bottles of the golden Piels Joe Mulligan so despised.

CHAPTER 24

⸺◆⸺

O N THE WEDNESDAY following the long July 4ᵗʰ weekend, Taylor walked into the office and found Novak bouncing like he was on a pogo stick.

"He's calling in five." Novak repeated the sentence as he bounced.

"Calm down. Who's calling? About what?"

"He would only talk—"

"Stop jumping around or we're not having a conversation."

He stood still, though the energy seemed to vibrate inside him. Novak—with an open, smiling face and hair slicked back in the fifties style he refused to give up—wore a dark suit as he had since his days working on the business desk at the *Messenger-Telegram*. They said reporters ended up dressing like the people they covered. Certainly explained why sports writers looked like overgrown twelve-year-olds.

"I was here, and Cramly was on the phone taking a story from Templeton. I picked up the next call. Man asked for you. I said you weren't in yet. He said he'd call back in a half hour. Could I give you a message? He said he has a Son of Sam letter. A new one. The third letter."

The phone rang. Novak started pogoing again.

"This is Taylor."

"You want the letter?" The voice was muffled, pitched high, like a strained falsetto.

"You are …?"

"Not important."

"With the cops?"

"Someone who thinks the truth needs to get out. What's in this letter is important."

"What do you want from me?"

"A fair and accurate story. The kind you write."

"Let's meet."

"There are complications."

"There always are."

"You want this or not?"

Taylor was instantly skeptical. He couldn't believe a letter from the .44-caliber killer was about to drop into his lap. He was no Breslin. City News was no *Daily News*. Sure, he'd received his fair share of tips out of nowhere. Nothing like this. Maybe the guy had a letter. Or maybe he knew something worth hearing. Or most likely, he was a nut looking for attention. Best to play along. Part of the job was sorting out the nuts.

"Yeah, I want it."

"All right, I'll call to set up a meeting."

"When?"

Click.

Novak stopped bouncing.

Raymond Associates' office door was locked. Both Lew and Samantha had to be out on cases. He wrote a message on a sheet from his notebook letting Samantha know he was going down to the meatpacking district to check out the address Joe Mulligan had phoned in, the address where he'd dropped off Denny Connell. He hadn't left notes every time he went out in the past, but she'd been so insistent Saturday, he'd decided this was better than a fight. Actually, anything was better than a fight. He'd been independent—alone—a long time, and it wasn't all it was cracked up to be. Lots of loneliness, the blues invading when he wasn't busy with a story. He had no interest in being independent of Samantha. He saw the blues and a yawning blackness behind them when he thought of losing her. He'd take the same chances, but keep her informed and hope that was compromise enough.

He knew one thing. This story had a bad spin on it. He was going to have to cross some lines to get at it.

He rocked on a downtown 3 train. This was the kind of trip he made with little hope of a return. How much of a waste of time would it be? In his mind, anyone who embezzled $25 million would already be on one of those tropical islands pictured in the windows of travel agents. *Gilligan's Island*, but with all the luxurious comforts. He took the steps up from the 14th Street station two at a time, walked west three long avenue blocks until he was in a neighborhood of industrial buildings. Slaughter houses, in the main. He found the address Mulligan had provided. The big garage doors used for loading were shut. A side door opened into a massive space, the concrete floor a collage of muted reds and less-than-reds, bloodstains of different ages.

The building had to be out of commission. An odor of dust and damp concrete. But not death. People were wrong about death. They said the smell of it hung around a place—around people even—forever. No. Even death faded.

The hooks for hanging sides of beef were gone. The whole space had been stripped. Meatpacking, like many commercial activities, had been fleeing New York to Jersey and places farther afield for more than a decade. His steps echoed as he walked to the back of the building.

A glow leaked from around the edges of a door in the rear wall. It opened to a stairway. Two flights led to another door and a hallway with what looked like four offices. A light was on in one.

Taylor knocked.

"Yeah."

Taylor stepped in and guessed.

"Denny Connell?"

A man in his early thirties in a sharp-cut blue suit that didn't belong in a slaughterhouse turned around from a file cabinet. He had long blond hair and a face that was more pretty than handsome.

"Who's asking?" His bass voice didn't match his face, and Taylor immediately wondered if Connell was the deep-voiced conspirator in the conversation Martha overheard.

Taylor took a seat without being asked. He kept his reporter's notebook in his pocket to see how this played out.

"I'm researching someone to handle investments."

The man sat down in a comfortable desk chair that also didn't fit in a slaughterhouse. "That's hardly likely." He looked Taylor up and down. "Whatever you are, what you make wouldn't pay a quarter of my fee."

"Doing the work for someone else."

"Oh yeah, who's that?"

"Edmond DeVries."

Connell—this had to be Connell—put a snub-nosed .38 on the desk. He chuckled. "He doesn't have anyone working on anything anymore."

"The family's looking for their money."

"What are you, some sort of low-rent PI? Probably all they can afford."

"Reporter with the City News Bureau."

"Wish you hadn't said that. A PI, maybe we could cut a deal. Publicity's another thing. We can't have that."

"*We*?"

"Figure of speech."

"Or maybe it took more than one person to embezzle the DeVrieses."

"You're not too stupid. Yes, an organization. Working several of these stupid rich families. So sad. Couple sentences, and you already know too much."

He picked up the gun.

"That's why you'd didn't leave. There's more than one score. Pretty greedy, given what you got."

Oldest play in the book. Keep 'em talking.

Didn't stop the cold from leaking into his stomach, which knotted up around the ice water. His shoulders tightened.

"You mine where you find the ore. DeVries was specially easy. His family already thought he was fucking miserable at handling the funds. Considered him a financial idiot. He was afraid he couldn't hang on to what he had. Had every right to be. Cooked up that plan to get out of the city. He was scared, running away. Too late. That's more than a couple sentences. You know all you'll ever need to know. Let's go."

"Where?"

"So many questions." He held the gun in a menacing, tight grip. "This is a good place to operate. Quiet. No sense making a mess here. There are people in my organization who take out your kind of garbage. Move, slowly. Out the door. Down."

Their shoes made hollow *klings* on the metal stairs.

Taylor checked behind, finding Connell a good three steps back. Too far to do anything before encountering a .38-caliber bullet.

"Turn around!"

The door to the slaughterhouse floor approached. Taylor saw one chance. A tight one, but the three-step gap might help him.

He reached for the door.

"Open it."

Taylor pushed, stepped onto the concrete of too many colors and dropped into a crouch on the other side of the door.

Slammed it shut, hard and fast.

The plan had been to try and catch Connell's leading arm in the door. He must have seen it coming. Slugs blew open three holes above Taylor's head.

"Naughty. Now I'm going have to hurt you before I have someone kill you."

The distance from where he kneeled to the door to the street now looked like a quarter mile. He'd get shot in the back trying to make it.

The door smashed into the shoulder he held against it, sending a shock of pain across his back. Connell hit it again. He was strong and had the leverage because Taylor had to stay low—and hope Connell didn't start shooting low. A third blow. Real agony. The door opened two inches before Taylor pushed through the pain to close it again. This was a war of attrition Taylor would lose.

Time for the old fifth-grade trick.

The next push came and Taylor fell away from the door to the left, leaving his leg trailing. The door swung open, smashing into the wall. Connell's momentum, with Taylor's leg for good measure, sent him flying, and he crashed to the floor.

Taylor moved in fast, kicked the hand with the pistol and sent it skittering across the floor. He punched Connell in the face—hard enough to send electric pain from Taylor's knuckles up his arm.

On his back, Connell lashed out with one leg at Taylor, who caught a heel in the gut, stumbled backwards, windmilled his arms, and kept his balance.

The scam artist scrambled for the gun.

Taylor leapt over him, snagged the revolver, and rolled up onto his knees. *Was that judo?*

Connell kept coming, slow, easy steps, now with a knife out. "Bet you have no idea how to use that fucking thing."

"You're right."

Taylor let Connell dance in closer.

He rose on one knee.

Closer.

The knife flickered in a shaft of sunlight coming through a hole the roof.

Closer.

Taylor hurled the pistol at Connell's face with all the force he could muster. This Connell did not expect.

The gun crashed into the bridge of his nose.

He screamed.

The revolver bounced on the concrete and went off with a roar. A bullet pinged somewhere in the slaughterhouse.

Connell, staggering blindly, held both hands to his bloody face. Taylor wasn't taking any chances. He stepped in, flipped him to the ground, and kicked him hard in the ribs for good measure.

A pile of old wire by the wall served to tie Connell's arms so Taylor could run and call 911.

Ten minutes later, the EMTs took Connell off.

TAYLOR SPENT THREE hours explaining the scene to the cops.

A bunco sergeant listened to everything Taylor had to say one more time and took charge of all of the paperwork in the office.

"You're saying you got hold of his gun and hurled it at him?"

"I'm a terrible shot. Believe me. Much better at throwing a Spaldeen—you now, in stickball."

"I know stickball. You disarmed yourself."

"If I hit him, he wasn't getting up."

The sergeant shook his head.

Taylor's press pass didn't have much effect on the man, but Connell's impressive rap sheet for running confidence games did. The murder cops were on the way to the hospital to see if there was any connection to the DeVries killing. After more interviews and much conferring, the bunco sergeant said they were holding off on any charges against Taylor while they sorted through what Connell was up to. It helped that Connell's gun was, of all things, legitimate and registered in his name, which meant Taylor didn't show up with the weapon. It also helped that he'd used the weapon as a projectile, though every cop who heard the story looked at Taylor oddly. Some chuckled. He was told not to leave the city.

Where the hell am I going?

Taylor wasn't concerned about himself. He was worried, more like panicked, that the bunco detectives wouldn't be able to figure out the paperwork and recover the DeVries millions.

Didn't help that the sergeant sent him away with the final words, "I wouldn't get my hopes up about the money."

He walked four blocks before he found a phone booth that wasn't vandalized. He called the DeVries number, and Audrey came to the phone. He told her what was up with Connell.

"Oh my goodness." Genuine concern. "Are you okay?"

"I'll be fine." Not really. Shoulders, entire back ached. Aspirin or Rolling Rock tonight. Or both. "Might mean some legal trouble if they're not convinced Connell's the kind of gentleman to pull a gun on a reporter."

"If there's anything we can do …."

"Thank you. You need to know, need to tell everyone, this doesn't mean the money's coming back. I don't know if the cops can find it. These aren't the kinds of con games they track. Even if they did, Connell may have put it out of reach. The only good sign is he stayed in the country to work more embezzlement scams. Maybe this organization of his still has the money in the U.S. Problem is, in my world, *organization* means organized crime. Few get money back from them."

"I don't care about the money. So much death. We'll be okay. What will these mobsters do next?"

"Don't know. Depends on what Connell tells the cops. And I'm not sure Connell can be ruled out as your father's murderer."

"He'd already taken the assets."

"He had more families to rip off. Maybe he thought your father knew something that would point to him. Something your father hadn't told anyone. Joe Mulligan gave me the address that led to Connell. Maybe there was another lead. It's pretty thin, I know, but I think he's still a suspect. He'd have acted through his gang."

"Might the organization come after you? You're the one who's upset things."

"Yeah, 'upset' is a good word. That's a possibility."

"What will you do?"

"Try and get the story before it gets me. You can help me with one thing. I need to talk to the whole family. Together. Go over all that's happened. Is there a time I can come over when—"

"Hold on." The phone went silent for a minute, then two, almost five. "Mother, Charlie, and I will be here next Wednesday evening. Mother's *finally* gotten out of bed. I've moved back in. Would nine suit?"

"That's a full week. This is important."

"I know. I'm so sorry. We're all running in different directions. What with Papa and the finances and the will. Charlie's so hard to pin down. I know it sounds weak of us."

"No, it's all right. I'll see you Wednesday. Maybe the bunco detectives will have found something in the paperwork by then."

"Bunco?"

"Cops who investigate cons."

Taylor walked to the subway. The "interview" with Connell had been a close call. Samantha was not going to be happy, even though he'd left the note. There was a lot of bad circling the DeVries family. Getting pulled into their orbit was a dangerous game, one where the usual rules didn't apply. What bothered him most: no connections. Criminal activity on this side and on that and he couldn't tie any of it together. Fact was, every connection he'd tried to make turned out to be a false lead. His stomach hurt from worry, hurt like it was in competition with his back. In that, it was failing.

Chapter 25

———◆———

Taylor worked his way through the day's stack of mail, most of it press releases that had nothing to do with the police beat. Covering cops. If he was getting a press release on something, he'd already missed the story.

Should dump them all in the trashcan without looking.

He had a reporter's paranoia. What if one of them was an actual story? Hadn't happened in the 12 years he'd been on the police beat. Couldn't rule it out either.

He was tired from sleeping badly. His back had woken him up and wouldn't let him go back to sleep. It ached now.

He tore open another envelope, this from the sanitation workers' union, bemoaning budget cuts. He reviewed for the fifth—or tenth—time what he had going on the DeVries murder and everything that seemed connected to it. Cramly wasn't complaining yet about the time he was spending on that crime, so that's what Taylor said he was working on. He didn't mention Martha Gibson. A Park Avenue murder would make a good story for the wire, get it the attention it needed, particularly as none of the New York papers had followed up after the *Daily News'* first story.

He was meeting with the whole DeVries family in six days. His big play to find out about the mystery man. Someone had to say something. If not, then a look, a movement, some kind of reaction, when they were all together in the same room. He'd have the staff in there too.

Then there were the loose ends. Denny Connell had stolen $25 million, a big crime in itself, and was now under police guard in the hospital. The cops were going to bring charges against him and *probably* not bust Taylor for assault. Did DeVries find out something about Connell—or actually track him down without Taylor's help? Maybe DeVries tried to get the money back while avoiding public exposure. That would have gotten messy fast, particularly as Connell already had new marks.

Finally, though separately, there was the Concierge, a story he'd stumbled over while working the murder. It was a damned good one, and needed lots of reporting. He wasn't giving it any time because of the killings.

He had to shake something loose, or draw someone out.

Damn, why can't the family see me earlier?

The copies of the *Amenia Times* still sat on the back corner of Taylor's desk. Taylor remembered DeVries' smile as he showed Taylor the farm, described his dream of escaping what would be to anyone else the good life. Connell had implied DeVries wasn't escaping but fleeing because he couldn't manage his affairs anymore. The truth from a liar? Maybe. It *was* Edmond DeVries' dream, and someone had shot him to death short of achieving it. That was a sad story, which made it a good story. The fall from a great height. Readers ate up that kind of news. As much as he liked DeVries, he'd write it that way if that was what the facts proved.

With only a half-dozen envelopes in the mail stack, Taylor came to a manila one, hand-addressed with stamps and Easter Seals; the return address was that of Martha Gibson's parents.

The envelope contained a handwritten note on blue onion-skin paper and four pages of typescript. He read the note first.

> Dear Mr. Taylor,
>
> I have been going through Martha's things. It has been a very painful experience, as you might imagine. She was a wonderful letter writer. Not that we didn't see each other all the time and talk all the time. I think she simply liked writing letters. It helped her put her thoughts in place. We both once believed she might do something with writing. But she needed to get the job she could with the economy so terrible. After that, she encountered those problems that made it hard to consider other options.
>
> I've included two letters she wrote to me. One to give you an idea for the kind of woman she was, and the other so you'll know more about the kind of trouble she encountered. We should have told you more. I'm sorry if you feel we deceived you in not admitting what we knew. But it is so embarrassing, even now, to talk about. Shame hides truth. She is forever in our hearts, and we wish something could be done about what happened to her.
>
> Sincerely yours,
> Margaret Gibson

Taylor turned to the first page, which had obviously been produced on a manual typewriter—the telltale jagged half letters, signs of uneven keystrokes, and ragged edges around other characters. The first letter was dated May 7, 1976.

> Dear Momma,
>
> Today was such a wonderful day. Thank you for coming to my graduation and the dinner afterwards. Even Abigail seemed to pull herself together for our family gathering. I do appreciate your talking about

me being the first in five generations or more to get a degree. However, you and Daddy must know that I would not have reached this day without you two. You both worked so hard. Intelligence is not in the piece of paper they gave me today. Wisdom certainly is not. You are both so wise; I can only hope I received some part of that wisdom to go with this degree. It is the wisdom that will carry me.

I have such dreams. I still would like to write, as we both know. Now is not the time. The economy is harsh. I will begin applying for jobs in business on Monday. I will use everything you have given me to make the best impression and get a job quickly.

A long paragraph listed jobs Martha had already "circled" in the *New York Times* classified section. Manning Corp was one of those. A second long paragraph described two graduation parties, consisting mainly of names, pleasantries passed back and forth and the plans of other graduates, who all to a woman or man couldn't wait to start looking for employment. Every line was optimism. The letter continued:

I have so many dreams. I know I can help the both of you. I truly believe I can get Abigail away from the influences that are making it so hard for her to make a fresh start. I did not pay her enough attention during my years at City College, a fault I intend to correct immediately. I dream beyond that. Once I really get settled, I'll start back on my writing. Most writers have begun that way and so will I.

The future looks golden to me. We have all worked so hard. Thank you to you and Daddy. I will see you next Sunday for dinner, still smiling.

With much love,
Martha

The second letter looked to have been done on the same typewriter, or the same make. It was dated December 10, 1976.

> Dear Momma,
>
> I left my job at Manning Corp several weeks ago. That is why I have not been over to dinner. That is why I am not picking up the phone. I was fired. My boss harassed me. He wanted to—I so hate using the words, even in a letter, but I could hardly speak them to you—he wanted sexual relations with me. Demanded them. Of course, I refused. I don't know how to describe the way he touched me while I was still there. I worked so hard to get that job, but I wasn't doing what he wanted so I couldn't keep it. I thought about Abigail and the things she must do to pay for her habit. I feel terrible guilt for that. Maybe it's because of my guilt that I've let her move in.
>
> I won't, I can't be more specific about what happened at Manning. That golden day, graduation, has turned to gray and my diploma seems to be a dark, faded thing, crumbling up. I am full of shame. Terrible shame. I know I should go to the police. But can I? A Black woman claiming that her White boss, a rich man, assaulted her. Where will that end up?
>
> A high school friend has a job as a maid on the Upper Eastside. She's going to make an introduction, as I left Manning without a reference, among other things. I'm going to go for that. I need to eat. Perhaps I'll be able to look for work in business at some point, when I can hold my head up and look people straight in the eyes.
>
> I will be over soon. But please write and promise we will not talk about this. Please let me try and move on.
>
> With much love,
> Martha

He set the letters to the side. Ricky MacDonald needed to be interviewed again. The letter needed to be part of that conversation—to make sure MacDonald had a rock-solid alibi for Martha's murder.

THE *NEW YORK Post* was based in a dingy building on dingy South Street in a dingy neighborhood downtown. Once, all the city's many papers—when there were many—were downtown, though most were located on Park Row, called Newspaper Row. The *Post's* headquarters formerly housed the *New York Journal-American*, the building bought by former *Post* owner Dorothy Schiff in 1966 when the *Journal-American* folded with several other papers after the disastrous printers strike.

Taylor had been invited down after the Murdoch executive from DeVries' party made the call he'd said he'd make. Taylor had finally decided to test what his gut was already warning him against. His head needed an answer.

The *Post's* assistant city editor, who'd introduced himself as Gorton, sat behind a steel desk in the newsroom. The odor of printing ink mixed with pine-citrus cologne. Taylor liked the ink better. He missed it.

Gorton was an Australian. Taylor knew from old friends who were hanging on at the paper that the men Rupert Murdoch had installed in key posts were called the *Gangeroos*. This had to be one of them.

"I went back and read some of your stories at the *Messenger-Telegram*," Gorton said. "Not sloppy or lazy."

"Is that what you were expecting?"

"That's what the boss thinks about the work of a lot of American journalists."

"Wasn't aware the true home of journalism had moved down to your little country."

"You must be American if you think Australia's small."

"Smaller population than just the New York area. Imagine that's why your *boss* came here. Small-time to big-time, right?"

"Are you looking for a job or here to bust balls?"

"Not sure. Someone suggested I talk to you."

"Don't know anything about this City News Bureau you're at now. Except your boss keeps calling on me. Why should I subscribe to it?"

"His name's Henry Novak. It's his job to sell you. I write the stories."

"You got anything good on Son of Sam?"

"No. Working something different. Woman murdered the same night as Virginia Voskerichian."

"Why the fuck would you do that?"

"Big city. There's more than one story in this town."

"This is *the* story. Everything else is dressing the window. That's what the boss says."

"You quote the boss a lot. The problem for your boss is the *News* looks to have its hook into that story of all stories. The killer's writing them love letters."

Gorton appraised Taylor with dark eyes. "Look, I can see you helping out Steve Dunleavy. The boss has him on Son of Sam full-time. We're going to catch up with the *News* and pass right by them."

"Help out?"

"Chase down leads. Dig up material he needs. You'll like him. Started as a copyboy on the *Sydney Sun*. Started like you, mate."

"Mate? What are we, pirates?"

Gorton ignored the crack. "Neither of you are like these Princeton pricks."

"One of us isn't a prick, at least."

Shaking his head, the man picked up the phone and asked for Dunleavy.

Taylor already knew Dunleavy in passing. An Australian, he had arrived from London in the mid-sixties and worked a bunch of jobs for British and Australian papers. Hanging out in all the press bars. Lots to say. He was most recently on the

Star, Murdoch's supermarket tabloid, and moved to the *Post* as soon as the mogul bought the paper. He had hair piled like a pompadour, wore the suits of a Wall Street man, and was a Murdoch favorite. Taylor had already figured out from reading the paper that Dunleavy was tasked with catching up with the *News* on the serial killer.

Gorton dropped the phone back in the cradle. "He's out."

"I got a call yesterday from a source offering a third Son of Sam letter."

Gorton brightened measurably. "You have it?"

"Not yet. Waiting for the second call."

"If so, we'd be interested."

"Okay. A deal, then. You get the letter. I write the story I'm working on. Call it a sidebar on all the other murders going down in this city."

"Who's dead? Who did it?"

"A young Black woman. Shot. I've got leads. Former boss at a shoe company. Or she might be connected with a Park Avenue murder."

"Not our sort." He waved his hand at the meaninglessness of it all. "We want Son of Sam and anything about him. That crazy maniac is selling papers like lollies at the beach, mate. I can probably get you cash for the letter—and the job working for Dunleavy would be a cinch."

"Why isn't it your story? Because a Black woman was murdered?"

"We're looking for a different reader now."

"What do you do on a day when there's no Son of Sam news?"

"Oh there's always something we can pull together." *Always something you can invent.* "We're covering other stories too. Crime's a priority. Crimes people care about."

"I've read some of Dunleavy's pieces in the *Star* and since he got here—and the rest of what's running in this poor broken-down old paper now. You boys seem awfully patriotic given your short stay here."

"Best country in the world, America." Odd-sounding with an Australian accent.

" 'Facts are stubborn things. Whatever may be our wishes, our inclinations, or the dictates of our passion, they cannot alter the state of facts.' "

"The fuck is that?"

"John Adams. He was a president of *ours*. Something a patriot would know. You and the boss will need that for your citizenship tests. You might try using more facts in your paper too." Taylor stood. "That's why it wouldn't work for me here. Facts."

"We're going to be *the* paper in this town, mate. The boss wants nothing else. He gets what he wants. Fuck the facts. He'd tell you that. We're in the entertainment business. That's what papers do. You'll come begging."

"More pirate talk. I've been covering cops in these five boroughs for more than a decade. The only Sydney I know runs a deli on Sixty-Fifth Street. This is a serious city of serious size. What'd you cover down there? A knifing at the pub once every couple weeks. Kangaroo-nappings?"

"Always Kangaroo jokes."

"You ever wonder why?"

"Call about that letter. We can make a deal. I don't care how big an asshole you are."

I'd rather do a deal with the devil himself.

Taylor left the newsroom—though not without a wistful look at the ranks of reporters working stories—and the building. The *Post* had failed his test quicker than he expected. He'd have done the trade—if he ever got the letter. He'd love to get Martha Gibson's story in a big paper. All a dead *if*. Everything he'd heard about the paper had turned out to be true in a 15-minute meeting. Should the guy with the letter ever call back, and should he not be some nut, Taylor would make sure the City News Bureau had the biggest scoop in its short history. Facts were the only choice Taylor knew how to make. Novak would never ask him to play fast and loose with the facts. Not even Cramly. Facts built the story, and the story was his way to act as witness for a victim. And let others do the same.

CHAPTER 26

———◆———

TAYLOR LEANED AGAINST the Empire State Building, as close as he could get to the entrance without being noticed. He wanted to see people coming in. He held copies of the *News* and the *Post*, one inside the other, and at this point was only scanning headlines as he kept watch. Both papers had begun counting down the days to the anniversary of Son of Sam's first killing—eighteen-year-old Donna Lauria on July 29, 1976. Murdered in the Bronx, and her friend Jody Valenti wounded. The tick tock of fear. The psycho *would* strike again at the end the month. It wasn't implied. It was run-for-the-hills fear-mongering. The papers parsed and re-parsed the letter to Breslin for a clue, interviewed and re-interviewed cops in the Omega Group, consulted shrinks, astrologers, and psychics. Taylor expected chicken entrails next. You had the distinct impression the papers wanted the killer to attack on July 29. Would be disappointed if he didn't.

This was all about selling newspapers.

Taylor hadn't worried once about circulation during his entire career. That was a job for publishers, which was probably one of the reasons the paper he worked for went out of business. He'd stupidly figured if he wrote the best stories—stories people didn't know, *needed* to know—the rest would take care of itself. It didn't, and yet it didn't change his view on what the job was about. If you chased what readers wanted, not what they needed to know, you'd do anything. Bend facts. Break them. Hell, run porn, the light stuff at least, like Murdoch did in London.

He'd twice tried to see Ricky MacDonald in the office without luck. Now he was staking out the building. MacDonald was unconnected to the crimes against the DeVries family, but his history with Martha Gibson left him on the list for her murder.

MacDonald spun through the revolving doors into the building. Taylor waited a minute, then entered and stepped onto an elevator.

Three women sat in folding chairs in the makeshift waiting area in front of the little round desk of Ricky's mother. The women were Black, young, and good-looking, each in her own way. He walked right past the blue-haired mother into the maze of stacked boxes.

"Where are you going? Where *are* you going?"

Ricky MacDonald, on the phone, spoke pleasant sales patter into the mouthpiece while laying angry eyes on Taylor, who plunked himself into the chair in front of his desk.

The mother stopped yelling when she saw her son was on the phone.

Taylor whispered to her, "I've got material evidence. I'd get on the phone with the lawyer brother and get him over here. Now."

She moved fast for an old lady.

MacDonald hung up. "What the fuck are you doing here? My brother said the next visit would be trespass. Harassment." He picked up the phone.

"Relax. Your mother's already calling." Taylor threw a copy of Martha's letter on the desk. "Read that."

MacDonald did, a hungry look on his face that nauseated Taylor. He tore it up.

"It was a Photostat. I've got the original. So you're a pervert and a sleazebag. But what matters to me at this moment is whether you killed Martha. Some one pays for *that*. My story could include that letter. I've got a witness who saw you attack her. I've got her sister's word on Martha's experience here. I want proof you didn't kill Martha Gibson. An alibi. Or I *write*. Then I'll be done here, and I can go take a long shower."

MacDonald threw the pieces of the letter in the trash and yelled, "Mother, we don't need Harry." He looked at Taylor, who couldn't tell if the man was pissed off or scared or both. "What was the date?"

"Early hours of March eighth."

Face transforming to that of a petulant child, he flipped through a black 1977 appointment book. A smile spread across his face, adding an element of greed to the petulance in his expression.

"Louisville, Kentucky, meeting with Jim Daniels of Daniels & Sons Shoes. We had dinner."

"Call him."

"I'm not calling—"

"Call him or I write. We talk to the cops about your extracurriculars. Let me listen."

Taylor leaned close enough—but no closer than necessary—so he could hear. His stomach squeezed, queasy. Aftershave that was more stink than scent. Is that why they called it musk? It seemed to be the type worn by men lacking confidence with women, the job, life.

MacDonald went through all the salesman preliminaries. Taylor's stomach churned. He wanted this to be over fast.

"Getting things right for the expense account," MacDonald said. "We had dinner on March Eighth?"

Daniels confirmed the dinner, time, and place. More sales

pleasantries were exchanged, though Taylor was already back in the chair when MacDonald hung up.

Taylor yelled for the ladies waiting for appointments. They arrived and stood, eager, looking to be the one.

"I know you all want jobs," Taylor said. "I'm a reporter. This man is a pervert. He assaulted a previous female employee. He seems to target Black women. I'm sorry to give you that news. Make whatever decision you like."

Anticipation turned to revulsion in two, who turned and were gone. The third paused and left more slowly. Taylor guessed she was taking her chances.

"God, how I wish I could come back and do that every day."

"We had a deal."

"We did. I'm not including the letter in my story. I wouldn't do a story on what you did anyway. I'm not dragging Martha's name through it. That's a justice her memory doesn't deserve."

"You lied. Now, you're crossing the line. You're going to ruin me. This is some … some kind of slander. Office romance. Happens all the time. You're going to hurt my business. That's defamation."

"You learn those big words from your brother? Tell him to come at me with whatever he's got. I'll tell him what you've been doing. I'd suggest you have him read Martha's letter before contacting me. Unfortunately, you tore up your copy. My final gift. Reporters, we make lots of calls. We're fast at it. I'm calling every secretarial service in midtown and telling them about you. They don't want to be in any news stories."

"You're a … you're a—"

"I'm nothing you need to worry about. You're a shit bag taking advantage of these women. Remind Mom. Tell Harry. This is a game that doesn't play in the courts. Not my way."

On the ear-popping decent in the elevator, Taylor opened his notebook and crossed Ricky MacDonald off the murder list. Taylor had already proven there wasn't a drug connection. That boosted the odds Gibson's murder was tied in with the

DeVries family, with the killing of Edmond DeVries. Yeah, but odds were nothing unless he figured out who was the goddamn connection and why it happened. Martha hadn't known if the person who came out of the sitting room had seen her. Was hearing that one conversation enough to get her shot down? Or was there some other tie he wasn't seeing? He'd get his all-important read tomorrow night when the DeVries family would be together to hear the story. He had to.

CHAPTER 27

———◆———

IT WAS LIKE the Greek Orthodox God of his mother decided the thermometer was a joke. The temperature had jumped to 93, with forecasters promising the same for the next three days at least. Much of July had been like this, the phrase "hazy, hot, and humid" worn to uselessness by the weathermen. A clockwork violent thunderstorm crashed through the city almost every afternoon, doing nothing to clear the air—in fact, somehow making it stickier. No storm this afternoon, but the meteorologist on all-news radio 1010 WINS promised an evening version. New York, always changing.

Taylor and Samantha walked up Park Avenue, a thoroughfare that highlighted the way New York could change on you—extreme wealth on the same street as desperate poverty, separated only by blocks farther north. If they kept walking, they'd be in Harlem.

The sun disappeared, yet the fading light did nothing to cool the hot, thick air. The heat somehow seemed worse in the dark, as if nothing could make it go away.

Taylor's undershirt had again failed in its job and soaked through to his dress shirt. He'd hoped to run back to the

Murray Hill apartment to change, but stories kept coming in at the office, as the heat wave drove people to rob, rape, and kill. He'd spent the day filing on one explosion of violence after another. Domestic dispute, wife stabbed, assailant in custody. Gunpoint mugging with a cop coming up the block—cop was shot. Bodega owner murdered for nine bucks and a Colt 45 malt liquor. On and on.

As they walked, Samantha's auburn hair, in a ponytail because of the humidity, swung back and forth. She was beautiful any way she wore her hair, and putting it up gave him a different view of her face, which was glowing—or dripping with sweat, depending on which side of the feminist-language line you fell. *Sweat* was Samantha's preferred word, he knew from early experience. Her time as one of the first few hundred women to ride on patrol in the NYPD hadn't made her a feminist, she claimed. It had taught her she didn't like being treated like shit. Taylor wasn't sure what the difference was, but he sure didn't want to argue about it.

He signed in at 8:50 p.m. at 827 Park, the doorman a guy he hadn't met before, and waited as the man called the apartment. They rode up in the elevator. Taylor had phoned ahead and specified the sitting room, which triggered a lot of back and forth. "We don't have company in there," he'd been told three times. Still, he'd insisted.

The pressure of the coming encounter tightened his throat. This was his shot, maybe his last shot. The DeVries household's reaction to the conversation Martha overheard had to shake something loose. The detective at the 19th Precinct wasn't even returning his calls now and had had him thrown out when he tried to pay a visit. Taylor did learn the cop's name was Dick Moore, so a dick in name and action.

He swallowed to try and loosen his throat. He had to sound confident and in command.

The sitting room was well named; it had a lot of seats.

Mrs. DeVries sat on a short sort of couch Taylor would call a loveseat, though he guessed they had another name for it here, probably because this was the original model. She wore a black dress and white blouse—half mourning at this point? Her face was composed, her beauty oddly more obvious than in happier times. Audrey was next to her, her head leaning against her mother's shoulder. She wore jeans and a peasant blouse. Charlie stood near a window that was framed by white drapes that looked like foam. He smoked, peering at Taylor with what might be anger, or maybe annoyance at being sidelined for the beginning of his night out. Taylor was a little surprised to see Bobby Livingston in a heavy leather chair, a cigar in an ashtray on the side table.

Audrey must have caught his look. "Bobby's so close to the family, we asked him to be here."

Nothing in the room matched. Intentional, no doubt. Matching furniture was for the middle class, striving for that living room set from Sears.

Bobby got up and shook both their hands with a big hello. Audrey and Mrs. DeVries offered hands from where they sat. Charlie didn't move. Taylor would watch Charlie extra close because Taylor had already told Charlie what Martha had overheard. Back at Studio 54. As the family member with the closest thing to motive, it would be telling if he'd shared the story or kept it to himself.

"I want to thank you for finding Connell," said Mrs. DeVries. "We're hoping …." She let her hopes trail off.

"I know. As I told Audrey," her warm brown eyes looked at him, "it may take the police a long while to track down the money."

"At least he's caught—"

"At least." Charlie stubbed out the cigarette. "*At least.* That buys us jack shit. What the hell do you want with all of us?"

"He's helped us," Audrey said. "Be civil."

"He's helped us to get a story. Which is all we need right now."

"I want to ask you all about something that may be related to Mr. DeVries' death. Could we get the staff in here too?"

The butler, standing at the door, looked like he'd suddenly been plugged into a wall jack.

"You want *all* of us together in the sitting room?" Charlie said. "Together? What is this, some kind of old-lady mystery? You going to lock us in here until we figure out James did it."

The electric current running through the butler—through James—increased.

"Believe me, I've never interviewed anyone in a sitting room, Park Avenue or elsewhere. I want to ask everyone about something important I learned about Martha Gibson. It's easier if I do it all at once rather than one by one."

Audrey sat up at this, while Mrs. DeVries blinked slowly twice, as if she was trying to remember who Martha was. After a couple more blinks, she told the butler to go get everyone.

Samantha watched him leave. Having moved to one side of the room, she'd listened with bland interest. Nothing obvious—undercover in plain sight. She'd give him a good second read on what was said and how people reacted.

Carol Wheelwright, James, the housekeeper Mrs. Frist, the cook, and a temp filling in for Martha (based on the maid's dress she wore) stood at the edge of the room. They looked around but not at their employers. Carol fidgeted. The cook's head went down. The family didn't seem nervous, but Mrs. DeVries' and Charlie's demeanors had changed, her back straighter, Charlie's anger mutating into concern. Or anxiety? Audrey remained intently focused on Taylor.

"Thank you for taking the time. A week before she died, Martha heard something here at work. She was changing the flowers outside this room. She heard two people talking in here. One, a so far unidentified man with a deep voice. The other person was speaking too softly to make out. If the man wasn't from this apartment, it's my assumption the second person had to have been. The man said, 'We can't wait any longer. The money's going to be all gone. All of it—' "

"Oh my god," Audrey said. "Martha couldn't even *guess* who this man was?"

"She said she didn't know the voice. That's all we'll ever get from her. Hard to be sure. She may have been scared afterwards."

"This is getting so ridiculous," Charlie said. "How do we know you're not making it up? That your source didn't? That you have a source?"

Taylor made a point of not looking at Carol. It wouldn't be hard to figure out the person Martha shared with was another member of staff. He also made a point of not yet calling Charlie on the fact that he already knew the story. Mrs. DeVries' face remained a mask. He couldn't tell how she was reacting. Audrey had gone white, lips pursed, like she was trying to figure out another question to ask.

Charlie continued to push back. "This is some stupid game of Clue," he said. "Or that silly play we saw in London. *Mousetrap.* Let us end these theatrics."

"Please go on," said Mrs. DeVries.

"As I said, the other person in this room spoke low. Martha thought perhaps he or she was sitting at the far side by the windows there. When that person talked, the man got angrier. Here's more of what Martha heard from the man. 'I don't care. He might as well be throwing the money out the window. The crazy things he's investing in. Still writing the same checks to charities when you're going to be the charity. He has to be stopped.' The other went on for a bit. The man ended with, 'All right. As long as we take care of him by then. Final and done. No frittering away what's left.' Martha heard steps coming toward those doors." All eyes moved to the doorway. "She hurried back down the hall. She had no idea if she was seen."

Taylor opened his notebook to a blank page. "To me, there are three key things here. Martha may well have been murdered because someone thought she overheard the conversation. Second, a threat was made against Mr. DeVries. 'Taking care' of someone usually has that meaning. Finally, a question. Who else would be in this room with someone but one of you three? Who else has direct interest in the money? Of course, not to rule absolutely anything out, one of the staff could have been in here instead. I doubt that as much as James does." He paused and had to keep from smiling at James' pale face. "One side point. I told Charlie all this at Studio 54. *His* theatrics tonight are a mystery to me. He already knows the story."

"Goddamn you." Charlie crossed the room halfway. "How can you say this? To us? To my mother? I was trying to protect her."

The lights flickered. Like a short circuit.

Total darkness.

CHAPTER 28

———◆———

A COUPLE OF screams, followed by shushing.

"I'll call downstairs to see what's going on." That was James.

"Let's get candles lit." That was Mrs. DeVries. "It must be a brownout because of the heat."

Taylor tried to move toward the windows while not knocking over an end table worth a month of his salary. But he couldn't tell the windows from the wall.

This shouldn't be that hard.

A crash behind him. "I'm so sorry," said one of the staff.

A candle flared to life and reflected light off the windows he'd been hunting. Outside was as dark as the sitting room. The Upper East Side was black, as was the entire area as far uptown and downtown as he could see. Queens had disappeared.

Taylor turned around. "Looks like a major blackout. All of the city that I can see."

"Must have been the heat and the air conditioning."

"Thunderstorms up north."

Taylor didn't want theories. "Can someone please find a transistor radio?"

"There's one in my room," said Audrey.

She went with Carol, who had a flashlight, and came back. Taylor tuned to 1010 WINS.

"The blackout is citywide and includes parts of Westchester County. Con Ed has yet to provide a statement. Lightning strikes were reported north of the city in Westchester."

Everyone started talking at once: questions about staffers' family members, distances from home, and food going bad. Sweat trickled down Taylor's back. The room was warming up fast.

"Okay, okay everyone." Mrs. DeVries stood for the first time. "This has happened before. Let's wait and see what happens. It may not last that long."

The '65 blackout went on for 13 hours. That was in November.

Waiting made sense, though. This might be a major news story, but Taylor needed to know where to go to cover it. The city was massive with the lights on; the dark made it a world without edges or boundaries. WINS kept reporting. "The cause of the outage may have been a lightning strike near the Indian Point Nuclear Power Plant in Buchanan. Civilians are out in some intersections of the city directing traffic stranded on the streets when the power went out."

There had been all sorts of Good Samaritan acts during the '65 blackout. Would be nice if a little of that New York returned tonight.

The butler served snacks on little silver plates.

"Worse ways to spend an outage," Samantha said, holding some form of hors d'oeuvres.

"There are. Imagine there are some mighty unhappy people on subway trains and in elevators right now."

The heat from the dark air outside continued to seep into the apartment now that the air conditioners were stilled. Taylor took off his jacket. Carol opened windows. The noise of traffic rose from the street, striking Taylor's ears as odd, with everything else stopped. Cars moved up and down the avenue, providing the only illumination.

The announcer broke off in the middle of a piece on the status of the hospitals. "We're starting to hear scattered reports of looting in Harlem and Brooklyn. No details yet."

"May I borrow the phone?" Taylor said.

Mrs. DeVries nodded.

Dial tone. *God bless you, Ma Bell.*

He dialed the City News Bureau and was surprised to hear the voice of night editor Howard Nicholson.

"Thought you'd leave soon as the lights went out."

"I'm a newsman." *Maybe. Once.* "Good you called. The general manager at WINS reached Novak. They'll pay two hundred fifty dollars for any stories we can phone directly in—"

"You mean anything I can phone in."

"Yeah, yeah. They get 'em exclusive, which is easy enough. The facsimile machine ain't sending anything tonight. Novak says you'll keep fifty bucks and I get twenty. Combat pay."

"Now I know why you stuck around. What combat are you going to be in?"

"Gimme a break for once, Taylor. You're getting yours."

"You're going to *earn* yours. You stay by that phone. You're my clearinghouse. People will be calling for me. I call and you're not there, no double sawbuck for you." Nicholson started making noises to interrupt that Taylor ignored. "The looting's the first story. I'm heading to Harlem. I'll get interviews, descriptions, what the cops are doing, and call that in to WINS."

He hung up and turned around to the room, the same people, but all different. Some in shadow, some lit by flickering candles. Features shifting or exaggerated.

"Interrupted by a blackout. The ultimate no comment. You heard everything I said. Someone in this room was with the man making threats against Mr. DeVries. 'Final and done.' Dead is final and done. Maybe it was more than one someone. Maybe it *was* someone from the staff. I need to cover the blackout. Martha Gibson and Edmond DeVries were killed because of what was said in this room. Does anyone know anything about who was here? Charlie?"

Charlie grunted something—maybe it wasn't even words—and charged at Taylor. He fell when Samantha hooked his leg.

He got back to his feet. "Assaulted by these scum in my own house. I'm done with this. I'm done with *all* of this."

He ran from the room. The door to the hallway that led to the stairs shut with a thump.

"Isn't it possible someone else was here?" Audrey said. She didn't appear angry, more apprehensive and bewildered, like she believed the conversation happened, but didn't know what to do about it. "It's such a big apartment. Guests visit. We're not always here. We're not always watching every room."

"Anything is possible. Some things are more probable, I'm afraid." He wrote his office number on a pad next to the phone. "Call my office and let me know when Charlie turns up. If anything else happens. There'll be someone there all night."

Mrs. DeVries shook his hand. "I don't know what to say." Which was true, because she said nothing else.

Taylor and Samantha went through the secret door in the foyer and took it slow down the fire stairs.

THE APARTMENT BUILDINGS on Park formed a canyon down which flowed a river of light from the cars still in the city when the outage hit at about 9:30 p.m. The first cab he actually got to pull over didn't want to go to Harlem because he could get $50 taking stranded commuters home to the burbs. And because it was Harlem. The driver had WINS on. Most everybody would have immediately tuned to that station or WCBS AM, the other all-news outlet. Taylor offered thirty bucks and promised to put the cabbie's story on the radio. The hack decided he could get more commuters after the short run.

At the next intersection, a woman in an evening gown cut

low in the back gracefully directed traffic, almost dancing. About every third light had a volunteer.

The radio reported trouble along Eighth Avenue on the west side of Harlem. Taylor told the driver to take 96th Street. The transition from the quiet dark of the city to the quiet dark of Central Park was eerie for the very reason you usually went from light to dark when you entered the park. Now it was more of the same.

Heading up Eighth, they saw trouble three blocks ahead at 114th Street. Flames flicked out of two buildings at the north end of the block, the light dancing off the street in tiny flashes that looked like a hallucination.

The cabbie hit the brakes. "End of the line, bub."

Taylor and Samantha walked the last three blocks. As they got closer to the shops under assault, Taylor understood the source of the hallucinatory flickering on the street. Glass from smashed store windows covered the pavement. Security gates had been peeled away like the openings of giant sardine cans so people could get into an appliance store, a jewelry shop, and a grocery. Men, women, and children emerged from the stores with armfuls of merchandise. Two men marched north with a couch.

"Oh my God," said Samantha, "it's chaos. The whole city has fallen into chaos. It's not one psycho killer. It's everyone. Everyone's giving up. The minute the lights go out, all hell breaks loose."

This could go any direction. Taylor flexed his fingers. Stay ready, focused, aware, but not afraid. There was a big story in front of him.

They stopped at the edge of the pillaging.

"Back when the city almost went bankrupt, I kept saying nothing could kill New York," Taylor said. "Now New York is killing itself."

A man of medium height walked toward them with a portable TV that came up to his eyes.

"Sir. Just a reporter." He held up his notebook. "Why is this happening?"

"We're taking it because they ain't giving. No jobs. No help. It's shopping day."

"Aren't these businesses part of the neighborhood?"

"Neighborhood? What the fuck do they do for the neighborhood? Nothing. Even the stores owned by Blacks are getting hit. None of them give back. You're not going to fuck with me, are you?"

Taylor kept notebook and palm up. "Just doing a story."

"Maybe we don't want a White boy doing a story."

With that, he walked past.

As they moved closer, they caught angry looks.

A boy and a girl, Black, the same size, like twins, skipped out of Monty's Sweets and Treats. They ran before Taylor could get close enough to ask a question. The boy turned. "It's Halloween in Harlem."

A teenager ran up to the fire callbox and pulled the handle. A patrol car came down the block from the north and pulled on to the sidewalk, rolling down it at medium speed to move people away from the stores. As soon as the car left, the crowd closed in on the storefronts again, some to work on gates that hadn't been ripped open.

There was too much to report here, but Taylor already had enough to phone in his first stories. The combat pay was a nice bonus. Getting the story out counted for more.

He took Samantha's hand and walked south a block. "Strange in New York when dark and quiet means you're safe."

Bang!

Taylor and Samantha crouched low.

"I spoke too soon."

She pulled out the Colt. "Gun?"

"Maybe a firecracker."

The crowd kept pulling merchandise from the stores.

CHAPTER 29

———◆———

TAYLOR CALLED THE radio station and gave reports on three different scenes. The blackout as experienced in a certain Upper Eastside apartment—leaving out the DeVrieses' name. The cab ride and volunteer traffic cops. The looting on Eighth Avenue. He'd never done broadcast before, so he just wrote stories with short sentences and read them out of his notebook. The WINS editor recorded the three, asking Taylor questions at the end of each read. He made Taylor wait to talk live on the air about the looting. Taylor told the anchor what he was seeing and what people were saying. He refused to give an opinion on the cause, the role of race, or if the looters were all "just thugs." He said he didn't do speculation.

"Pretty old-fashioned approach," the anchor said. The line went dead.

The rampage moved a block south. More people flooded onto the street from the apartments above the stores and the side streets. When a group couldn't get a security gate free, a flaming bottle went into S.W. Schwartz Men's Clothing, setting the biggest fire so far.

Cheering.

Taylor had never witnessed anything as ugly and chaotic—not even during the race riots of the sixties. It made him think of war. A warzone. Was this what Billy had to deal with every day? *Don't be so fucking dramatic. I can stand at the edge of this. Get away if necessary.* Billy was never safe. Armed and dangerous but running toward men who wanted to kill him, who did kill him.

"Let's go up the left," he said. "Looks less ... crowded."

"It's like they're having a party. A shopping party."

"Did you see the looks we're getting?"

"Yeah, I see those."

"We need to be careful. We're not welcome. What's a shopping party now could turn into something deadly real fast. For us. For them. There's three working-structure fires and no FDNY on the scene."

Traffic in and out of the stores in the new block under attack was heavier, now that there were fresh pickings.

Taylor and Samantha hunched down again when something crashed through a window. Other side of the street. Party maybe, but the crowd was finally balanced. It could tip either way—keep taking stuff or start hurting people. A shadow dashed to the right, making Taylor turn, then one to the left. The anxious energy of the street was inside him, his neck sweating, his eyes tingling from trying to focus on bodies, shadows, moving in and out of beams of flashlights and flickering building fires. He wasn't afraid, but he was as worried as he'd ever been on a street in New York.

Two patrol cars came down the street, abreast this time, with a bullhorn announcing anyone breaking and entering or stealing would be arrested. The blocked cleared. Again for only a few minutes.

Three stores up, a crowd had started to form around the front of Jobson's Pharmacy. Yelling. Two or three arms waved clubs.

Samantha started that way and Taylor went with her.

"Give it up, old man. We're here to take what we want."

The old man in question was actually more middle-aged and sat in a lawn chair in front of the store. A shotgun lay across his lap.

"We've been in this neighborhood for two generations," the man said. "I'm not losing my business because the damn lights went out."

"What the fuck you do for us?" An echo of what the man with the TV had said. Was it a real grievance—or an excuse?

"I give to all the community organizations. The churches. I have special senior citizen prices."

"All for shit. You're not the only one with a gun."

"No he's not." Samantha shouldered her way through the crowd, her revolver in clear view without quite being aimed at anyone. She definitely had a different view of their odds than Taylor did. "Seems there's enough available so that this gentleman can be left alone."

Grumbling in the crowd. Not much movement.

She held her hand out to the old man. "Samantha."

"Monty Jobson. Thank you."

"Haven't done anything yet."

"You're helping. The police, they drive by and keep going."

"You going to stay with him?" Taylor said.

"Seems the one bit of good I can do here. See how long it plays out. I need to do something with all this going on."

"Now I'm the one who's worried. Should we be splitting up?"

Samantha turned to Jobson. "You know how to use that thing?"

"Served with the 101st in Europe. Learned it's best not to be outnumbered if you can avoid it."

She stepped closer to Taylor. "We'll be okay here. I know what I said, but I can't expect you to stay inside during a blackout. Any other night, you'd be out here by yourself."

He kissed her. "I'm going to get more interviews. Please be careful."

"Both of us."

"Just no Alamos, okay?"

"Right now all's we have is a complete breakdown of law and order." One dark chuckle. "Hasn't turned into a total frenzy yet."

Taylor discovered Nicolae Bernath in the back corner of a big furniture and lumber store. It was cleaned out. The shelves had been wrecked.

Bernath said he came to the U.S. after World War II. "For twenty-five years, I've helped all the children—Black children, White children, Catholic and not Catholic, Jewish and not Jewish. All kinds of children. Wood and supplies for school projects. I survived Auschwitz. The only difference is *they* wore boots and here they wear sneakers."

Back on the street, another police car rolled by, stopping as a tall teenager walked by with a box of stereo gear.

"Where'd you get that?" the cop at the wheel asked.

"Found it on the fucking street."

"That don't make it right." The cop looked at Taylor and shrugged. "Need to see him take it from the store to arrest him. Tell ya, they're grabbing anything now."

Taylor went back to check Samantha's position sooner then he might have, but he was worried. The crowd had thinned markedly, off to easier pickings. He went two blocks for a working phone, called in his latest to the station, then dialed the City News number.

"Anything?"

"One call, from Audrey DeVries," said Nicholson. "She said Charlie phoned her, drunk and scared, really scared. He told her to get out of the apartment. She wasn't safe. He wouldn't say why. He said he was done, going. He was getting money from the church ... no, from the chapel. He knew no one would be there now. He was getting it and leaving. She begged you to call her."

In the middle of the damn blackout.

First, he *had* to call their neighbor, Max.

"How's the neighborhood?"

"Quiet in Murray Hill. Hear it's chaos other places."

"You hear right. Can you use your key, open the windows and make sure Mason has enough water? I hate to ask but—"

"We'll take him out. Like I said, it's dead down here. I mean that in a good way."

"Thanks, Max. The old New York lives."

"Not enough of it."

Audrey picked up on the first ring.

"He's never sounded like that."

"That drunk?"

"So drunk and so rattled at the same time. Do you know what he's talking about?"

"Have you heard of Our Little Chapel?"

"Awful place."

"He ever mention any other chapels?"

"None. He's not religious in the least."

"Then he's going there for money."

By the time he got back to the pharmacy, it was Samantha, the owner, and a uniformed cop wearing a riot helmet and carrying a baseball bat. The crowd was gone.

"This is Todd," Samantha said. "We were in the academy together."

Taylor shook his hand. "You the reinforcements?"

"Lot of brush fires at one time," Todd said. "We get one block under control and another goes up."

"We're going to be all right here." Samantha's face was serious, confident.

"There's something up with the murder story. With Charlie." Taylor considered leaving out the location, but decided against any backsliding. "He's at that *chapel* I mentioned, but there's no one else there now."

She hesitated a moment, likely running through what they each faced. "You go. Charlie's not the sort I worry about. Todd's deputized me. We're going to try and keep what's left of these two blocks safe."

"Thought only a sheriff or a marshal could deputize." A pinprick of jealousy.

"It's a bit informal," Todd said, with a laugh. "To be honest, we really should be deputizing. The commissioner called in everyone who's off duty, but a whole lot didn't show. Not sure if they didn't hear the call because of the power cut or they're pissed off."

"The contract talks?"

"Yeah."

Taylor pulled Samantha over. "One last be careful."

"I will. I was a cop. A good one."

"I know. But it's insane out here."

"That's why people need to step forward. Why we both need to do something."

"Don't think we're going to get enough of them to make a difference this time. Leave messages at my office. I'll be back here as soon as I track down Charlie."

He jogged over to Broadway. He was sure there wouldn't be cabs—empty cabs—but he checked anyway, and to his everlasting surprise, a city bus rumbled toward him. The one city service still operating. He ran to the stop and the bus door opened.

"Let's go. Last run of the evening. Thank God for that. Was almost in three accidents at those dark intersections."

The dark city, usually a bright mountain range of buildings sloping down from midtown toward Harlem, rolled past. It was as if the city itself had vanished. That was until he looked closer. A candle danced in one window, then another. Candelabra. A flashlight played across the wall of a third-floor room. Silhouettes at windows watched the blackened city from flicker-lit apartments—or maybe just sought slightly cooler air.

Taylor arrived at the former church huffing, a stabbing pain in his side after the 12-block run from the nearest bus stop.

Something—a flashlight probably—briefly played across the stained-glass window at the front.

A white flash. Followed by the report from a gun. A second shot. Taylor ran from the front to the walkway he'd used the first time, next to the rectory. He slowed and eased along the path in the midnight darkness, again his hand on the outside wall, stopping every few steps. A car parked at the rear of the church took off. He found the entrance door and pulled. It was open.

A man lay on the floor where the gambling tables had been. Charlie was on his back, his hand full of bills, the money held up to his chest. The bills were red. His shirt was red. Soaked. A puddle of blood formed beneath him. He'd been shot bad. More than once, going by the shots Taylor heard. He went down on one knee next to Charlie.

"Who did this?"

"Got too crazy." His voice was a hiss. "This place. Doing everything he said. He wanted more. Couldn't. Too much."

"Who, Charlie, the Concierge?"

A nod of the head. "He wanted everything. Warn Audrey."

Charlie stopped breathing. He had no pulse.

Great night to need a cop.

He waited an hour—an hour while a big story went on all around him—for the police. Another half hour before a detective could take his statement. The detective worked fast. He had another shooting to investigate.

Once allowed to leave, Taylor walked south, taking notes on the scenes he witnessed, interviewing people, phoning in stories as he got them. He might have been missing for almost two hours, but the lights were still out and the radio station wanted anything he could give it. He crisscrossed blocks, then went over to East Harlem, where the looting was worse, if possible. He headed west, back to the neighborhood where he and Samantha had started. Samantha had left about an hour earlier.

The pharmacy owner said, "The cop arranged a ride for her."

No subway. The buses gone. The cabs not interested. Taylor zigzagged south toward the apartment, looking for looting (too much), hoping for Good Samaritans (not enough). Watching, interviewing, phoning. His voice was hoarse. His legs hurt so much he thought about sitting down somewhere, but knew he'd fall asleep wherever that was. The sun started shoving the darkness up the buildings and off the city as he arrived at their building. Samantha was fast asleep, still wearing her clothes. Taylor convinced Mason now was not the time for big, happy greetings. He dropped into bed in the same state of dress.

The power was still out.

CHAPTER 30

———— ◆ ————

THE OPEN WINDOWS at the City News Bureau brought no cooling breezes. The office was as stuffy and humid as any subway train Taylor had been stuffed into in the middle of August. Cramly was down to his crewneck t-shirt. Taylor refused to give in. Somehow, keeping his dress shirt on was the flag he flew for civilization. The thermometer hit 90 at noon, heading up.

Silence. That was the strange thing coming from outside. The honking, car and truck engines, air conditioners—the general rumble of the city on a workday—were absent. With power still out in most places 15 hours after the blackout, many offices were closed for the day. Many workers stayed home.

Taylor got in after four hours of sleep to find Nicholson still working—those WINS bonuses were motivators—along with Cramly, Novak, and Templeton, the wire service's other reporter, an alcoholic who did the light lifting. Samantha walked with him because Lew Raymond couldn't get in from New Rochelle, and she volunteered to staff the office for emergency private investigation calls during the blackout. They'd both laughed at the idea of what that might be. What wasn't lost last night? Taylor understood her dedication to the job. It mirrored his. They'd kissed at her office, and she'd extracted his now regular promise to let him know what dark holes he was heading down.

"They're not all dark."

"Lately, I don't know."

Power came on in a handful of neighborhoods. People in so many buildings continued to suffer. Pumps to push water up into apartment buildings needed juice, so those folks were without electricity *and* water. Food went bad in refrigerators.

Daylight had sent some of the looters home with what they'd stolen, but not all, another sign of the total loss of control that twisted Taylor's insides. The city he'd believed was the most civilized in the world, even with its faults, wasn't civilized at all. The cops battled to control the pockets of pillaging.

He made calls and collected statistics of the type a disaster correspondent should handle, not a police reporter. More than three thousand arrested. Crammed into every corner of the boroughs' jails and holding cells. The courts had ground to a halt. Upwards of one thousand businesses had been looted, 418 cops injured, 18 seriously. The NYPD had been flooded with 45,000 calls during the blackout. The FDNY went out more than 23,000 times, most for false alarms, though 900 were real, 55 severe. Some still burned as of Taylor's last check. Bottom line: the blackout cost the poor, broke city $1 billion.

He typed up interviews, statistics, politicians' statements, and each announcement as a neighborhood gained power. The work wearied him. City News was back to regular operation, or at least trying to take care of all their radio stations and newspaper clients. With only phones and no facsimile, he had to call each subscriber and dictate what he had.

Taylor didn't know how to push the story beyond the blizzard of numbers. He covered murders—one person's life, a disaster for one family. A catastrophe of this size was about so many other things. Investigations of Con Ed, demands from

politicians that looters get the harshest possible sentences—
everybody was law and order now—judges saying they couldn't
process the arrested fast enough, and allegations that a total of
ten thousand off-duty cops had ignored the commissioner's
call to come in and help. Politicians, unions, the justice system.
This was the whole city's story, not one person's. If the city was
dying, he didn't want to cover it.

Didn't help he couldn't keep his mind off Charlie DeVries.
The story he'd been after for months was as hot as it could be.
Everything, suddenly, pointed to *The Concierge*. The story
would run, if he could write it. A rich White man had been
killed to protect a criminal conspiracy. Charlie's death, where
he died, what he said, made the Concierge *the* suspect. Problem
A, No. 1: who the hell was he?

Charlie ran from the apartment after Taylor confronted
the family. Ran and died. What terrible mistake had Charlie
made? Was he involved in his father's murder? Or next in line
for some reason?

Though desperate to start tracking down the Concierge,
Taylor sat chained to his desk, taking stats, statements,
and accounts of misery. A staffer from the office of former
Congresswoman Bella Abzug—one of five Democrats
challenging Beame in the Democratic primary for mayor—
called in with four paragraphs of charges against Con Ed.

When the phone sat still for a full half hour, Taylor picked it
up and called Jersey Stein in the Manhattan DA's office.

Stein, usually even-keeled no matter what the bad guys or
acts of God threw at him, was tense. "Unless you're on fire or
already shot, can't talk."

"Wanted to see how it's going."

"Seven hundred plus arrests in Manhattan. No paperwork.
Cops brought them in and had to go right back on the street.
Can't arraign without paper. Cells jammed to the rafters.
Which means the public defenders and civil rights people are
coming up our asses."

"Got it. Quick one. You ever heard of a guy who operates under the name 'The Concierge'? Supplies drugs, whores, other illegal services, probably some legal ones, to high society folks on the Upper East Side."

"Nope. Funny, though—the name, that is, if I thought anything was funny right now. The gang unit has been trying to get inside some sort of organization working those games in the same neighborhoods. The group isn't connected to any of the traditional families. Smaller gangs, either. Our guys are having a tough time getting intelligence because its roots are deep into the community."

"Protected by the customers?"

"Yes."

"So maybe this 'Concierge'?"

"Maybe. Who knows?"

"Good luck with the paperwork. The city's a fucking mess. All from a blackout."

"That was only the trigger. The conditions that drove people to loot were always there, and it really didn't matter if it was the shooting of a kid or the lights going out. The point is, we have people unemployed, inadequately housed, drinking, and in the summer, in the street. We've created a huge class of poor, disaffected people who have no place to go. That's your mess. New York is slipping down … a kind of slow drift as we become inured to the invisible cancer. My damn paperwork won't change a thing."

Taylor knew Stein was one of the few *justice* guys in the cops and robbers business—rather than a law and order guy. But he'd never heard Stein sound this down. He'd never heard him say *damn* or any swear word.

"Can I use that?"

Stein always said no.

"Why not? My boss isn't going to say it. Quote from an official in the criminal justice system."

At 2 p.m., power in the office came on.

Templeton turned to Cramly. "I want to compare the 1965 blackout with this one."

Cramly's eyebrows rose and his mouth half opened. Incredulous Templeton had a story idea.

"You can remember '65?"

"I was on the *Journal-American*. Just after five on Tuesday, November Ninth. Lasted thirteen hours in eight states, plus Ontario. This one's totally different. Everyone's saying it. Not only the weather. People helped each other then. If they needed a light. Whatever they needed. People laughed, smiled, dealt with it, got through. No looting. No fires. New Yorkers believed they could cope with anything back then. They did. Now they don't."

Cramly, pausing presumably to take in the facts Templeton had somehow dredged up from his half-pickled brain, said, "It's all yours." He picked up Templeton's coffee, which was usually laced with bourbon. "It's a good story. You get your *coffee* when you're done. Call around to find some people who lived through both. Get them to say what was different and why."

The butler answered Taylor's call, sounding sad and formal at the same time.

"I'd like to speak to Mrs. DeVries."

"Sir, this is a house crushed by tragedy."

"It will be crushed by more if she doesn't talk to me."

"She's gone to bed. I will try." A pause, though not all that long. "She is not taking any calls. She asked me to make sure I told you she blames you for what happened to Charlie. You and your accusations."

"Let me speak with Audrey. She's in danger. Charlie's last words to me."

"Audrey left this morning."

"Left? Where?"

"We don't know. She was afraid from the time you departed. When the news came ... she took off."

"She needs protection. The police. Or private. The family can afford private, can't it?"

"You should have thought of those things before saying what you said."

Saying what I said? I didn't murder him. I'm just too many steps behind the killer.

CHAPTER 31

———◆———

Friday was another day of collecting more on the blackout and sending stories out. The only change was working air-conditioning and the facsimile machine. The toughest part was finding something new. Taylor counted 17 different stories in the *Times* about the disaster, including the top four on the front page.

He knocked off at five with the excuse he wanted to get up to Harlem to view the destroyed blocks in daylight. He really needed to visit Carol Wheelwright to talk about Audrey. Every one of his non-blackout calls today had been an attempt to find Audrey. James the butler had even hung up on him once. He wondered if that was a first.

Worry wove itself like cords through his body, then went piano-wire tight.

He checked the looted blocks. Boarded-up shops, glass everywhere, kids searching through shards for some bit of dropped merchandise. The storeowners talked anger or fear.

There was too much loss to take in; he wanted to leave and pursue one murderer and help one young woman stay alive.

He realized this was the real reason he'd never make it at

the *Times*. Vast panoramas of destruction weren't for him. You couldn't tell those stories like you could tell one human being's. They were grocery lists of numbers and quotes from the good and the great. There *was* a story, an important story, in one murder, one mugging, one swindle. The *Times* was Panavision; Taylor was the close-up.

"These three blocks are done," said a man from the community association. "The businesses barely held on in the good days. They can't rebuild, and they all employed local people. It wasn't just Jewish and Italian businesses. Shops owned by Blacks were torn apart. The neighborhood attacked itself."

A good quote, and it went into the notebook, his hand on autopilot.

Ten minutes later, Carol let Taylor in. "My brother's checking the neighborhood. He's been doing it every few hours for two days. No one's interested in his baseball bat."

"Did you have any trouble during the blackout?"

"The block was quiet. Even the merchants out on our part of the avenue were spared. My brother and some other vets, they all had their bats."

"How are things at the DeVries place?"

"Haunted by grief. It's thick in the air. You can almost taste it. No one's talking about the blackout at all. You wouldn't know there was one." The pitch of her voice rose to anger. "No, it's the night Charlie died. No one else got hurt. No one else lost out."

"Mrs. DeVries blames me."

"She's scared of the truth."

"What truth is that?"

"I don't know. Something bad. I feel it. It's all coming down on that family. Charlie ran from it. He knew something. Or he did something. He ended up dead."

"Do you think Mr. DeVries did something that got him killed?"

A sad smile. "That's hard to imagine. He was a good man. Kind. Charlie was not his father's son, though. Whatever happened to him, he brought it on himself."

"I need to find Audrey. She's in danger. Where would she go?"

"Had to guess, one of her good friend's."

"Who?"

"I'm not supposed to give out that information."

"This is about saving her life. Her mother's in bed doing nothing, from what I can tell. Audrey needs protection. She might know something about the man who killed Charlie ... even if she's not involved in any of it."

"You know who did it?"

"Man who goes by the name of the Concierge."

Her mouth flattened to a thin line, and her eyebrows drew together in a frown.

"You know who that is, don't you?"

"Heard the name. People need something, that's who they call. Any time of day. We're staff. We're invisible. We see. We hear."

She took a pad from the side table, wrote on it, and tore the sheet off. "Those are the five women in Audrey's group. They've been friends since they were little, somehow stayed together in that world they live in, which is as cutthroat as you can imagine."

"Call me if you hear anything from her. James won't listen. Try and convince him to get some security. Or to convince Mrs. DeVries."

"That won't be easy."

Taylor worried about what Carol had said all the way back to the office. He decided to handle things himself. He called the One-Nine, got the lieutenant on the phone and explained the connection between Martha Gibson and Edmond DeVries and the warning Charlie had given.

"I'd tell your detective, but he doesn't want to listen to me. I warned the detectives at the scene of Charlie DeVries' murder. Audrey is in danger. Probably her mother. Anyone in that apartment. The stories won't be so good if there's another body at that address—and police had good notice to provide protection."

"You threatening me?"

"No, explaining how news works."

"How am I supposed to provide manpower with everything going on?"

He had to keep from laughing. "There hasn't been any looting on the Upper Eastside. If I had to lay odds on your top location for crime right now, I'd say it's the DeVries place. Having a uniform around regularly would be a good idea."

The lieutenant hung up without thanking Taylor for the suggestion. Taylor spent an hour using the phone to chase after the first two women on the list of Audrey's friends, calling their houses, the names of friends *they* were visiting, and a hair salon. Every time, he'd missed them.

He dialed the number for the doorman at the DeVries building.

"Seen any cops lately?"

"Funny you ask. Patrolman showed up a half hour ago, went upstairs to the DeVries, now is hanging around the front."

SERENA FOWLER, THE third friend on the phone list, was at home. "A reporter?"

"Audrey will know me."

"I'm sorry, she doesn't—"

A bit of shuffling and Audrey came on the line.

"Are you all right?" Taylor said.

"No. Frightened to death."

"Please meet me. Do not come alone."

TAYLOR, AUDREY, SERENA, and Bobby Livingston, who'd also been at Serena's, sat in the back booth of the Oddity. Grandpop brought over mugs, filled them without asking and put a stainless-steel creamer down next to the black wire-metal rack of sugar packets.

"Where's Samantha?" Grandpop said.

"She's working." Taylor smiled, "like I am."

Grandpop waved the coffee pot, the black liquid swishing inside. "My grandson has a wonderful girlfriend—Samantha."

"She still is. We won't need menus. Thank you, Grandpop."

The old man moved off.

"Your grandfather's a bit protective," Bobby said.

"Of Samantha more than me."

"This is his place?"

"Yeah. Different sort of Upper Eastside."

"Bobby didn't mean anything," Audrey said.

"Nothing to worry about. We've all got different beginnings. It's the endings that worry me. First, you need to be somewhere safe."

"She's safe at my parent's place," Serena said. She was a blonde, with features too sharp to be pretty. The find of face he figured aristocrats would call aristocratic.

"How many people know she's there?"

"Well, our friends."

"These." He slid the list across the table.

"Yes, and some others," said Audrey.

"For everyone of those, multiply by three. I got the cops to put a uniform on Audrey's building. That's your safe bet."

Bobby sipped black coffee. "How'd you do that?"

"Explained the concept of bad PR."

"You would have thought they'd twigged to that already."

"Our apartment is so grim," Audrey said. "With mother in her room, yelling at everybody, blaming everybody."

"Maybe Serena can join you. I can't get an officer put on another building."

"Certainly," Serena said. "I'll make the calls for some others. We want Audrey safe and comfortable."

"No, only you. As far as everyone else knows, she's still at your place."

Taylor looked at the placid face of Serena Fowler and

wondered if she was brave, stupid, or clueless—the life of the insulated. Two people who lived in that apartment and one who worked there had been murdered. Audrey, on other hand, looked grim and scared. That glowing smile from the dinner party might never have existed.

"Good. Second, the Concierge."

No one spoke.

"Whoever he is, he was behind Charlie's murder. The other killings, I can't say until I find out more. What do you know about him?"

"We *know*," said Serena, "you're not supposed to talk about him unless someone provides the proper introduction."

"This isn't a cotillion. People are getting killed. Charlie pointed to this gangster—gangster to the rich, but gangster nonetheless. I need to track him down."

"That would be dangerous," Bobby said. "No one knows who he is. No one's ever met him. He takes care of things, and he does it fast."

"Has he killed anyone before?"

Audrey opened her small blue-leather purse and rummaged around in it.

Serena shook her head. "Never. He provides things, that's all." She was getting defensive. "Some of it's illegal but it's stuff you can get elsewhere in town. He probably makes it safer."

"Safer? He's the definition of a criminal enterprise. Guilty under the RICO Act."

"What is that?

"Racketeer Influenced and Corrupt Organizations Act. The law for mobsters. The killer's club."

Audrey finished digging and handed Taylor a card with a phone number on it. "Never used it. Don't even know why I kept it. You call this and use the code word 'Thomas.' "

"Does everyone have the same code?"

"No, it's the name of who escorted you or you escorted to the debutante ball. Thomas Carlton had my arm."

"What about older people?"

They all laughed.

"The balls have been going on as long as there's been a New York," Serena said.

"So, somehow this person has all those lists."

"They're not hard to get. It's what society's about. Lists. Who's on. Who's not."

"If I call in, Audrey, they'll know it's not you."

"Say my name too and use Thomas' full name. Some people have their help call. Different women answer the phone."

"Who delivers?"

"Guys on bikes like they're bringing Chinese food."

Taylor closed his notebook. "Audrey and Serena, you go straight to the DeVries' apartment. I'll make double sure the patrolman stays on duty."

Taylor watched the group leave, said goodnight to Grandpop, and rode the 6 Train downtown. At the apartment, he fed Mason and took him for a long walk. The air was still, warm, and wet, what Taylor imagined a jungle would be like, without the added benefit of pollution. He tried to get his head out of the story for a little while by focusing on what Mason was up to. They meandered, but thinking like a dog only worked so long. He turned for home.

After he and Samantha ate, he called the DeVries apartment. James spoke with him long enough to tell him Audrey had not showed up. Not at all. Taylor's gut turned to a bag of ice. Bad news was coming at him. He called the doorman at 827 Park. Yes, the cop was there. No, Audrey hadn't come through. He'd been at the podium the whole time.

At least doormen pay attention.

Serena was hysterical when he reached her at home. She'd arrived from the precinct and was about to leave a message at his office. The three of them had walked to Park Avenue when they were knocked down from behind. Audrey, screaming, was dragged into a white car—Bobby thought a Ford. The car took off south. She couldn't identify the kidnappers.

He tried the precinct. They had nothing but Serena and Bobby's report.

He dialed the number for the Concierge and gave the code word *Thomas Carlton*.

"How may we assist?" said a woman's voice, deep and smooth.

"Audrey DeVries is having a little party. She'd like to get a couple bags of pot and two ounces of cocaine." He gave his address.

"That's a new one for us."

"She's at a friend's. The gentleman has a small place where he likes to host parties outside the neighborhood."

Samantha went to bed. She had an early meeting in the morning on the divorce case with an Army vet who had a surplus mine detector. He was willing to go up to the Adirondacks and sweep the two acres. He missed the excitement of the hunt.

Taylor sat on the couch, Mason at his feet, aching to open a beer, but if he opened one Rolling Rock, he'd open 12. People dead or disappearing, and he wasn't any closer. He stared at the front door. Sometime around two, his eyelids closed and opened, closed and opened, closed. He woke up at five.

They hadn't come.

They had Audrey.

CHAPTER 32

———◆———

STORMING IN ON people never worked. They threw you out. Or had you arrested. Or shot at you. Evangeline DeVries left Taylor no choice. Saturday morning, he rode the subway uptown to do some storming. He knew the butler was off. Didn't matter. James would have been on his ass if he got in Taylor's way this morning. The elevator door opened, and Carol stood there, surprised, worried.

"Why are you here?"

"Which way to Mrs. DeVries' bedroom?"

"She's not seeing—"

"To her room."

Carol frowned, led the way down a hallway, stopped at a door and retreated as soon as Taylor put his hand on the crystal knob.

"Carol?" Mrs. DeVries rolled toward the door. "What in the name of God are you doing here? I'm not seeing anyone."

"I'm not *seeing* the rest of your family. Two are dead. Audrey has been kidnapped. What's the Concierge have against your family?"

"Which Concierge?"

"Right, you're the only person on the Upper East Side who hasn't heard of the villain. Did Charlie run up some kind of debt with him? Did your husband take a loan because of the missing money?"

"How do you know my family's business?"

"It's a story. Worse, it's a tragedy. I'm trying to figure out what's going on. We are both running out of time now that they've grabbed Audrey."

"I don't know," she cried. "I'm broken. I can't handle any of this. You're in here haranguing me. *Haranguing*." She fell back onto her pillow, tears streaming down her face.

"The reporter again." Detective Dick Moore walked in with his partner. "Were you invited?"

"No, he wasn't." Half a sob. "He's harassing me."

"So maybe I get to drag you in for harassment. That will be a pleasure."

"I already told your lieutenant: the murders of Edmond DeVries and Martha Gibson are linked. A mobster calling himself 'The Concierge' did Charlie in. Same guy must have abducted Audrey." The mother rolled over and moaned. "What have you got on the Concierge?" Taylor asked.

"What I got, I tell my lieutenant, and we tell the DA."

"Means you have jack shit. This is not the time for the standard *Dick Moore* power trip. Do that when less is at stake. Three-quarters of her family is gone." He pointed at the back of the sheer black nightgown, which he hadn't noticed before because of the blankets. Odd dress for mourning and a daughter kidnapped. Probably totally out of her head with grief. "At this point, I've got more than you do."

"Nothing about you worries me."

Moore stepped in, swinging a mini Billy club that appeared from his trench coat. Taylor dodged to the right so the rod struck his shoulder instead of his skull. He avoided a concussion, but his shoulder lit up with the bright fire of pain.

Searing pain.

Moore slugged him in the stomach.

"That's for embarrassing me with my lieutenant by demanding a patrolman over here. He doesn't think I know what's going on around this place. Guy who never leaves his desk."

Taylor crumpled to the ground, his breathing whistling over his teeth, his stomach muscles tightening.

"Oh God, no violence in here." Mrs. DeVries' voice climbed in pitch and lost its strength at the same time, sounding like wind in the trees. "Please."

"I'm sorry, ma'am. He should never have bothered you. Do you want to press charges?

"No, just leave me alone."

"Get him out of here."

The junior partner pulled Taylor to his feet, shoved him down the hallway, and pushed the elevator button. The door opened. The detective threw him at the back wall.

Taylor hit with his injured shoulder, yelled and dropped to the floor.

"Take out the trash," the detective said to the operator.

"Wrong elevator," the operator said dryly. He closed the doors. "I thought you were a friend of the family.

"Depends on who you ask." Taylor gasped for another breath.

The operator and the doorman got him into a chair in the lobby.

"That detective doesn't have the lightest touch," said the doorman, "does he?"

"That detective doesn't know what's going on, and it's pissing him off."

"Do you?"

"Not as much as I should. At least I know that much."

IN THE EMPTY offices of the City News Bureau, Taylor swallowed two aspirin with a paper cone of water from the cooler. He rotated his shoulder, groaned, rotated again, winced. A look under his shirt showed blue-black bruising on his stomach. The pain would be with him for a long while, but he'd gotten lucky. He wasn't going to have to spend the better part of a Saturday in a New York City hospital emergency room, purgatory's location here on earth.

The next two hours were spent dialing anyone he thought could help, often at home, scoring him few points with cops, ex-cops, prosecutors, and their wives. When he ran out of people to call, he still had nothing. The Concierge was a ghost. The clock moved past one in the afternoon. Taylor had covered kidnappings before. If a call didn't come soon, it wasn't a kidnapping. He hoped Carol had the presence of mind to let him know if that call did come.

He couldn't find a sitting position where his shoulder didn't burn. His pulse thumped in his temples. The harder he thought, the less there was to focus on. Smoke blown by the wind. The straining turned into an ache above his eyes. The aspirin was having no effect.

He stared at his desk. Out of ideas. The stack of the *Amenia Times* still sat there. He'd read a couple. Coverage of the Grange and a 4-H meeting. A police blotter with a lost cow and a one-car accident involving a fence post. The story on the monthly town board meeting covered two full pages in the old-fashioned eight-column layout. His vision blurred reading that one.

He read another copy, hoping the distraction would help. Didn't.

The phone rang. It was the muffled, high-pitched voice from the first call. "Do you want the third Son of Sam letter?"

Now, of all times?

"How do I know it's real?"

"Same weird handwriting. You can check it out with your sources. He wrote this. Meet me at the Blarney Rock on Eighth."

"Which? There are three."

"Forty-Eighth Street. Be there at eight thirty."

"How'd you know I'd be in the office?"

"I saw you come in."

Taylor worked to keep any reaction out of his voice. "Eight thirty then."

Prickling along the back of his neck. He was being watched. Worse, he was actually considering chasing the letter with Audrey missing and his story pretty much a lost cause.

Taylor walked to one of the office's two windows. Below was the roof of the *New York Times* building, which sat behind the Paramount Building on 43rd Street. It was Templeton's favorite joke. "City News looks down on the *Times*." It wasn't funny the first time. The haze was a feverish yellow and the sun a smear far larger than its usual disc. No sign of a thunderstorm from the west yet. Meant nothing. The sky over New Jersey could turn Armageddon in minutes.

He made up his mind and turned from the window. When you didn't have a sure thing, or even decent odds, you played the long shot. He'd go get the letter because of what it was worth in information that might lead to Audrey—and save his story. If the letter were real, the cops would have to deal with him. Cooperation from the 19th Precinct on the Concierge and the DeVries murder. Everything they had on Audrey. Jersey Stein had already told him there was an investigation into a gang on the Upper East Side. Had to be the Concierge's operations.

Worst case, the walk would clear his head and maybe give him a new idea to work on. Because he was coming up with shit sitting here and couldn't stand sitting anymore.

He'd be tromping all over the tenets of his profession. A reporter who got that letter should write the story as fast as possible and slam it on the wire. Taylor didn't give a crap about the Son of Sam circus. He wanted to find Audrey before she was another body. He wanted to report who killed the DeVrieses, father and son. He wanted to tell Martha Gibson's story, how the gears of villains ground her up because she'd had the bad fortune to stand outside the wrong room in a rich family's apartment.

All a fair trade.

CHAPTER 33

———◆———

HE LEFT THE office and headed for Sardi's, right around the corner on 44th Street. He wanted to kill the time waiting for his 8:30 meeting in a New York place that represented the time before the blackout, psycho killers, the Concierge, and the destruction of the DeVries family. Sardi's was that.

In the same location since 1927, the restaurant—white tablecloths standing out against the red booths, with hundreds of caricatures of celebrities on the walls—had been serving dinner before and after the theater through all the decades when New York was the capital of everything. Rather than a national joke. Old New York all around him, Taylor took a seat at the bar and ordered the pork chops. He limited himself to a couple of beers, paid, walked west to Eighth and turned north toward 48th Street for this meeting he didn't expect much out of but prayed would give him everything. Going made him feel like he was doing something, an empty gesture that had the advantage of being a gesture.

From a corner phone, he called Samantha at home and told her he didn't want her to come along and spook whoever had the letter—if they had the letter. Samantha said she'd go to the office and wait to hear from him there.

The blue neon light of the Blarney Rock sign bled into the haze—much like the sun, though on a smaller scale. The name of the place always made Taylor wonder if the owner of the chain was really Irish, since the object in question in Ireland was the Blarney Stone, not the Blarney Rock. On the other hand, could be an inside joke. *Blarney* itself was jokey conversation usually used to deceive. A con. Below the neon were the words "Great Beer, Excellent Food, and Fine Company." Now *that* was blarney.

The sickly haze transformed to a gray and somehow more pleasant cloud of cigarette and cigar smoke. He approached the bar, which was populated by a handful of the usual lushes in this sort of dive, and took a seat with empty stools on either side of him. He didn't want a drunk laying into his ear now— or anyone listening in on whatever transaction was about to take place.

He ordered a Fresca. A shimmer of white in the corner of his eye. Not a color he'd expect on a regular patron; they were all in grays and browns. The shimmer sat down next to him as he was putting money on the bar. He turned to find the frightened eyes of Audrey DeVries, dark circles under those eyes.

"Audrey." He might have yelled it but kept his voice as quiet as possible for fear she would panic and run. Or do a shimmery vanish. "How'd you get here?"

She grabbed his forearm.

"It's all gotten so terribly desperate." Not Audrey, but a deep voice on the other side of Taylor. "None of us really knows what to do."

Taylor turned slowly. Doing anything fast right now seemed a bad idea. Bobby Livingston straddled a barstool, back straight as a board. For the first time, Taylor realized how deep Livingston's voice was. Next to him stood Mrs. DeVries, who though sad, didn't look scared like her daughter.

"What the hell is going on?" Taylor said. "*You* have the letter."

"Let's not get all rushie. Welcome to our what's-left-of-the-family meeting." Livingston pulled his hand out of a tan silk jacket to display the grip of a pistol. "Nothing rushie at all. Things have gotten too messy. We need to clean them up tonight. Drinks first. Evangeline?"

"Something strong."

"I'm afraid what's strong in here may not be up to the standards you're used to. I so hate coming to the West Side. All grubby and cheapsided. It's why I quit going to the theater years ago. Audrey?"

"Nothing."

"Oh, you must have something, dear." Menace in his voice.

"A glass of wine. Anything."

"Taylor?"

"Fine with what I've got. You're the Concierge."

"You see," he turned to Mrs. DeVries, "I told you he was smart. Surprising for his profession."

"Maybe. Maybe not. I don't get it. I got the call about the Son of Sam letter back on July Sixth. Charlie hadn't been murdered yet."

"You may be smart for what you do, but you're in a chess game now. I'm playing moves ahead. Always. You're a pawn on the board. You were already a bit too uncomfortably close back then. Asking the wrong questions about Martha. Then Charlie, that drunk ass, invited you to the Chapel, and one of those idiot girls mentioned the Concierge to you. Poor thing. I didn't *know* then that you'd become a real threat, but I thought I'd set the bait in case I needed to take steps to trap a real threat. If you hadn't been so pesky, you'd never have heard about the letter again. I knew anything with Son of Sam would be catnip to a reporter. You couldn't resist, could you?"

"Martha, Edmond DeVries, Charlie ... they were all a threat to you?"

"Martha was, of course. For what she heard. Her sister's

boyfriend, McGill, took care of her. Convenient that was his business. Bobby Livingston knows a lot of good people. The Concierge knows a lot of bad people. Edmond, I eliminated for the money. Evangeline and I have big plans for it. We're an item, you see."

Livingston reached for her hand, which she offered, slowly, almost unwillingly, then winced from what must have been a hard squeeze.

"I didn't want my children harmed," Mrs. DeVries said. A defensive answer to a question Taylor hadn't yet asked. She looked at the space between Livingston and Taylor. "We were supposed to take care of Edmond, that boob, and get what I was due. It's out of control. You need to get this under control, Bobby."

Livingston's knuckles whitened. A cracking as he squeezed her hand harder. Mrs. DeVries uttered a low cry.

"Let's keep things civil and quiet." Livingston picked up the gin and tonic he'd ordered. "Don't want to make a mess here." He looked at Taylor. "Charlie was the one who lost his nerve. We brought him in on all our plans. Then he lost it. I'm hoping for a reconciliation with my lover over that incident. We'll see. That's business for later, between her and me."

"What money can you be getting if Denny Connell embezzled twenty-five million?"

"That's why we had to act. The fool DeVries let that little scam artist rip him off. Rip *us* off. It was all going to be gone."

"Wasn't ever your money."

"Let's not slice things fine. It was Evangeline's, so it was mine. Between real estate, financial assets, and a trust, there remains sixteen million or so. As for the twenty-five million, the Concierge has his ways and means. Connell's going to be given some options by a couple folks I've contacted in Rikers. The money comes back to us, or embezzlement becomes a capital crime for Mr. Connell. Oh heck, I'll probably have him killed anyway." A laugh of real enjoyment. "I despise loose ends."

Taylor shook his head and sipped the Fresca. "You're a Livingston. Why'd you need to become a pusher and a whoremonger? A killer?"

"Keep your language more respectful."

"You're not going to shoot me in here."

A sly smile. "Old money doesn't age well these days. It fades. Then it's gone. Like that. I told you I was from a distant twig on that family tree. We were like the DeVrieses, though with even less, and that going faster. In fact, my father made Edmond DeVries look like a financial mastermind. I knew his type when I met Evangeline. I explained how it all was going to go down for her. Neither of us had any interest in a radical change in our lifestyles."

"Like getting jobs?"

Livingston ignored the comment like he'd probably ignored the idea his whole life. "I was already in business when we met. I got started supplying my fellow students at Choate, you see. Got caught. Expelled. I came back to Park Avenue and realized there was a much bigger market here and an incredible advantage in using intermediaries. I called myself 'The Concierge' as a joke at first—a joke that became serious. The rest of it was customer demand. Women. After-hours parties. People would call and ask if the Concierge could help. He always could. He couldn't go on forever, though. Getting caught back at school taught me that. Detectives were nosing around. Evangeline and I were together. We were *deeply* in love and decided divorce would be wrong for her financially." He stroked her cheek with his fingernails and she winced as if she'd been struck. "The DeVries fortune would be more than enough funding so the Concierge could retire. Or perhaps bring his exceptional services to some continental city. Your nosing around only confirmed how right I was. Now finish your drinks, and we'll go for a little walk. Mother and daughter arm in arm in front of Taylor and me."

It was only when they stood up that Audrey let go of his arm, not before squeezing so hard her fingernails dug in, like he was a life preserver she was being forced to give up.

CHAPTER 34

———— ◆ ————

TAYLOR GLIMPSED THEATER marquees to the east as they crossed streets. Foot traffic on the sidewalk was light. Legitimate visitors to the neighborhood were in those theaters watching *Beatlemania*, *The Gin Game*, *Your Arms Too Short to Box with God*, *Godspell*, *Annie* and the other shows that kept Times Square from becoming solely a district of porn and theft. Hookers—most wearing tight, tiny dresses, one in a bikini—were working corners on Eighth, though it was early for that commerce. Their numbers would double as the theater people left and the cops did little.

The sun had set. For another evening, the heat remained.

They passed an old-fashioned porn shop—only books and magazines offered. The four of them could be theatergoers themselves, though woefully late for their show and apparently in no hurry.

Taylor had finally found—stumbled on—his connection. Little good it did him. Shit, more than one connection. Livingston was having an affair with Evangeline DeVries, and he was the Concierge. The deaths were tied together in one murderous knot. Livingston puffed on a cigar and walked behind Taylor, off his shoulder.

When they'd first met, Taylor had taken Bobby Livingston for a pleasant version of New York's young and wealthy. Something like Audrey, though she was the most down to earth of all those he'd encountered. He'd gotten Livingston wrong. Completely. The bad call of the year. Of the decade. Taylor had covered murder over money and sex before. But Livingston? Proved the worst could come from the best sort of circumstances. The mask off, Taylor could see the meanness in him, along with tremendous avarice—a cool, sane desire for wealth gained by selling drugs, women, anything clients wanted, and killing.

Taylor was sweating more than the heat warranted. His stomach turned in on itself. He'd been caught off guard. He didn't know what exactly Livingston had planned, but giving Taylor all that info meant a bullet at some point.

He needed a plan. Focus on escape, not on what Bobby might do. So far, they hadn't come across a cop walking the Eighth Avenue beat. If they did, how would that play out? He could shove Livingston to the ground and scream "Gun!" Bullets would start flying. Whose? The cop might react too slowly. There were no guarantees. It'd be like playing Russian roulette—with people instead of bullets.

Plan B: Some sort of break and run? Yell at the women to take off. No, that looked worse. They all couldn't get away. Mrs. DeVries might not want to, could freeze. Livingston didn't seem the type to hesitate in the least. An even lower odds version of roulette. He didn't have a move from judo to deal with a gun held behind him inside a coat pocket. Bobby, a smart man, was keeping far enough away.

Fuck judo. I'd need a bazooka for the shits infesting this city.

They turned down 54th, the art-deco Studio 54 marquee sticking over the sidewalk.

"Let's cross the street, why don't we," Bobby said.

They walked by a couple of small restaurants—one French, one Italian—that were near empty. They'd served the prix fixe dinners before the shows. Waiters stood around waiting for the after-theater crowd.

They passed a parking lot and reached its ramp.

"Up."

The four of them climbed the steep deck past the first level.

He's going to kill us in this garage. Need some kind of move. Might mean roulette.

The second level.

Audrey turned her head around.

"There's nothing back here, honey," Livingston said.

She kept looking, a tear running down the right side of her cheek.

"Turn around. Or I use this now."

At the top of the ramp, parked facing down the steep slope, was a light-blue VW Beetle. The top level was totally packed with cars. Lots of folks drove in for a show so they could get out of Times Square as fast as possible.

"My car?" Audrey asked, surprised and confused, like it was a vision.

"From your pseudo-hippy period. Getting with the people didn't last long. Never understood why you kept it. Had one of my guys bring it over."

Livingston stepped away from the group. "Stand behind the car." He unlocked the VW, pulled a big, short-barreled revolver out of his pocket and signaled Taylor to get in the front seat. Taylor couldn't take his eyes off the gun, even as he sat behind the wheel.

"You know what it is, don't you?"

Livingston led Audrey around to the other side and ordered her into the front passenger seat. The door slammed. Taylor's hand automatically rested on the stick shift. Audrey's returned to clamp on to Taylor's upper arm.

Livingston was back on Taylor's side of the car, crouched down to look into the window. "You did recognize it."

"Hard not to. It's in the paper every day. Charter Arms Bulldog Forty-Four."

"We're not all avid readers of the crime pages. Audrey here works at the *New Yorker*, after all. They're still catching up with Prohibition. Who uses this gun?"

"Son of Sam."

"Correct. We've got here a nice car that easily could have come in from the outer boroughs."

"He's only killed in the Bronx and Queens."

"Indeed. Won't this get the cops going? New angles. New media coverage. Such excitement. The car's not on the street either, but of course, I couldn't really pull this off curbside in Times Square."

"Bobby." Evangeline DeVries took a step closer to him.

"Hold on, dear. I'm explaining things. Audrey's close to the perfect age. Hair's a little short. But I've read the stories. The cops have no real idea who this guy is or what he's up to. Son of Sam, he keeps making changes. Finally, the topper for our little scene. A reporter caught in the middle of Son of Sam's murderous campaign against the beautiful young women of New York. She is beautiful, isn't she?"

Evangeline again. "Bobby, please."

"The ballistics won't match," Taylor said.

"I did think about that. The cops, the press, the whole city is wound tight like a spring. They're going to decide Son of Sam has two guns. A dead couple is going to be found in this car, and they're going to be the new victims of the city's favorite psycho-killer. As I understand it, he always comes to the passenger side, gets the girl and then sometimes her beau. They'll be no sometimes this time."

CHAPTER 35

———◆———

LIVINGSTON STOOD UP and walked toward the rear of the VW.

Taylor turned to watch.

"I said Audrey must stay safe," said Evangeline DeVries. She pulled on Livingston's arm.

"I told you, honey," Livingston smacked her across the face, "Audrey doesn't want to go along with our adventure. She's become a liability. You don't want to become a liability too, do you?"

He strolled around the back of the car and appeared outside Audrey's window, waved with his fingers and went into a shooting crouch.

The black end of the barrel pointed at Audrey's head. The bullets in the other chambers were huge, even from where Taylor sat. The warheads of ballistic missiles.

She screamed, threw her arms up for protection they couldn't give, and hunkered down.

Evangeline flew into Bobby.

They tumbled to the ground.

"Duck all the way down … now!" Taylor said.

He jammed his foot onto the clutch, shifted into neutral and released the emergency break. The car started rolling down the steep ramp, picking up speed fast.

The gun went off.

Audrey raised her head and turned. "Mother."

In the rearview mirror, Evangeline slid slowly off the hood of a Cutlass, leaving a smear of blood.

"Get your head back down!"

Second level.

Livingston started running down the ramp after the rolling car.

Taylor scrunched his head as low as he could and still steer.

First level.

The VW's rear window blew in, throwing glass all the way to the front seat.

The street came at them fast.

The needle on the speedometer pushed to thirty. He could not brake. There would be no way to regain momentum.

They shot onto 54th with a Yellow cab no more than two car lengths away.

The cabbie hit his horn and brakes at the same time.

Taylor started a turn, but not fast enough. The cab caught the VW in the rear, sent it spinning toward the far curb. The vehicle, facing forward, jumped the curb and hurtled toward the front doors of Studio 54.

Taylor slammed on the brakes and braced himself with the wheel.

The car rammed through the doors with a jarring crash, raining down more glass, and traveled a full length into the entryway before stopping.

"Are you all right?" Taylor opened his door.

Blood ran from Audrey's nose and a gash on her forehead. "I'm not shot. That'll do."

"Move it if we want to avoid that happening."

Out of the Beetle, they ran down the entranceway and

turned into the dark, empty club. It was probably another hour before opening.

Taylor looked back. A shadow moved down the hallway from the front door. Bobby would be coming around the corner any second.

"We won't get across this big a space in time. Other side of the bar."

They hopped up on the bar and dropped down behind.

"Well, well. What a nice place to finish things off." Bobby's voice from where they'd come in. "Quickly, though. You've attracted a whole lot of attention. Somewhere near. Couldn't have gotten far."

Now what? Cops and fire were going to get here soon. If they could survive that long, they'd be set. If Bobby found them before that, they'd be dead, and it wouldn't matter how much evidence this asshole left behind. Not for Taylor and Audrey, at least.

Steps came toward the bar.

I've got to stall.

The lowest shelf behind the bar was long, deep, and empty. He signaled for Audrey to crawl on to it. She barely fit.

With his lips almost touching her ear, he whispered, "Don't move, no matter what."

Two more steps from the other side.

Taylor picked up a shot glass, edged up for a glimpse, found Livingston turned toward the dance floor, and hurled the glass as hard as he could back down the entrance hall. The gun went off.

Fucking trigger-happy.

Taylor ran low to the other end of the bar, came around the corner, and stood up. Livingston faced the entrance, gun up.

"She got away, Bobby boy. Out the front door. We split up."

He turned. The .44 was steady, the smile transformed into an angry sneer.

"Then I'll kill you and hunt her down. You're the smarter

one. It's not always about class and money. I've learned that in my business career. I'll find her and finish all this."

"You'll be finished long before that. She's going to tell your whole story to the cops. You've got nothing over her anymore. You wiped out her family."

Livingston raised the big gun higher and stepped closer to Taylor.

"How about I don't care? How about I put a bullet in your head."

"Long as you saved one for yourself."

"I'll get out of this. I've been raised to manage this system of ours."

Movement behind Livingston. A bulky man wearing a Mets cap emerged from the hallway.

"Hay! Who the hell ran that VW in front of my cab? We pushed it to the side, and I need to report this—"

Livingston spun and fired, hitting the cabbie in the chest.

Taylor closed the distance as Livingston was bringing his arm back around. Taylor hurtled into him. The gun roared as Taylor tackled Livingston to the floor.

The world went silent.

One bullet left if he didn't reload.

Taylor wrestled with Livingston. All his concentration was on the gun hand. He slammed it once, twice onto the wood dance floor.

Again. As hard as he could. Something cracked in Livingston's wrist.

Livingston might have been yelling. His mouth was open wide enough. Taylor was deaf from the gunshot. Livingston let loose the gun's grip. Taylor leaned and stretched and swatted the Bulldog away.

Taylor paid a steep price for that move. Livingston elbowed him in the throat, sending him onto the floor, gasping for air. Livingston landed on top, punched him in the face.

Everything spun.

Taylor bucked. Livingston stayed on top and hit him again. He bucked again but without as much strength. One more punch, and he'd be out of this.

Taylor's left hand was free. He grabbed for Livingston's face, reaching for his nose, an eye, anything. Livingston bit his thumb hard. The hand fell away to his chest bleeding. If there was pain, it faded, because Taylor was fading from gray to black. Livingston pulled back for the final punch.

Taylor heard the first sound since Livingston's revolver had deafened him. Another gunshot. Half of Livingston's scalp flew into the air like some theatrical string had pulled it. Blood splattered on Taylor's face. Bobby Livingston collapsed onto Taylor, which did nothing to help him catch his breath and clear his head. He pushed to move Livingston off. Couldn't. Worked to take in air, let it out again. Spit blood out of his mouth. Woozy spinning.

Audrey appeared in his fuzzy field of vision, almost a magic trick, holding the .44-caliber revolver in one hand, her grip tight like she was certain she'd need to use it again.

The first thing he wanted to do was thank her for not following his orders. His jaw wouldn't work.

"Are you okay?"

He tried again and got four words out. "Help … get him off."

In the end, she did all the pushing and dropped the body into a puddle of brains and blood onto the floor.

"Thank …" he took another raspy breath, "you."

"You saved me first."

"Put the gun down. Cops coming."

By the time he was able to sit up, five patrolmen came in, guns out, followed by an engine crew.

There was some discussion about sending Taylor to the hospital, a suggestion he fought with impeded speech and gestures. He didn't want Audrey going into the precinct by herself. There were two bodies here and one across the street. Bad enough. Worse, this was a complex case. Bobby Livingston had done a merry dance all over the Upper East Side. For Audrey's sake, Taylor wanted to make sure the detectives heard the same story from both of them—that he put the story in front of them, clear and clean. It was his job, after all. There were things he knew that she could not know about the case.

While they were all conferring, he got Audrey to call Samantha, who arrived within five minutes and bullshitted her way onto the scene.

Precinct first, he told her, then he'd get checked out. Must have been the look in his eyes, because she didn't argue. In fact, she backed him with the cops.

The ME's people were starting to do their work, and a lieutenant—a sure sign how serious this was—invited them all to the precinct. Didn't sound like an invitation.

A slender man in a black silk tie walked into Studio 54.

"What the fuck happened to my club?"

.44-CAL. KILLER
SHOOTS 2 MORE

Wounds B'klyn Couple in Car
Despite Heavy Cop Dragnet

—*Daily News*, page 1, August 1, 1977

CAUGHT!

—*New York Post*, page 1, August 11, 1977

'Son of Sam' Case Poses Thorny Issues for Press

—*New York Times*, page 1, August 22, 1977

CHAPTER 36

———◆———

SON OF SAM didn't "celebrate" the July 29th anniversary of the killing of Donna Lauria with a shooting. He waited until two nights later and attacked a couple in a car in a parking area facing Gravesend Bay, Brooklyn. Stacy Moskowitz died from a bullet to the brain. Her date, Robert Violante, was permanently blinded.

The *Post's* Steve Dunleavy managed to escort the victims' parents into a private room in the hospital and shield them from the rest of the press. He shoved a TV crew out of the room to keep things private. He got his scoop. The story began, "For 13½ hours a *Post* reporter stood at the side of four courageous people in a painful and often stirring vigil—praying, talking about God, and swearing at an unknown madman who has launched a guerrilla war against the young and beautiful of this city."

His nauseating invasion went on from there. If he didn't know already, Taylor was now certain he'd made the right decision. There was no good reason for him to work at the new *New York Post*.

An item as innocent as a parking ticket put on a car near the murder scene led to a man named David Berkowitz in Yonkers. Two Yonkers cops had already been working to link Berkowitz to the shooting of a dog, a fire set in Berkowitz's apartment building, and strange letters to the dog's owner and another couple. Berkowitz was arrested for the Son of Sam shootings.

The circus stayed in town.

During Berkowitz's walk into 1 Police Plaza, the scramble by seemingly every photographer on the East Coast launched cameras into the air, sent photographers crashing to the ground and had them taking pictures of the backs of each other's heads. One cameraman stepped in front of the police car and was almost flattened. The police escort had to push and shove to inch Berkowitz through the crush.

On the day Berkowitz was being arraigned in Brooklyn Criminal Court, four journalists were arrested for breaking into the gunman's apartment. Two days later, an attorney who somehow ended up on the initial team representing Berkowitz was being investigated by the U.S. Attorney for pedaling 90 minutes of taped interviews between him and Berkowitz for newspaper serialization and book rights. The price: $100,000.

The August 22nd *New York Times*, today's paper, carried a front-page story on how the press had handled the case, concluding the *News* and the *Post* had gone beyond reporting by "transforming the killer into a celebrity."

No shit, Sherlock.

Taylor turned to the jump as he ate his fill of his grandfather's bacon and cheese omelet. Samantha sat across from him at the Oddity with eggs sunny side up and sausages.

Even the comics had joined this circus, which had grown well beyond three rings. The *Doonesbury* strip was parodying Jimmy Breslin and his role in the story with a Son of Arnold and Abigail Lieberman calling the *News'* promotion department trying to get some attention. The *News* wouldn't run the strip. *The Post*, though it didn't have the rights, published a few of them on Page 6, including one in which Breslin wrote an open letter to Hollywood because negotiations for the movie rights had broken down. It appeared under the headline BRESLIN TO TINSELTOWN: DROP DEAD.

Audrey DeVries slid into the booth next to Samantha. She'd asked to meet at the Oddity. She'd said on the phone she liked the place. That didn't surprise Taylor. Everyone fit in at Grandpop's diner, from cabbies to the ladies of the Upper East Side.

Her face was too pale. She'd lost weight. Sadness radiated off her.

"Thank you for getting together," she said.

"Of course."

"I was talking to one of my editors at the *New Yorker*—"

"You're back at work?"

"I had to go in. Sitting around thinking was crushing me. Friends don't know what to talk about. I can tell they're working on things to say and that brings on more of the crush. I moved out of the apartment. I'm with my aunt. The crazy one who moved to the Westside." The barest hint of a smile. "I was telling my editor about your Martha Gibson piece. He'd like to do a story on a murder that happened while the city was obsessed with David Berkowitz."

"I don't think I write in your style. I don't know what your style is."

"Write it your way. Will you, please? This is the first story I've pitched that he's been interested in. A story on Martha would be a small step for me. In a lot of ways."

"I can put something together. You'll go over it with me before you turn it in?"

"Deal."

Things weren't going in the direction he'd expected, hadn't for almost two years. Maybe he should let the worrying go for a bit. His series on the DeVries family had been picked up by every City News client, plus some papers that weren't subscribers. Now, the *New Yorker*, of all publications. Novak had even mentioned there might be more work and money from WINS. They liked his "gritty newspaper style," which Taylor took as an insult—the gritty part. He got over it quick enough. He was, by accident, cobbling together a hodgepodge of ways to report his stories. This could be the answer in a city that bounced lower every time he thought it hit bottom.

"You want something to eat?"

"I've got to get back to the office. I bury myself in the work—to keep a little of it at bay. It's Friday, and I'm the only one who hates it. Weekends are awful."

After she opened the glass door, stepped outside and turned downtown, Samantha said, "She must be pretty strong. She's going to need more than work to keep going."

"How do you heal from that?"

"Time heals—"

"A favorite line of my mom's."

"What about the city? How long for it to come back?"

"Not sure it's done hurting itself. Being hurt. Self-inflicted wounds by its own people. Attacking their own in their own neighborhoods. In some ways, all that was worse than Berkowitz. Dodging bankruptcy wasn't even a beginning of the city's recovery." He shook his head. "I can't wait for this summer to end. Let the next thirty days go by quickly. Cooler weather. Autumn. A fading of *some* of the fear."

"Should we move somewhere else?"

"I couldn't. Could you?"

"No way. Thought I should ask."

He closed the paper. "I liked that beach out on the Far Rockaways. Let's spend the afternoon there."

"You'd skip a day of work?" Her incredulous tone was only half feigned.

"Wouldn't want to miss this balmy eighty-degree weather."

Taylor stood. They both waved to Grandpop and walked toward the door.

Photo by Domenica Comfort

Rɪᴄʜ Zᴀʜʀᴀᴅɴɪᴋ ɪs the award-winning author of the critically acclaimed Coleridge Taylor Mystery series (*Last Words, Drop Dead Punk, A Black Sail, Lights Out Summer*).

The first two books in the series were shortlisted or won awards in the three major competitions for books from independent publishers. *Drop Dead Punk* won the gold medal for mystery eBook in the 2016 Independent Publisher Book Awards. It was also named a finalist in the mystery category of the 2016 Next Generation Indie Book Awards. *Last Words* won the bronze medal for mystery/thriller eBook in the 2015 IPPYs and honorable mention for mystery in the 2015 Foreword Reviews Book of the Year Awards.

"Taylor, who lives for the big story, makes an appealingly single-minded hero," *Publishers Weekly* wrote of *Drop Dead Punk.*

Zahradnik was a journalist for 30-plus years, working as a reporter and editor in all major news media, including online, newspaper, broadcast, magazine and wire services. He held editorial positions at CNN, Bloomberg News, Fox Business Network, AOL and *The Hollywood Reporter.*

Zahradnik was born in Poughkeepsie, New York, in 1960 and received his B.A. in journalism and political science from George Washington University. He lives with his wife Sheri and son Patrick in Pelham, New York, where he writes fiction and teaches kids around the New York area how to write news stories and publish newspapers.

For more information, go to www.richzahradnik.com.

FROM CAMEL PRESS AND RICH ZAHRADNIK

THANK YOU FOR reading *Lights Out Summer*. We are so grateful for you, our readers. If you enjoyed this book, here are some steps you can take that could help contribute to its success and let you stay in touch with the Coleridge Taylor series:

- Please think about posting a short review on Amazon, BN.com, and GoodReads.
- Check out Rich's website and join his mailing list at www.richzahradnik.com.
- Spread the word on social media, especially Facebook, Twitter, and Pinterest.
- "Like" Rich's author Facebook page: www.facebook.com/RichZahradnik and the Camel Press page: www.facebook.com/CamelPressBooks.
- Follow Rich (@rzahradnik) and Camel Press (@camelpressbooks) on Twitter.
- Ask for your local library to carry this book and others in the series or request them on their online portal.

Good books and authors from small presses are often overlooked. Your comments and reviews can make an enormous difference.

Discover the Coleridge Taylor Mystery Series, Books 1-3

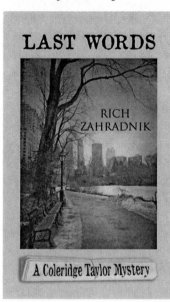

LAST WORDS

RICH ZAHRADNIK

A Coleridge Taylor Mystery

In 1975, newsman Coleridge Taylor roams New York's ERs looking for the story that will revive his faltering career. While investigating the death of a society kid up to no good, he tries to protect a homeless man on the hit list of three goons and soon finds his own life in danger. If he doesn't wrap this story up soon, he'll be back on the obits page—as a headline, not a byline.

Pres. Ford refuses to bail out NYC, but newsman Coleridge Taylor has other worries. He needs his next scoop. He thinks he's found it when a mugging leaves a punk and a cop dead. Only the punk was a good kid, and the NYPD thinks Officer Samantha Callahan abandoned her partner. Taylor falls for Samantha. A bad move. Her story has a mighty undertow, and Taylor is already in over his head.

"Taylor, who lives for the big story, makes an appealingly single-minded hero." —Publishers Weekly

DROP DEAD PUNK

RICH ZAHRADNIK
FINALIST, FOREWORD BOOK OF THE YEAR AWARD

A Coleridge Taylor Mystery

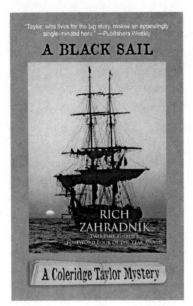

A BLACK SAIL

RICH
ZAHRADNIK
TWO-TIME FINALIST
FOREWORD BOOK OF THE YEAR AWARD

A Coleridge Taylor Mystery

Coleridge Taylor is covering Operation Sail. A police reporter, he'd rather do real stories, and NYC has plenty in July 1976. When a dead housewife is fished out of the harbor wearing bricks of heroin, Taylor believes he's stumbled upon a war between drug cartels. Flanked by his ex-cop girlfriend, he pursues his big story but sees it grow more twisted and deadly by the hour.

Keep Reading for an Excerpt from
LAST WORDS

1

———— ◆ ————

THE DEAD SITTING on his desk could wait.

Instead of going back to the office, Coleridge Taylor stopped at the newsstand on 23rd Street and looked at the front page of the *Daily News*. MAYHEM IN QUEENS spelled out in two-inch type. Another story that should have been his. The *Times* led with a dull speech by President Ford. It made him miss Nixon. Nothing like a crook in the White House to sell papers. He spent a nickel on a pack of Teaberry gum, folded a stick into his mouth, pulled his field jacket tight against the wind, and turned east toward Bellevue.

Taylor spent his long lunches making the rounds—precincts, ERs, firehouses—the same rounds he'd done when he was the paper's top police reporter, before they'd banished him to obits. Unless he caught a break soon, his career would be over. He'd be a has-been at thirty-four. As he walked, Taylor rapped his pen on his notebook, a nervous habit that kicked in when he was looking for a story, and now he was running out of time. In a week, Worth and Marmelli were going to review the work he'd done since his demotion and decide. A permanent job writing obituaries or back out on the street. He didn't know which was worse, but if he kept dodging obit duty, that meeting wasn't going to go so well.

Gusts off the East River buffeted him as his long strides carried him up First Avenue. His arms were long, too, while his high cheekbones and strong jawline added to the impression that Taylor was all angles. He slipped the notebook and pen into his coat and stuffed his big hands into his pockets. Bellevue towered over FDR Drive and the muck-brown East River. He went up the driveway to the ER entrance.

The waiting room was empty. Unusual for New York's medical center of last resort. The nurse behind the reception desk, Barbara Cortez, was a bit on the chubby side and smiled no matter what she had to deal with.

"Anything good?" He leaned in.

Cortez was one of those women who looked better the closer you got because of her kind dark eyes and smooth olive skin. "We're going to be busy in about ten minutes. Three kids up in Harlem. All gun-shot."

"What happened?"

"A detective sees a kid pull a knife at 131st and Lenox. He shoots. More shots. We've got another race riot."

This sent a jolt through Taylor's gut. "They're driving them all the way downtown? What's wrong with Harlem Hospital?"

"The cops ordered it. They didn't want protestors going over there and making things worse."

"Ten blocks versus more than a hundred? Those kids could die." Taylor took out his notebook and wrote down the intersection and what Cortez had said about the order to bring the boys downtown. He circled this last fact. If something stuck out, he noted it.

"I just treat whoever gets here alive." Cortez shrugged. "I thought you were doing death notices."

"Obits."

"Aren't they the same?"

"One you pay for. One you don't."

Taylor headed down the corridor, away from the ER. Few things bothered him more than walking away from a big story. Cops shooting black kids was a very big story, and every police reporter in town would soon descend on the ER. He couldn't be there when they did.

The gray hospital walls matched his mood as he wound an aimless route around the hallways and ended up in a back corridor. A black orderly, tall with graying hair, pushed a gurney with a body under a sheet in the other direction.

"That one of the boys from Harlem?"

"No. This one's white and no cop shot him. Young. Homeless. Found dead on the street."

"How'd he die?"

"Like I said, homeless." The orderly stopped pushing.

"That's not a cause of death."

"What it's been for five others in the past two weeks. This wicked March freeze is catching them all off guard."

"*Five*? Dead from exposure?"

"That's right. I've got to get this one into the cutting room." The orderly pushed past, and Taylor followed him into the autopsy room.

"Where do you think you're going?"

"I'm going to write about this kid."

"The homeless don't get stories in the paper."

"First time for everything."

The orderly rolled the gurney onto an elevator. Taylor stepped on, too. The orderly read his press pass. It expired in three months, and if Taylor couldn't get back on the police beat by then, he'd lose it and all the access it gave him. Doors all over the city would slam shut. The thought chilled him.

"Coleridge Samuel Taylor."

"Just Taylor." He hated the literary ornamentation of his name.

"Name's Jackson."

The autopsy room looked like any operating theater with its

silver-domed lights, trolleys of medical instruments and glass-fronted metal cabinets. The acrid smell of disinfectant was even stronger here.

A second orderly came in and helped Jackson shift the wrapped body onto a table, both of them grunting.

"Jesus, this body is frozen stiff," Jackson said.

The second orderly shrugged and left, as if moving bodies was his only job.

"You said he died of exposure, right?" Taylor leaned in.

"Yeah, but he feels like …." The orderly frowned. "The last time a body came in frozen solid like this was when a jumper went into the Hudson back in January." He pulled the sheets open near the neck. The corpse was still dressed and the orderly fingered the material of the outer clothing. "The coat and sweater are cold but *not* frozen." He slid his hand inside the sweater. "The undershirt feels like it's iced right to him. The skin *is* frozen."

"That doesn't make sense." Taylor looked from the orderly to the body on the slab. "It's like he froze from the inside out. Or his outer clothes were put on *after* he froze." He made a note of this. "Be interesting to hear what the pathologist makes of it."

"Not much if he thinks he's cutting a homeless boy. How are you going to do a story on a dead nobody?" The orderly sighed and turned away.

I'll find out what makes him a somebody. Getting frozen in your underwear and dressed by another person might do the trick.

"You gotta be a big somebody to get your death notice in the papers here."

This victim's story already bothered him. The boy was going to disappear. Taylor was watching it happen. No last words for the family. No notice taken anywhere by anyone. It had happened before, with Billy. This was going on now in Taylor's city. There was no excuse for it.

"When did the body come in?"

12/17

CPSIA information can be obtained
at www.ICGtesting.com
Printed in the USA
FSOW01n0829150817
37480FS

9 781603 812139